For Linda,
I hope you enjoy
this creepy collection of stories.
A pleasure meeting you at VCON!

Bryce Raffle

CONTENTS

FOREWORD

LEANNA RENEE HIEBER

THE TERM DREADPUNK WAS BORN OUT of love, snark and reclamation. Derek Tatum, track director of the DragonCon Horror Track, asked authors Cherie Priest and myself about a tongue-in-cheek term to attach to Victorian Gothic work to ensure that not everything with top hat, corset or waistcoat was lumped automatically in with "Steampunk". We settled upon Dreadpunk because the engine, the furnace, the terrible beating heart of the Gothic is dread, correlated with the prolific 19th Century tradition of "Penny Dreadfuls". Dreadpunk's compass needle is the centuries-old Gothic literary tradition, but it is a cross-genre enterprise reimagined by modern voices.

The term "Steampunk", thanks to author K.W. Jeter and his colleagues, was born from a literary tongue-in-cheek counterpoint to the term Cyberpunk. Dreadpunk exists in relation to the other established genre terms. If Steampunk is 19th century inspired science fiction powered by steam and alternate technologies, then Dreadpunk's steam is dread; the narrative is powered by a slow-mounting fear of what's happening, what's perceived and what may happen next. It is further driven by a psychological focus and its genre core is historical horror.

Cherie Priest (Boneshaker) rightly says that true Steampunk must have "punk" at its core, not a decorative concept. Punk, in its original subculture, strove to question manmade power structures and sought to upset, dismantle, and reveal the divisive and exclusionary natures of imbalanced power dynamics. The appeal of good Steampunk is when it subverts the repressive Victorian age, its strict gender roles and violent colonialism, offering instead reclamation and innovation. Good Dreadpunk ought to question similar historical restrictions and politics. Due to Dreadpunk's roots in the Gothic and "Penny Dreadful" literary tradition, it seeks to illuminate the intimate inner-workings of fear, isolation, and repression. It toys with the concept of freedom. It seeks to unsettle the foundations of life as triumphant over death.

Powered by dread, motivated by the human desire to seek resolution, the tradition of the Gothic- and so then of Dreadpunk- is to be a mirror to the human psyche, as gorgeous as it is terrible. This genre swings on a pendulum edge of beauty and horror. Its inexorable momentum is what keeps me writing in this genre and always drawn to read it.

Here in DeadSteam, you'll encounter an engaging array of themes, conventions, points of view and settings spun into unique webs of intrigue and horror. You'll find meticulous homage to familiar monsters and a hearkening to classic authorial styles. There is an economy of modern language that keeps these stories from being weighted down by overwrought prose so associated with the historical Gothics. Instead these authors' terrors, real and imagined, cut straight to the bone.

While some stories dance that razor-thin line between pleasure and horror, between sanity and madness, others let the paranormal rule in spectacular displays, allowing for the great Gothic question of who is or isn't a reliable narrator. Still others keep alive a genre parallel to Steampunk and feature unique alternate technologies and innovative gadgets.

Quite often in the Gothic genre, the reader is thrust into knowing terrible realities before the characters; a device that makes the reader complicit in the unfolding horror. There is a fraught involvement, then, between audience and action. So does Dreadpunk in its Gothic heritage, draw the reader into the inevitable. One cannot, as is the case with many of our narrators in this volume, look away. The Gothic confides in you, dear reader, you are bound to its unfolding. So you shall be in these pages. Dreadpunk is an invitation into the inner recesses and you are magnetized to their depths.

Descend to the tracks. Open the door. The coffin. The letter. Crawl into the cave. Run. Hide. Confront. Acquiesce. Avenge. It is all inevitable. Enjoy this perilous, dark and stormy journey.

Leanna Renee Hieber

BURKE STREET STATION

BRYCE RAFFLE

THE CITY WAS FROST AND FOG. Icy crystals formed on the windows of the train station. Breath drifted up in hazy clouds like puffs of cigarette smoke as Theodore tried to warm his hands, blowing hot breath onto his stiff, cold fingers and rubbing his hands together vigorously. When that failed, he thrust them back into his coat pockets, cursing under his breath. His threadbare coat offered little warmth. Drafts of wind found their way through the broken stitching and the tears in his sleeves like rats scrambling through the cracks in the station walls. A discarded page of newsprint, caught in the rushing wind, tumbled and turned in the air and landed, crumpled and torn, at Theodore's feet.

He stooped over, picked it up, and glanced at the

engraving of a wanted man. Even without a skill for reading, he knew what name was printed beneath the picture of masked man on the page. Anthony Tidkins.

Wanted, he read. That was one word Theodore recognized. *Crimes* was another, and then, finally... *murder*.

Rubbish. The newspapers always tried to make villains out of the radical thinkers of the world. The Resurrectionists, who named their organization after the sack-em-up men who provided the anatomists with subjects for their scientific endeavors, were scientists. They had provided the world with *aether*, revolutionizing air travel. They had brought Prince Charles back from the brink of death. They had devised the engines for the London Underground. Anthony Tidkins himself promised to cure death. Yet the newspaper men still called for his blood. Theodore balled up the page and shoved it in his pocket.

He pulled out his trick coin as he approached the gate. The station master was asleep at his booth, a little dribble of spit running down his chin. Typical. Theodore stuck his coin in the machine, waited for the gate to open, and then, with a light tug on the fishing line threaded through a little hole in the tip of the coin, it popped back out. Easy. He was in before anybody noticed what he had done. He pocketed the coin and started down the hallway.

Tap-tap, clack, tap-tap, clack, his shoes beat a rhythm on the stone steps. The sole of his left shoe was beginning to wear, and the heel of his shoe tapped against the heel of his foot as he walked. He puffed on his hands again, and peeked over his shoulder. No one was after him. He had done this trick a thousand times before. So why did he feel like there was someone watching him?

Clack, tap-tap, clack. Again, he glanced over his shoulder. The odd double-rhythm of his broken shoe was suddenly unnerving in the deserted station. Where were all the other passengers? Nice folks avoided this place like the plague, especially after midnight. The oil lamps that lit Burke Street Station were so routinely out of oil that he could hardly find his own feet in front of him, but still, Theodore expected to see other passengers. But where were the other vagrants? They should be sleeping in the dark corners of the hallway under blankets made of rags. And the boys from the blacking factory should be heading home from their long shifts, fingers stained black with powders and oil. But there was no one. Only the rats skittering through rat tunnels to keep him company.

Tap-tap, clack, tap-tap, clack.

Another set of footsteps began to follow his own, beating out a different rhythm. A steady *tap, tap, tap, tap.* He paused to listen, and nothing but silence greeted him. He glanced over his shoulder. Nobody there.

He continued onward, and again, a second set of footsteps started up behind him. He paused to listen. This time, they didn't stop.

Tap, tap, tap, tap.

Whoever it was, they were getting closer. Closer and closer, louder and louder, tapping out a steady rhythm as they approached down the long, dark hallway. He could almost make out the solitary figure in the gloomy, hazy light, but then the fog grew thicker, and whatever he thought he'd seen was gone. The footsteps kept on getting louder, though, and closer. He turned and ran down the hallway.

A long flight of steps delved deeper into the darkness of Burke Street Station, down, down toward the platform. The train was already rumbling, announcing its approach. It vibrated through Theodore's toes to the tip of his spine, rattling his bones.

He grabbed the railing all but flew down the staircase. The rumble of the train grew louder and clearer.

"Shit," Theodore cursed. Taking the steps two at a time, he hurtled down the steps and didn't stop when he reached the bottom.

Nails on a blackboard. The tines of silverware scraping against a ceramic plate. The screaming madmen at Newgate Asylum. The anguished cry of a mother weeping over her stillborn babe. Theodore had heard these sounds all, but not one compared to the shrill screech of an automatic train rolling into Burke Street. Iron wheels grinding against iron tracks. Hot metal sending up sparks, belching out steam as black as sin. The carriages rattling and clanging against one another. The hiss of hot coal burning in the engines. The shriek of brakes as the train ground to a halt. If it went on long enough, it would surely drive a man mad. Theodore covered his ears with his hands, pressing them against his head to muffle out the deafening noise, and waited for the thundering train to come to a halt.

When it did, he realized it must have drowned out the sound of the steadily approaching footsteps he'd heard in the hallway, because he could hear them again, and they were closer. So close he half expected to feel someone's hot breath on his neck. He whirled around, but there was no one there. Silence greeted him like an old friend. His heart hammered against his chest.

"There's no one there," he muttered to himself. But he didn't sound convinced.

A smell lingered in the air, as if something foul had passed through. The smell was familiar enough, the breath of a man with rotting teeth. It was a foul, cloying stench. He spun around again, and this time found himself face to face with the man to whom those dreaded footsteps belonged.

Only he wasn't a man. Not really.

They found his body under a dusty alcove in a dark corner, as far from the tracks as it was possible to get without leaving the station entirely. No lamps lit this corner of the platform, but the boys were accustomed to the darkness. They could spot the trail of blood from a mile away, even in the gloom of Burke Street.

Thomas leaned over the body. "Is he..."

"Dead?" said Fish, the smaller of the two boys. Unlike Thomas, who was fat and dressed in layer upon layer of ragged clothes, Fish was skeleton-thin and shirtless. He wore nothing more than a dirty pair of trousers and an oversized pair of fish-eyed goggles that made his eyes look bigger than they were. His feet were bare and covered in a year's worth of grime. "Well, I don't fink 'e's gettin' up any time soon."

"S'pose not," said Thomas.

"Check 'is pockets," Fish urged.

Thomas shot Fish a dark look and scratched the top of his head. He looked down at the body, then back up at Fish. "Why don't you check 'em?"

Fish raised an eyebrow. "This ain't the first time you've seen a deader, is it?"

"No."

"Well then..."

"I don't like the look of 'im," said Thomas.

Fish wrinkled his nose. He didn't like the look of the dead man either, but curiosity urged him forward. "Bloody coward. I'll do it then."

His stomach twitched in complaint. He had seen bodies washed up on the banks of the Thames. He and Thomas had gone through their pockets and plied gold out of their teeth. Hell, his goggles weren't bought new. But none of the bodies they'd looted had looked quite like this. The deader's mouth was wrenched open as though he'd died in screaming terror. His face was ghastly pale and horror-stricken, his eyes were wide and white, unblinking. Grisly strips of meat hung from his shoulder blade where his arm had been. The flesh around the wound had turned black and hard, like a scab. "Let's see..."

He bent low over the body, took a deep breath, and peeked into the dead man's coat pockets. There was something sticking out of them. A piece of paper. Just as he was about to reach out and grab it, a hand clamped down on his ankle. He screamed and pulled away.

Thomas howled with laughter. It was his hand on Fish's leg.

Fish punched the bigger boy in the shoulder, scowling. "Bastard."

"Shoulda seen your face!" Thomas howled.

"Idiot." He turned back to the corpse and grabbed the piece of paper from the coat pocket. "Shit, Tom. Look at this."

He passed the crumpled newspaper clipping to Thomas, whose laughter died immediately, the last few notes of his barking laugh echoing against the stone walls as though he was laughing at himself.

"Anthony Tidkins," he said.

"The Resurrection Man," said Fish.

"You think that's who killed 'im?" asked Thomas.

Fish tightened the straps on his goggles. His eyes refracted inside their bug-eyed lenses, making his every blink look like the shutter of a camera. "Who else?"

A look passed between the two boys, the sort of look that could only be shared between those who had seen enough death to know the gravity of it and be impressed by its finality. There was no childlike wonder in their eyes as they considered the corpse at their feet, no boyish delight in the macabre spectacle set before them, only the grim reality of maggots spawning in a dead man's mouth.

These boys slept in underground places. They lived in the dark corners of Burke Street Station and beneath the bridges along the Thames, deprived of sleep by the fiendish things that prowled the night. Worse than the disease-ridden rats crawling upon their bodies as they slept, worse than the drunkards stumbling over them as they made their way home from the brothels and the public houses late at night, worse than the clanging and rattling of the automatic trains arriving at the station like clockwork, were the stories whispered by the boys who slept in such places.

"When the Resurrection Men get you, you don't come back," said Thomas.

It was a phrase they'd heard whispered before, but until now they'd thought nothing more of it than the stories of ghosts and vampires lurking in alleyways, stories meant only to frighten them. Now, as they looked down upon the corpse at their feet, they had to wonder if the stories were real. Had the Resurrectionists gotten him, or was there something else lurking in the tunnels built for the automatic trains?

Fish stood, bouncing on the balls of his bare feet with nervous energy. There was a trail of blood on the platform that led down toward the tracks.

Whatever had killed the young man, the trail it had left behind could not be clearer. "I guess we go that way," he said, pointing into the darkness.

"I guess so," Thomas agreed. But he didn't sound convinced.

It was hours after the young man's death that Scotland Yard arrived at Burke Street Station with their oil lamps, and later still that the detective inspector determined that if he were to solve this case, he would need to call upon his old friend, Sir Roderick Steen. That was unfortunate. Sir Roderick was nothing if not a braggart, determined to rub the detective's nose in his own shortcomings while flaunting his intellect like a peacock touting his bright plumage. That said, the man did have an uncanny nose for sniffing out clues, and a particular expertise when it came to the Resurrectionists. This murder had Anthony Tidkins' scent all over it.

Sir Roderick sniffed and looked away. Dragging his Yorkshire Terrier along by his leash, he walked swiftly in the opposite direction. "I truly don't know why you've summoned me here, Detective, if not simply to ruin my breakfast," he complained. "Come, Bailey." The dog sniffed, as if in agreement, his ears perking up.

"Well, isn't it obvious?" said Taggert, pursuing the artist as he walked away. "This is clearly the work of Anthony Tidkins and his ilk."

Sir Roderick snorted. "Certainly not." He looked

at the body out of the corner of his eye. "Looks more like he ran into a pack of rabid dogs. Tidkins is more clinical, in my experience. This lacks the surgical precision of Tidkins."

"Then what about one of his accomplices? Mr. Hyde, perhaps?"

Sir Roderick gave pause to run his violet-colored glove along his chin. "Yes, I suppose Hyde could have done it," he said, "though I find it unlikely."

"Won't you at least look at the body?" Taggert chewed on his mustache.

"I've seen quite enough," said Sir Roderick. Bailey let out a whimper, tongue hanging out of his mouth. Sir Roderick sniffed and turned back to the inspector. "Very well, if you promise me that's the last you'll say about it, I'll take another look. Oh, and do stop that dreadful habit. You're turning your wonderful mustache yellow. Come, Bailey."

The Yorkshire terrier wagged his tail and followed at Sir Roderick's heel. He kept his nose to the ground, sniffing as he walked. Sir Roderick crossed the platform and stooped over the body.

Taggert stood, frowning, over the artist's shoulder as he conducted a swift examination. It took an incredible amount of effort not to chew his mustache, but he'd had just about enough ridicule from Sir Roderick for one day. He resisted.

The corpse was a gruesome mess of ravaged flesh, the rotting meat beginning to attract flies.

"He was just found this morning, you say? He

must have died well before that, given the advanced state of rot."

"You think he was killed elsewhere?" said Taggert, twisting his mustache with his fingers now.

"Must have been." Sir Roderick looked up. "Did you find his arm?"

"No," Taggert replied. "Why? Do you think it's important?"

"Perhaps," said the artist, pinching his nose as he gazed at the body. "Perhaps."

Taggert snorted. "Well, that's helpful."

Ignoring him, Sir Roderick returned his attention to the cadaver before him. Taggert watched as the artist poked and prodded the man's neck, inspected his fingernails, rooted inside his pockets, and even pried his jaw open in order to inspect the inside of his mouth. Next, Sir Roderick pulled back the young man's coat and peeled off his shirt. It made a sound like wallpaper being stripped from a wall, as a thick layer of blood and skin tore away, clinging to the shirt like glue. What remained of his arm was black and grey, with hues of green and violet, like an infected wound.

"He was eighteen or nineteen years of age. He had blue eyes, blonde hair."

"Brown, I would have said," said Taggert.

"You would have been wrong."

Taggert frowned. A few minutes in Sir Roderick's presence and that had become his default expression.

"His head has been darkened by soot, but there are patches where his natural color shows through.

This young lad was a chimney sweep. Not a terribly elegant job, nor one that pays well, but he was not entirely unemployed as I would have guessed. He was terribly malnourished. If whatever killed him last night hadn't done so, I'm afraid he'd not have been long for this world anyway."

Sir Roderick stood, and Taggert met his eyes. "So what do you think *did* kill him?" he dared ask.

"I've no idea," Sir Roderick answered plainly. "But..."

And there it was. The bastard had discovered something else, some hidden clue he'd spotted, some hidden knowledge to keep for himself, like an older brother keeping a favorite toy just out of his little brother's grasp. The worst thing was that it was always something *obvious*, something Taggert *should* have spotted on his own.

"...perhaps we should follow the trail of blood."

"Yes," said Taggert with a sigh. "Perhaps we should."

Down in the deep dark of Burke Street Station's railroad tunnels, Fish reached up to adjust the bulbous lenses of his goggles. There was a dial on the side of each lens with only two settings, marked *D* and *N*. He switched each lens to *N* as he delved deeper into the underground, and his vision took on an absinthe-colored hue, while the evanescent shadows resolved into shapes. The red orbs blinking in the dark corners of the tunnel became the eyes of rats, skittering out of their holes. The ground took shape beneath his feet, and the railroad tracks stretched out into the distance.

"There," he said, bending down to point a finger at a spot on the ground.

"I don't see nuffin'," said Thomas. "Can't see a bloody thing down 'ere."

"It's blood," said Fish. "Lots of it."

Thomas looked strange through the green lenses of his goggles, pale and ghostly. There was a look in his eyes that unsettled Fish.

"Let's go," he said, hurrying down the tracks. "We don't want to be down these tracks when the trains start rolling into station."

He started off and listened for Thomas's footsteps to join his own. After a minute, he realized his friend still wasn't following. He stopped and turned around. "Let's go, what are you—"

He broke off. Thomas was right where he'd left him, but he was frozen, statue-still, his gaze fixed in place. Fish sighed as he started back. "Blood coward," he complained, marching back toward Thomas.

As he approached, it soon became clear that his friend had seen something. Whatever it was, it had unsettled him. He was muttering under his breath, repeating the same words over and over. Fish couldn't quite make out what it was, but he cupped his hand around his ear and put his ear close to Thomas's lips.

"Don't let him get me. Don't let him get me. Don't let him get me..."

"Don't let who get you, Tom?" said Fish.

Thomas broke off from his muttering and looked away from the spot on the wall he was staring at. "Fish?" he said, as if seeing him for the first time.

"What is it? What did you see?"

Thomas grasped Fish by the shoulders. "Whatever killed the man in the station," he said, shaking him roughly as he spoke.

"Anthony Tidkins?" said Fish.

"No. Something else," said Thomas, his eyes wild, unfocused.

His nails dug into Fish's shoulders, cutting into his skin. Fish's teeth rattled, as Thomas shook him like a rag doll until the goggles came loose from his head and clattered on the ground. The world went dark.

Endless blackness surrounded Fish.

"Don't let him get me," Thomas whispered. Though he still had a tight hold on Fish's shoulders, Fish couldn't actually see him. He couldn't see a thing.

Something growled in the darkness, low and snarling, like a rabid dog. There was something else with them in the tunnel. Something foul, like meat gone bad. It was close. Footsteps on the dirt floor preceded the clang of hard leather shoes on the metal railroad tracks. Then searing pain as Thomas's nails raked his shoulders, grasping for purchase as he was dragged away.

"Don't let him get me!" Thomas screamed.

"Thomas!" Fish reached out toward the sound,

but he was grasping at air. His friend was gone, as quick as that, dragged off into the shadows. "Thomas? Where are you?"

He was met with silence. He bent down, reaching around in the dark for his goggles. Instead, he managed to grab on to Thomas's hand. It had gone cold, his fingers stiff.

"Get up, Tom," he said, lifting his friend by the hand. It came up too easily, like reeling in a fishing line when the fish has escaped the lure. There wasn't enough weight attached to Thomas's hand. "Bloody hell!"

He let go and scrambled back, feeling as if he might vomit. It wasn't Thomas's hand. It was a severed arm. Probably belonged to the man they'd found in the station. "Shit," Fish swore, pacing animatedly, his hands shaking with unbridled energy. Every bone in his body was screaming at him to run, just run, but he couldn't go anywhere if he couldn't see.

It took him a minute before he could try again, groping along the pitch black ground one inch at a time. When he finally found them, he discovered that the glass had cracked in the fall. He put them on anyway, and found he could see again. There, lying on the tracks, was the bloody arm, grey and necrotic, half-eaten by rats and god knew what else. And there was something lodged in the arm that looked an awful lot like a tooth. A human tooth.

Of Thomas, there was no sign. Fish was alone. Then again, not quite. He heard a noise behind him and started off again.

☠

The amber light of Detective Inspector Taggert's kerosene lantern did strange things to the fog that had followed him into the station from the streets above. The darkness was so thick that even the lantern's light couldn't push its way through it, but got caught up in the fog like a moth in a spider's web. Taggert, therefore, had only the dimmest impression of train tracks beneath his feet, and a trail of blood along the floor, glimpsed only through the passing wispy clouds of fog.

The fog moved quickly; the underground passageway's design was that of a wind tunnel. Whatever scientific phenomena caused it Taggert could hardly hope to explain, but he wrapped his coat more tightly around his neck, and paused for a moment to hold his hat steady on his head.

Sound traveled oddly in the tunnel, too. Distant wind from some place down the tracks sounded like the baying of a wolf. Falling rocks sounded like gunfire. For a moment, Taggert thought he heard the sound of moving water, almost like rushing rapids. There were subterranean rivers running through this city, rivers known to the ancient Romans but forgotten in time, and sewer tunnels running parallel to the trains. But that wasn't the sound. No, it was something else. Moving more quickly than white water, and without the gurgling, burbling quality of liquid. It had a more mechanical quality to it. A low rumble building in amplitude and pitch. And beneath that, an awful screech like...

A train on the tracks!

"Bloody hell!" Taggert cursed.

Lantern swinging, Taggert started to run. He didn't know if he was running toward the train or away from it, but he knew one thing for certain. He needed to get off the tracks before he ran into it. "Shit, shit, shit!" he shouted as he ran.

Steen was supposed to have talked to the station manager, convinced him to halt the trains on account of police business. Clearly he had failed to do that. He cast a glance over his shoulder as he ran. He could have sworn he saw two beady eyes, gleaming in the darkness, staring right at him, like the distant lights of a train bearing down upon him.

Taggert wasn't built for running, but he tore down the tracks like the hounds of hell were on his heels, dirt and dust flying as he raced down the tunnel.

The sound of the train became clearer. It couldn't have been more than a hundred yards away, and it was getting closer by the second. Ninety yards, Taggert guessed, then eighty. Bloody automatic trains moved fast. Seventy yards turned into sixty, and there was still no sign of escape. He needed to find a service tunnel, or to reach the next station, something, anything to get him off the tracks.

The train was surely no more than fifty yards away now, barreling toward him, screeching and clanging, a hundred tons of iron and steel, with no conductor to pull the brakes even if he spotted Taggert before it was too late. Forty yards, and no sign of escape. His lungs were about ready to collapse, breathing in stale air and dust, but he pushed himself to keep running. How far was it now, thirty yards? Twenty?

He risked a glance over his shoulder, and then stumbled to a sudden halt. There was no train. What the hell? He could still hear it rushing toward him. Was it merely the acoustics playing tricks on him? Bloody hell, he'd *seen* the lights in the distance. They'd looked like eyes, but they *had* to have been the train's lanterns.

He took a moment to catch his breath, but he knew he had to keep moving. Even if the train wasn't as close as he'd thought, it would eventually catch up with him, and he didn't want to be on the tracks when it did.

He cast his lantern about, still in pursuit of a side tunnel, a door, some sort of passageway that didn't include train tracks. He was so intent on finding a means of escape that he almost missed it entirely. Almost. But not quite.

He moved the lantern over to where he'd seen it, stooped over to get a closer look, and his mouth fell open. "Bloody hell," he muttered.

It was an arm, detached from the body, and here, the trail of blood ended. There was a human tooth lodged in it, as though someone had actually been eating it. He put a hand on his stomach and willed himself not to vomit, but bile rose to his throat, and he spat onto the tracks.

"What kind of animal..." he said, his speech trailing off. He could feel someone watching him, looking at him. He spun, swinging the lantern, hoping to catch them off guard. "Who's down here?"

Whoever it was, they scrambled deeper into the darkness. A pile of rocks fell away, the noise echoing eerily in the tunnel. And as the rumble of the train faded into the distance, he could hear their grunts and groans of effort as they scrambled over a mound of rocks.

"Who goes there?" Taggert shouted. No response. He wiped the sweat from his eyes. His lungs were aching, but he started running again.

Rats scattered, out of his way, as he raced toward his quarry. There was no sign of any person or creature, but as he scrambled over the mound of rocks he'd heard them climbing over earlier, his lantern fell upon something of interest. A door, open just a crack, still swinging on its hinges as though used only a moment or two earlier. He pushed it open and stepped through the doorway.

Fish pushed open the door and stepped inside the room. "Tom," he called, half-whispering, half-shouting. Through the cracked lenses of his goggles, he surveyed the room, terrified of what he might discover. Thomas's arm ripped from his body like the other victim? The Resurrection Man himself, Anthony Tidkins, masked like a plague doctor, mouth dripping with blood and cheeks filled with human flesh? But no, the room was deserted.

The room was filled end to end with copper pipes, valves, and wheels. An enormous furnace took up one end of the room, alight with the orange with the fiery glow of burning coals. Fish wiped sweat from his forehead and ducked beneath an iron pipe that ran from wall to wall a few inches beneath the low ceiling. He stepped over a row of pipes jutting out of the floor, his eyes darting back and forth as he whispered Thomas's name. He wanted to find his friend, but he didn't want to gain the attention of whoever else that might be down here.

"Thomas?" he said, spinning back toward the door.

For a moment, he thought he'd unwittingly pressed some lever or valve, as the very floor began to vibrate and dust fell from the ceiling, but he'd slept beneath the streets long enough to recognize is as an approaching train. He crept deeper into the room, which bent around a corner, giving way to what must have been a storage room. It was cluttered with stacks of dusty boxes and shelves lined with mildewing books. He rounded the corner and had to shove one of the boxes out of his way to get into the room. Blood smeared along the floor as he pushed the box aside. It was fresh. He looked up in alarm. Thomas must have come this way.

"Tom?" he called.

There was a blur of movement, the outline of a figure behind a stack of boxes. Something fell to the floor, echoing like the blast of a shotgun in the confined space. Fish crept closer.

"Is that you?"

He headed toward the source of the noise, toward the figure in the dark, his neck itching as he eyed the blood on the floor. If it was Tom, why wasn't he answering? Was he too badly hurt to call out a response? Fish hurried forward, knocking over another box filled with old books, and stepped over the resulting pile of fallen, tattered pages. From behind the stack of boxes, where he'd seen the figure moving in the darkness, a pair of eyes stared back at him.

"Tom?" he said, rounding the corner.

It wasn't Thomas. Lips lined with blood, flesh falling away from his cheeks, eyes white with cataracts, a dead man stared back at him. Bones exposed through gaping holes in his rotting flesh, skin blackened and necrotic like the corpse in the station, the man who stood before him looked like he'd dragged himself out of a grave. There was no question that he was dead, but he was moving about as though he hadn't figured that out just yet. The dead man swallowed whatever it was eating and made a sound in his throat like the low growl of a feral dog. He reached down, picked out another piece of red, raw meat, and shoved it in his rotting jaws.

Unable to move, his breath coming quicker and quicker, Fish could scarcely tear his eyes away from the dead man's awful visage, but he finally managed to look down at whatever the corpse was feasting on.

His eyes widened. He tasted bile.

Thomas's eyes, wide and frozen in an expression of horror, stared off into space. His familiar face was mutilated, the jaw chewed clean off and spattered with blood. His head was not attached to his body, and the dead man was scooping meat out of

Thomas's upturned skull, as though scraping soup from a bowl.

Fish covered his mouth and tried not to vomit or scream. He stepped back slowly, cautiously...right into a heavy wooden box. He landed on his back with a wheeze. Thomas's head hit the floor with a sound like a wet pumpkin dropped on cement. He scrambled back, grasping at the walls in a clumsy attempt to get back on his feet.

Hissing and biting as it shambled toward him, the dead man outstretched a rotting hand and made as if to grab him. He ducked, and the creature's fingers grazed his hair. He shook free, wriggling uncomfortably as he pushed himself back to his feet.

Then he just ran. He darted across the room in a flurry of movement, leaping over and ducking under the pipes that crisscrossed the room without slowing down. The door swung open. He was too bent on getting away to even stop and question what that meant. He just flung himself at it. Escape. Run. That's all he could think of. Escape. Run.

Run!

A pair of hands clamped down on his shoulders, seizing him so hard he couldn't move.

"Calm yourself, son!" said Detective Inspector Taggert, seizing the poor boy by the shoulders and holding him still. "Steady, lad, steady."

The boy, dirty, bare-chested and barefoot, thin as a skeleton, was a fighter. He kicked, scratched, and even tried to bite Taggert, but the policeman held fast.

"Easy now!" Taggert shouted when the boy stomped on his foot. "I'm not going to hurt you! I am Detective Inspector Taggert, with Scotland Yard. Whatever's got you so worked up, you don't have to worry about that any more, son. I've got you."

He met Taggert's eyes, his own bulbous and round through the fish-eyed lenses of his goggles. His breathing slowed. "It's still in here," the boy whispered.

"What is?" Taggert peered over the lad's shoulder, but he saw nothing. The room was silent but for the rumble of the train.

"The deader, sir," said Fish.

Taggert blinked. *Deader?* "Where?"

The boy pointed a finger. Still, Taggert couldn't see a thing.

"Stay here. I'm going to go take a look."

"If it's all the same with you, sir," said the boy, his breath still rushed and ragged, "I'd rather not be left alone down here."

Taggert shrugged. "Suit yourself. Just stay behind me, and don't make a sound, lad."

The boy nodded, and Taggert headed into the room. Ducking low beneath the pipes threaded through the ceiling, and stepping over those jutting out of the floor, he slowly made his way forward. Whoever was down here, they were likely responsible for the death and dismemberment of the young man in the station.

He drew his billy club. He felt hot air on his neck and swung.

The club clanged against an iron pipe, the sound ringing out like a gong. Steam hissed out of the pipe. Taggert's breathing slowed. Just the piping. He crept forward. There was something scuttling around in the dark. He swung his lantern toward it. There was someone there, a figure in the darkness, dressed in rags.

"Stop!" cried Taggert, wielding his baton, "Scotland Yard!"

A pair of eyes looked up at him in the dark, and it took all his wits not to stumble back. There was something strange about his eyes. They were white and pale like the eyes of a ghost. Something about his skin, too. It was rough and raw as if it were actually rotting away. He must have had some condition, leprosy or something of the like. The man—the *deader,* as the boy called him— growled at him, like an untamed beast, and darted across the room.

"Stop right there!" Taggert called, and started after him. "Bloody hell," he grumbled.

Leaping over the protruding pipes, he cleared the room in half a moment's time, but the creature was already gone. "Which way did he—"

"That way!" said the boy, pointing a finger.

Taggert turned just in time to catch a blur of movement as the deader headed out the door through which they'd entered the room.

"I can't let him get away," said Taggert. He sprinted toward the door with the vagrant boy at his heels. He bounded out the door, onto the tracks. A blazing white pair of eyes rapidly approached from the distance. This time Taggert was certain of what they were.

"Train!" he shouted.

The creature was still on the tracks, with the automatic train barreling down the tracks toward him and nowhere to run. Grabbing the boy by the hand, Taggert stepped back through the doorway, and pulled the lad inside. Not a moment later, the train whipped past them, ripping the hat from Taggert's head. The boy tightened his grip on Taggert's hand, so tightly his nails dug into his palm.

It rumbled past, iron screeching along the rails. When the last carriage finally passed them, the boy loosened his grip on Taggert's hand. He patted the boy's head, stooped down to pick up his hat, and stood. "Come, lad, let's go and see what became of our *deader*."

"It would have been a comfort to have seen the body, mangled and dismembered though it would have been, given the atrocities he had committed." Taggert raised a steaming hot cup of tea and blew on it before drinking. They had chosen the Pickwick Club, which was popular amongst the men of Scotland Yard, and settled into a table near the back so as to enjoy some modicum of privacy, though Taggert could practically feel the eyes of the other gentlemen upon him as he described what he had seen in the underground tunnel.

"It *would have been?*" Sir Roderick Steen repeated. The artist was seated across from him. "What do you mean?"

"Only that there was no body," said Taggert. "I am half convinced that the man truly was a *deader*, a phantom, impervious to the dangers of the living world, unable to be struck by a locomotive—or a policeman with a billy club. Of course, deep down I know that's impossible. I suppose he must have found some crevice or cranny, flattened himself against the wall of the tunnel as the train roared past, or something of that nature."

"And what of the urchin boy?" asked Sir Roderick.

"I thought it fitting to let him go," Taggert answered. "After all, he obviously had nothing to do with it, wouldn't you agree?"

"I would," said Sir Roderick, spooning yet another lump of sugar into his tea and stirring it vigorously. "You were right, by the way..."

"I was?" said Taggert, and then, catching himself, added, "I mean...or rather...yes, of course, I was."

Again, he blew on his tea to cool it down. He set the cup on the table. Still too hot. As he stared into the swirling steam from his cup, he began to feel that he was missing something, like he was the butt of some joke he didn't quite grasp. He reached for his cup of tea. "Sorry. Right about what?"

"The involvement of Resurrectionists," said Sir Roderick.

Taggert spat out his tea. "Bloody hell, that's hot!" he cursed. He reached for his napkin, face red. "And no, surely I was wrong about *that*. The Resurrectionists are men of science—albeit a morally corrupt sort of science—not cannibals. We have reason to believe that Anthony Tidkins has committed unspeakable acts of murder, but nothing to suggest he actually eats the flesh of his victims. Not that I don't consider him capable of it, but it's not his style, is it? What was it you said earlier? That the killing lacked *surgical precision*? This was more like an animal attack than a scientific experiment."

Sir Roderick reached for the sugar, took another spoonful, and stirred it into his cup. "You're *certain* the poor lad's head had been chewed upon? And that there was a human tooth lodged in the arm of the other young man?"

"Undoubtedly. We were unable to locate the arm, but I had the remains of the bodies taken to the morgue, where the chief medical examiner agreed with my assessment that the bodies had both been *chewed* upon." He paused, feeling the eyes of the gentlemen at the adjacent table upon him. Even the paintings on the wall seemed to be staring at him. He lowered his voice to a whisper. "The poor boy I met in the service station was scared half to death."

Sir Roderick leaned forward, lowering his voice as well. "You say this boy claimed the culprit was a dead man."

"Yes," said Taggert. "A *deader*, risen from the grave to commit gross acts of violence."

"Isn't that exactly the sort of scientific pursuit our own villain, Anthony Tidkins, might attempt?"

"You don't mean—" Taggert began.

"Yes," said Sir Roderick. "The man who killed the young man at Burke Street Station, and the boy in the tunnel, was himself a victim. The victim of one of Anthony Tidkins' vile experiments. Brought back from the dead by the Resurrection Man, an act so heinous, so juxtaposed to the laws that govern life and death, that the results could be nothing but an *abomination*. The cannibalism and the violence, then, are to be expected."

Taggert spluttered. "You must know how absurd that sounds, Sir Roderick."

"I do," said Sir Roderick, "but then, so does the idea of a man impervious to a collision with a train." He sipped his tea, signaling to the waiter and calling for another bowl of sugar to be brought to the table.

The waiter bustled over, not with the sugar, but with a note in his hand. "This just came in, sir," he said, "straight from Scotland Yard."

He set the note down on the table in front of the detective. Taggert shared a look with Sir Roderick before picking it up and reading it. A dark expression must have crossed his face then, for it caused Sir Roderick to lean across the table, nearly spilling his tea. "What does it say?"

Taggert had to read the note once more to be certain of what he'd just read before he could answer. "It says that one of the bodies in the morgue, that of the young man whose arm was ripped off, has disappeared."

Sir Roderick's eyes widened. He adjusted his cravat and fell silent for a moment. The waiter came, set a fresh bowl of sugar upon the table, and left, before Sir Roderick said another word. "Disappeared?" he repeated.

Taggert nodded. "As though he simply got up and walked away. But that's impossible, isn't it? A dead man doesn't just get up and walk away. It's just not possible," he said.

But he didn't sound convinced.

A Specter in the Light

David Lee Summers

THE LIGHT IN MY OFFICE GREW FAINT as I graded geology term papers late one afternoon. I debated between lighting the lamps and simply going home for the night—possibly with a stop at the Capitol Saloon—when something banged on the ceiling, startling me. I shook my head and smiled when I realized the new physics professor, Mr. Jones, was working late on one of his experiments. I decided to go upstairs and see whether Mr. Jones wanted to go to the Capitol with me.

I gathered up the term papers—not many as there were only eight students at our fledgling New Mexico School of Mines—and locked them in the desk drawer. Grabbing my coat, I went upstairs. I knew very little about Mr. Ike Jones other than the fact he specialized in electricity. Dr. Davis, the college president, had hired him away from the coal mines at Madrid to teach physics and electrical engineering. I found Ike Jones in his office connecting a wire to a contraption he had been building. The contraption consisted of two cylinders of wire nested one within the other. To the side of the cylinders were mounted two wheels with magnets. One of those wheels had a hand crank so one set of magnets could rotate within the other.

"Can I light a lamp for you?" I offered, unsure whether or not Mr. Jones could see well enough to accomplish his task.

"No thanks, Mr. Delay," said Jones, with a smile. "I'm just about finished."

"Please, call me Ted," I offered.

"Thanks, Ted. Call me Ike." He retrieved a glass tube from a cabinet next to the desk.

"I just came up to see if I could buy you a drink. We haven't had much of a chance to talk since you hired on a couple of weeks ago."

"I'd like that," he said. "But let's take just a moment and see if this works, shall we?" Ike handed me the glass tube.

"What is it?" I asked.

Instead of answering, he spun the hand crank. There was a buzzing and sparking from wire-wrapped cylinders and I almost dropped the glass tube.

"Steady on," he warned and I gripped the tube

more tightly. I nearly dropped it again when it began to glow. "Aha! It works!"

"It does indeed," I said, impressed. "I'd heard that people were working on electric light, but to actually see it..." I shook my head and handed the glass tube back to Ike. "How does it work?"

"The glass tube is filled with argon gas. The wire-wrapped cylinders are a type of generator devised by a fellow named Nikola Tesla about five years ago. The electricity from the generator excites the gas in the tube creating the light. One generator powered by a simple steam engine could light hundreds of these gas tubes."

I nodded. "That would be great for mining. You don't need wires to bring electricity to the tubes?"

"No. The electricity travels right through the atmosphere." He smiled again and grabbed his coat from the rack. "Still want to buy me that drink?"

"More than ever," I said. "You deserve it!"

"Good, I want to demonstrate this to Dr. Davis sometime this week. I'd like to pick your brain about some of the caves and mines in the area—I want a place for a suitably impressive demonstration."

"I think I can help you find a good cave," I said.

With that, he patted me on the arm and we went back downstairs.

That night, amidst the smoke and noise of the Capitol Saloon, I told Ike about a cave I'd discovered in nearby Socorro Peak. "It's deep enough that you can get fully out of the light of day, but close enough you don't even have to ride. We could walk up if you had a mind to."

Ike nodded, then took a swallow of his beer. He wiped the foam from his mustache. "Can I get a hand on Sunday? I'd like to take the Tesla generator to the cave and test it out."

"Sure thing." I lifted my glass. "Here's to success. God knows the school needs it."

His brow furrowed, but he lifted his glass anyway. "So, why does the school need a success?"

"I thought you knew." When Ike shook his head, I explained: "Dr. Davis has been under a lot of pressure to close the school and move our departments down to New Mexico A&M in Las Cruces. A lot of powerful folks wonder why New Mexico Territory needs two land grant colleges. The fact that we only have eight students doesn't help matters any. Even Elfego Baca, Socorro's most famous lawman, has voiced his reservations."

"Ah." Ike's face brightened in apparent under-standing. "So, if we come up with something that innovates mining, Dr. Davis will have an easier time keeping the school open."

"That about sums it up," I said.

"Then here's to success." He raised his glass again.

That Sunday, after church, I arrived at the school to find a small wagon hitched to a horse out front. I let myself into the building and went upstairs.

There, tall, skinny Ike tried to lift the generator all by himself.

"Be careful," I said. "You'll hurt yourself."

He surprised me by lifting the coils and taking a couple of steps my direction. I took some of the weight and helped him carry the generator downstairs.

"You're stronger than you look," I commented as we loaded the generator onto the wagon.

"I've been working as a mining engineer my whole life." He shrugged.

"So, what made you come to a mining college?"

"I thought it might be a little quieter life here in Socorro than in the mining camps. Maybe it'd give me a chance to settle down—get married—have a normal life." He pulled out a handkerchief and wiped his brow. "Of course, if the school closes after this year, I may be back in the camps."

I nodded sympathetically. Not knowing what else to say, I darted back inside to grab helmets and carbide lanterns while Ike grabbed the light tube. We rode in silence to the base of Socorro Peak and I directed Ike to the cave I'd discovered. We unloaded the generator, then I lit the carbide lanterns. I led Ike into the cave and we looked around.

"This is a surprisingly large network of caves," commented Ike.

A ways in, we found a place where the cave widened. "This looks like a good spot for your demonstration," I said.

He nodded. "Let's go get the equipment, then run a quick test."

Half an hour later, we had everything set up. He had me turn the crank on the generator while he held the tube. As before, the tube glowed with an eerie light. Reaching to his helmet, he turned the valve on his carbide lantern, shutting off the light.

"Do you think that's a good idea, Ike?"

"As long as you keep turning the crank on the generator," he said with a wry grin. He looked around. "I'm going to see what's down there." He pointed at a tunnel that led away from the entrance.

"Just don't go too far," I said. "I don't know how long I can keep cranking."

"Don't worry, I'll be right back." With that, he stepped down the tunnel and out of sight.

I don't know how long I sat there cranking that generator. I just know it felt like an awfully long time. Other than the squeak and whir of the rotating magnets and an occasional pop and crackle of sparks from the coil, it was utterly quiet there in the cave.

A long, low moan issued from somewhere deep within one of the tunnels.

Without thinking, my cranking slowed. "Ike, is that you?" My voice was little more than a whisper.

The moan sounded again.

I stopped cranking.

"Ted!"

When I heard Ike's voice, I realized I'd shut off his only source of illumination. I fumbled around for the hand crank. Finally, my sweating palms latched on and I began turning it again. A few moments later, I saw a spectral glow from the tunnel Ike had disappeared into. When Ike appeared shortly after, holding his tube, I released a breath I didn't even know I was holding.

"Is there some kind of animal down there?" Ike set the glass tube down behind some rocks.

"Not that I know of," I said, still turning the crank. "But, I suppose there could be."

He shrugged, then relit his carbide lantern.

"Sorry about letting go of the crank earlier," I apologized once Ike had the helmet back on his head.

"Don't mention it." He grinned. "Just don't stop during the demonstration tomorrow."

With both of our helmet lights on, I stopped cranking. "You bet." I stood and we returned to the entrance. Just as we stepped into the daylight, I thought I heard another moan from the depths of the cave.

The next day, I met Ike back at the cave. Shortly afterward, Dr. Davis and two students—both of whom had worked in mines up by Raton—joined us. Dr. Davis wore a hopeful expression made somewhat dower by his drooping, gray moustache. I was surprised to see Ike packing six-guns. I supposed he was concerned about the moaning we'd heard in the mine the day before. We lit our carbide lanterns and entered the cave.

We located the generator and Ike retrieved the argon-filled glass tube. He looked up and smiled. "Though this is hardly my invention, I believe this application of Mr. Tesla's generator and light will revolutionize mining. I hope you agree. Ted, take your position by the crank. Gentlemen, douse your helmet lights."

Dr. Davis looked doubtful for a moment, then complied. Once the darkness engulfed us, I began turning the crank. As before, the tube began to glow eerily. However as the light level came up, the hair on the back of my neck stood on edge.

There was a sixth person with us in the cave.

But, he wasn't really a person, exactly. He was more like a specter or a wraith dressed in armor like the Spanish conquistadors used to wear, with a metal breastplate and crested helm. His face was ghostly white with sunken cheeks. The remains of a mustache and goatee clung desperately to paper-like skin, reminding me of moss clinging to a tree.

I gasped and to my shame, I let go of the crank.

Someone screamed out. Another man yelled, "Ted!" I wasn't sure if it was Ike, Dr. Davis or both, but I fumbled in the darkness for the crank. Finding it, I resumed spinning. As the light level rose, we realized that the spectral conquistador was gone, along with one of the students.

"Charlie, take over the crank," Ike called to the other student. "Ted, come with me."

Dr. Davis lit his carbide lantern. "I'm coming with you," he said.

"No," said Ike. "I'm the one who's armed. Sir, you should get back to the school and get some dynamite. If we're not out in an hour, blow up the entrance so that creature won't get loose."

Dr. Davis, looking like he wanted to argue, bit his lip. After a moment he nodded and retreated toward the cave entrance. Once he was gone, Ike looked at Charlie. "Whatever you do, keep that crank going."

Charlie nodded. Ike handed me the glass tube and drew one of his six-guns. Looking at the dust on the cave floor, Ike pointed to a set of footprints and heel marks showing the path the specter had taken. We followed.

"What was that thing?" I asked.

Ike took a deep breath. "When the conquistadors came up El Camino Real, they must have used this cave to bury their dead. The generator must have reanimated one of the corpses—something like Mrs. Shelley described in her book, *Frankenstein*."

"Is that even possible?" I asked.

"If I hadn't seen it for myself, I would have dismissed it as fantasy," said Ike.

We were interrupted by another scream. We stepped up our pace.

Turning a corner we saw the specter bent over the student—Jasper—as though he was going to bite him. Jasper let out a noise that was little more than a pitiful squawk.

Ike raised his six-gun and fired. He missed the specter. Actually, I'm not really sure he tried to hit it, but the creature dropped Jasper and rushed at

Ike, who just had time to cock the hammer and fire again. This time the shot caught the creature in the eye, whirling it around. It toppled over and landed on the cave floor, raising a cloud of fine dust.

Ike helped Jasper stand. Meanwhile, I held the tube over the specter. There was no blood from the gunshot wound—just a fine spray of brown dust, marking the bullet's path as it exited the body. I felt that were I to touch the specter, it would simply crumble to dust.

"Ted, let's get out of here before Charlie's arm gets tired," said Ike.

"Or Dr. Davis seals us in for good," I agreed.

Working our way back through the cave, we collected Charlie and emerged into the light of day where we saw Dr. Davis looking at his pocket watch and tapping his foot.

"It's over," said Ike. "The thing's dead."

Two days later, Dr. Davis called Ike and me to a meeting in his office. "Mr. Delay, Mr. Jones," he began formally and I knew the news wasn't good. "I'm afraid the budget for next year isn't looking good. If I don't take steps now, the school will have to close next year, especially given the mounting political pressure."

Ike and I looked at each other and nodded, then looked back at Dr. Davis.

"Unfortunately, this means that I'm going to have to let one of you go now so I can show the SOBs in

Santa Fe that I'm taking steps to improve the budget situation. Also, unfortunately, word of the incident with the revenant or the specter or whatever you want to call it has spread like wildfire among the students."

"And you're afraid that might have further repercussions in Santa Fe," said Ike without malice. "Because of that, I'm the one to go."

Dr. Davis nodded.

"Can I go up and retrieve my Tesla generator from the cave?" asked Ike.

Again, Dr. Davis nodded. "Be careful," he said, with genuine concern in his voice.

"That goes without saying." Ike turned to me. "Care to give me a hand after the meeting?"

"Wouldn't miss it," I said.

In the end, Dr. Davis did his best for Ike. He paid him the rest of his month's wages and arranged via telegraph for him to have his old job back in Madrid. After the meeting, we returned to the cave for Ike's generator. We lit our carbide lanterns and went in. We found the generator in good condition.

"I'm curious about something," said Ike. Before I could say anything, he went back to the tunnel where we'd fought the specter. I followed him. I almost ran into Ike's back as he stood, staring at the place where the specter's body had lain. The body—even the armor—was gone.

SILENT NIGHT

DJ TYRER

PARIS WAS IN THE GRIP OF A WINTER as tight as the noose the Prussian military had thrown about the city; so cold that sentries had been found frozen at their posts. She was grateful to see the gendarme on duty beside the door, wrapped in great coat, cape and lengthy scarf. He turned his head to glance at her as she approached.

He gave a nod and she entered the building. A junior officer showed her through to Durand's office.

"Mademoiselle Castaigne," he announced, before closing the door behind her.

Durand gestured for her to sit. The Gendarmerie officer was seated behind a desk piled with files and loose papers.

Camille sat down, smoothed her dress straight and waited for him to speak.

"Disappearances," he said, without looking up at her.

"Again?"

"So it seems. Since our fellow subjects took it into their heads to chop down every telegraph pole they could for fuel, the Differential Recorder has slipped into error, especially as the Prussian shells have severed so many of the pneumatic postal tubes." He shook his head at the disorder. "But there is rumour and agitation. Talk of ghouls..."

He held up a hand to forestall her protest. "Yes, yes, I know you say the ghouls are too well fed at present to pose a threat to the living, but that doesn't quiet rumour and speculation – and their child is chaos. Such stories need to be quashed forthwith.

"What I do know for certain is that I sent two of my men to investigate a couple of days ago, and neither has returned."

"Well, that does pique my interest."

"It could be criminals or communards or cultists, it matters little, but if people are vanishing, the people need to be reassured." He steepled his fingers and looked straight at her. "Talk to Ste. Clair. He can tell you where the trouble is."

Camille nodded, rose from her seat and headed for the door.

The evening was unusually quiet and dark,

the chill having largely sent the siege into a state of hibernation. The Prussians had largely ceased shelling the city and there was, thus, little need for the French counter-battery fire. Most of the gas mains had been ruptured, so there were no lights and, with most of the population cowering away from the cold, there was none of the bustle Paris had known before the war.

Camille moved carefully along empty streets, a walking staff in her hand to test the drifts of snow for hidden shell holes. Beneath the cloak that was pulled tight about her, she wore a blouse under a rough woollen jersey, a pair of baggy men's pantaloons and sturdy boots. Her hair was pinned up under a woollen cap beneath the hood and her hands were enclosed in thick leather gloves that served as poor protection against the cold. Despite the layers, she shook. At least she could take comfort that there would be no tell-tale puffs of breath when stealth became a necessity: her lungs burned with the freezing air.

She was being shadowed. She couldn't see them, but she could sense their presence.

Her hand slipped under her cloak.

A figure stepped out from an alleyway ahead of her, heavily wrapped in scarves.

"Strange weather for a young lady to be wandering these streets," he said. He held a cudgel.

She gripped the handle of the revolver she wore. "I seek Ste. Clair."

The man tugged the scarf down from his face and chuckled. "It is I, Ste. Clair."

Her hand remained on her revolver. "Durand said you could show me where these disappearances have occurred."

Ste. Clair seemed to shiver; he hadn't before. "I showed his men the way. Neither has returned. It is a bad place. My outfit used the ruins for business, but my men kept vanishing. The homeless, too. Now, none go there."

He turned and pulled his scarf back up. "Follow me."

Their destination was a jagged maze of ruins centred upon the stark, shattered spire of a church, which was missing one side; the Prussians had found that they made easy targets.

"In there," he said. "I will go no closer. The dead walk within."

"It's possible. The exploding shells might disturb their rest."

Ste. Clair didn't answer, just slipped away into an alleyway, leaving her alone.

Keeping close to the remaining walls, Camille entered the ruins, probing ahead of her for any treacherous ground.

The night was growing darker. Camille paused and reached under her cloak. Hanging from her belt on the opposite hip to her holstered revolver was a second holster and, beside it, a heavy battery that powered the wand-like electric 'candle' she now drew forth to light her way. Steadier than the glow of a gas lamp, it lit her immediate surroundings with a harsh glare, but plunged the space beyond into deeper blackness. It was horribly conspicuous in the darkness, but a necessity.

She resumed her advance.

Rounding a corner, she spotted a figure huddled in a corner beneath a ragged blanket crusted with snow.

Slowly, she approached them. They didn't move.

Leaning towards them, she poked them with the staff. They remained still. Reaching out, Camille pulled the blanket aside to reveal the ice-white face of an old woman. No mystery, just another victim of the winter cold.

Then, she stiffened. A sound, the crunch of snow, and loose rubble underfoot. Somebody moving without care at being heard; not expecting to be heard.

Another crunch. She switched off her light.

Slowly, trying to make no noise, she moved forwards.

Pressing against what was left of a wall, she peered through a gap and caught a hint of a figure disappearing around a corner.

There was no way she could immediately follow them, so she considered climbing over the wall, but it looked too broken to do so safely or soundlessly. Instead, she turned her light back on and threaded her way between broken walls and over-teetering piles of rubble trying to locate footprints, but couldn't. She suspected the ruins were not as deserted as Ste. Clair claimed.

The shattered walls were stark in the light of her

torch and the darkness beyond its glow seemed to be waiting for the light to die. As she advanced deeper into the ruins, towards the church at its heart, she couldn't shake the feeling of something lurking just out of sight.

The shattered steeple loomed above her, a deeper darkness against the starless sky.

She shone her light towards the shattered church. Its roof was gone and there was a gash in its wall where a shell had exploded.

Pausing, she listened, but heard nothing but the soft sound of her breathing and a faint electrical hum from her light. She switched it off and said a silent, half-hearted prayer that she would avoid twisting her ankle in the darkness.

She crossed to the gap torn in the wall and entered the church. There was no sound, no movement, no hint it was anything more than an empty shell.

Turning the light back on, she blinked at the sudden brightness. Although any of the congregation who had fallen victim to Prussian shelling would doubtless have been removed, Camille could discern a number of bodies scattered about the church interior, perhaps as many as a dozen. Some were little more than mounds of snow, others had but a fine dusting of white frost upon them. As she shone her light about, she could spy men in civilian clothing and others in military uniform.

Camille considered the scene. There was a hole in the floor, where a shell had exploded down into the crypt. If there were any secret here, she was certain, it would be down there.

She searched for the stairs down to the crypt. As she looked about the church, she could not escape the unease that nagged at her. The night could hold a multitude of horrors and the dead could, on occasion, walk. She shook herself as if she might banish both the cold and the fear, but both remained.

Keeping close to the wall, she made her way round to where the stairs were. She kept glancing towards the dead, watching them for movement, but saw nothing, not even a twitch.

The top half of the door had been blown away. Moving what was left made more noise than she would have liked. Following the glow of her torch, she made her way down the stairs as quietly as she could. At their bottom, broken stones covered the floor and she almost stumbled.

The crypt was thick with rubble and the wreckage of pews, burying many of the tombs within. With difficulty, she began to make her way over the mounds.

Suddenly, there was a tug at her shoulder and she turned, revolver in her hand; her cloak had caught on a shattered length of wood. She pulled it free.

She was at the midpoint, now, and raised her torch high to illuminate the whole crypt. It was as silent and still as the tombs it contained. She waited for a moment... nothing.

Durand and Ste. Clair had her chasing shadows.

She turned and began to scramble back towards the stairs.

A sudden scraping sound made her turn again and raise her light once more. She could see nothing.

Crash! The sound reverberated about her in a deafening cacophony of echoes that destroyed the silence of the night. Camille was momentarily stunned.

The upper half of the shattered lid of a tomb almost below the shell hole in the roof had flown up and crashed down onto the floor of the crypt. A green glow came from within the tomb.

As she watched, something rose up from it, a collection of bones and bone fragments, within the diffuse glow, then assembled themselves into a human skeleton within a glowing flesh of ectoplasm. It landed gently on the rubble beside the tomb.

Camille raised her gun and fired, then fired again, but, although the shots seemed to hit it, they had no effect.

With curiously smooth movements, it stalked across the rubble towards her.

Camille turned and ran for the stairs, scrambling desperately across the loose rubble. The electric 'candle' slipped from her hand and clattered along behind her on its cord, casting wild and misshaped shadows about her. Then, the glass shattered and the only light was the sickly glow behind her. All she could do was scramble desperately for the stairs.

Bursting back out into the freezing night, she could barely even see the hint of the outline of the broken walls and piled debris.

She looked back. There was no glow in the stairway.

Then she heard noises. Clumsy footsteps and rough dragging sounds. She tensed.

A figure loomed out of the darkness. She fired and it seemed to jerk, but didn't fall.

More appeared, vague shadows reaching for her.

Dodging away from them, she felt something shift beneath her feet and, then, was falling forwards. The gun flew from her hand and she heard it clatter somewhere amongst the rubble a short distance away. Desperately, she groped for it, but her hand touched on nothing but stones.

A glow suddenly appeared. A green glow rising from the pit torn by a Prussian shell into the crypt. The entity was ascending from the crypt. The dead that had lain within the ruins surrounded her; amongst them, she thought she recognised a Gendarme uniform.

Rough hands seized her, began to drag her towards the pit. Camille fought against them, but their grips were unyielding and they were impervious to pain.

They deposited her before the pit and she sprawled upon the rough ground.

The entity loomed over her and reached out with tendrils of green ectoplasm that damply caressed the skin of her face like writhing worms. Camille felt a chill deeper even than that of the winter air flowing through her body and a terrible lethargy. She could feel her life-force draining...

Clawing at her face, she tried to pull the tendrils free from her skin, but they seemed to enter her flesh and her gloved hands seemed to slide through them like mist.

She swore, using words that would have shocked polite society. She was dying.

Groping beneath her cloak, she tried to grasp her stiletto dagger in a last desperate attempt to save herself. The cord of the broken torch slapped against her arm. She grasped it, a wild thought in her mind.

With a scream, Camille thrust the stub of the 'candle' at the entity. The shattered glass penetrated the ectoplasmic glow and there was a bright spark and everything went black, leaving only the cold.

Camille shivered herself awake. Her eyes flickered open and she winced: The dawn's light was like a bright furnace fire.

For a moment, she just lay still, face down in the snow. She felt frozen. Her limbs barely managed to twitch when she willed herself to move.

She sighed. This was it.

Then, she forced herself into a crouch, refusing to die.

She could barely feel her limbs and slapped at them to restore some circulation.

Bones lay scattered about her, more lay in the crypt below. Several bodies lay in her vicinity; two Gendarmes amongst them. She took a stone from a nearby pile of rubble and set about smashing several of the bones into fragments, hoping doing so would prevent it from manifesting again. Durand could send men, now, and see that they and the tomb were properly destroyed.

Detaching the cord from the battery, Camille tossed the broken light away and shook her head, then laughed. Maybe those savants who believed that science would conquer the supernatural were onto something!

Camille began to walk away, but groaned. She was in desperate need of a hot bath – a hot drink would probably have to suffice.

THE CASE OF THE MURDEROUS MIGRAINE

Karen J Carlisle

THE SPOON SANG AGAINST THE EDGE of the china cup, as Sir John tapped the last drop of medicine into his cup and waited for it to dissolve before quaffing the foul-tasting liquid. With a heavy sigh, he slumped back into his chair and retrieved the evening paper from the side table. The headlines announced:

Police Still Baffled Over Toff Killings

Searing pain raked its way over his right eye and

down his face. He grimaced, crumpled the paper and flung it back onto the side table.

Would he ever be rid of these migraines? He rose from his chair, fumbled in his jacket pocket for his pipe and crossed to the fireplace, where a silver tobacco box lay on the mantelpiece. Hands trembled as he filled his pipe and lit it from a taper near the fire. Tobacco smoke filled his lungs. A warm cascade of relaxation flowed across his chest, over his shoulders and into his neck.

A knock on the parlour door broke the calm. A slender young woman entered the room.

"Good evening, Sir."

"Good evening, Millie," mumbled Sir John.

"Have you another of your heads?" she asked.

Sir John nodded slowly. Every movement exacerbated the pain; it felt as if his entire brain hammered the inside of his skull, clawing to escape.

"Sit down, Sir," Millie instructed as she lit the wall sconces. A warm light flooded the room. Sir John winced and massaged his right brow.

"Sorry, Sir," Millie adjusted the gas to dim the brightness.

Amber light flickered, from both the fireplace and the wall lighting. She plumped up a tapestry cushion, replaced it on Sir John's armchair and ushered him to his seat.

"Those powders are not working as well as they used to," he whispered, as he eased into the comfort of the large padded leather chair. Blood thumped through his temples and whooshed in his ears.

Millie mouthed something about supper and a snifter of brandy for his head. Everything melted into a throbbing, incoherent mass.

☠

The heavy parlour curtains rattled. A shaft of sunlight glared across Sir John's face. He moaned and shifted in his chair. He always suffered the day after one of his migraines.

"Good morning, Sir." Millie's overly cheerful voice chimed. "If the neighbours saw you, they'd assume you imbibed an excess of drink last night." She smiled. "Or worse."

"At least that would mean I'd enjoyed myself." Sir John frowned. Unfortunately, he could never remember much when he suffered from 'one of his heads'. Blackouts, the doctor said.

He rested his head in his hand, shading his eyes from the light. Or perhaps it was fortunate he couldn't remember? It didn't matter. Whatever the neighbours believed, there was always one certainty: the episodes always ended extremely unpleasantly – exacerbated by Millie's excessively cheery moods.

Sir John glanced at his housemaid. She was a jovial girl, and always ready with his brandy or to fetch his powders. Her honey-coloured hair was pinned meticulously in an elaborate array of braids. How did she find the time?

She leaned across his desk. A gold necklace slipped from under her blouse and dangled in the air. A gold locket glinted in the morning sunlight.

He eyed its central ruby, surrounded by delicate engraving. It was worth a year's maid's wages. He raised an eyebrow. What other secrets was she hiding?

"That's a beautiful locket, Millie," he said.

Millie snatched up the trinket and pushed it back under her blouse.

"It's a family heirloom. I inherited it." She cleared her throat. "I brought the morning paper in for you, Sir." Millie passed it to Sir John. "It seems there was another one, last night."

"Another what, Millie?" Sir John groaned as he reached down between his jacket and the chair, shifting his weight as he pulled his pipe out of an awkward area. He placed it on the table next to him.

"Another murder. Lord Gilbertson, this time. That makes three in the past month. A girl could get worried about walking the streets if it weren't for the fact that it is Gentlemen who are being done in," she continued.

"They are bound to catch the blaggard eventually." Sir John opened the newspaper to the relevant article and skimmed the details. "It says here that all three murders have been within the district. Make sure you double check the windows and doors tonight."

Absent-mindedly, he reached his hand into his coat pocket, his fingers curling around a smooth round object. He removed it and examined the find – a gold fob watch, its crest emblazoned with two ravens. Not his. He shrugged and shoved it back into his pocket.

"Is there anything you need, sir?" asked Millie.

Sir John discarded the newspaper and dusted stray tobacco from his evening jacket.

"A strong cup of tea, I think." He straightened his cravat as he rose from the chair, noting the silver tray with most of the previous night's meal. He had no memory of eating supper, nor where he had acquired the watch. He rubbed his fingers over his moustache and wondered what else he had forgotten. This would not do.

Sir John cleared his throat.

"I'll dress for breakfast," he said.

Sir John dipped his nib pen into the inkpot on his desk. He signed the letter and placed it next to the afternoon tea tray. The teapot was still warm. He poured another cup, picked up the paper sachet of powder on the tray, and sighed as he slipped it into a small wooden box in the top desk drawer. He leaned back in his chair and fidgeted with the fob watch. Something bothered him...

Millie cleared her throat. Sir John flinched and slipped the fob watch into the drawer.

"Here are the old newspapers you requested." She placed them on the desk.

He glanced at the stack of newspapers.

Millie hovered near his desk. "Cook wants to know if you will be wanting anything special for supper?" she asked.

"No, I have a dinner engagement." He sealed the letter and addressed the envelope to his brother, Andrew, and placed it on a pile of papers. "Isn't it your night off?"

"Yes," Millie smiled.

Sir John nodded, picked up the top broadsheet and flipped through its pages.

Long shadows filled the hallway. Millie answered the front door.

"Delivery. Sign here," The plainly dressed deliveryman shoved a paper into her hand.

Millie signed the note. He deposited a well-worn trunk on the top step and scuttled back to his wagon.

"Here! Won't you bring it in?" Millie thrust her hands on her hips.

"I just deliver 'em," he replied as the cart trundled its way toward high street.

Millie scanned the street. A carriage clattered along the cobblestones in the same direction. The few passers-by took no notice of the housemaid on the doorstep. She tugged her gloves tight, grabbed the worn leather strap and yanked the trunk up the front stairs into the hallway.

She glanced into the library. Dishevelled piles of newspapers surrounded Sir John. A deep furrow etched his brow as he stared at the gold watch.

Millie smiled and quietly edged the trunk up

each stair, toward the attic. The door shut with a click.

The lamplighter moved slowly towards the house. His pole rang against each lamp. Comforting pools of light seeped from each lamppost, melting into the thickening mist. As he passed the window, he lowered his head and tipped his hat in Millie's direction. The Night Constable turned the corner, into the far lane. Millie smiled and closed the curtains. Sir John had gone out for the evening. It was her night off. And she had plans.

The fog was thicker than usual, restricting visibility to no more than several paces -- easier to slip along the streets unnoticed.

A hint of moonlight peeked through a chink in the gloom. The patch of light was low. The hour was late. Puddles of revellers dribbled out of the taverns. Bawdy tunes oozed from the music halls. Laughter and drunken clamours echoed through the streets, making the revellers easier to avoid. They made things too complicated. Too messy.

Patience.

The quarry had already been selected. Occasionally, an upper-class gentleman would venture out for a taste of the street nightlife. Alone.

They preferred not to draw attention, so sure they could look after themselves.

Waiting was the secret to success. Wait long enough and one would stroll too close.

A lone gong reverberated through the fog.

Tonight the wait was longer. Too long. It was past midnight. The potentials were thinning out.

Finally, there was movement up ahead in the fog... A shadow.

"Hello, dearie. Fancy some?" A long white limb flashed, from under layers of skirts. She reeked of rose water and lavender and gin. Her hair was tousled; her red bodice partly unbuttoned and pulled low over one shoulder. She adjusted her bonnet and glanced up. Her grin faded.

"Sorry." She slinked back into the shadows. "I thought..." Her voice faded as the distance between them increased. The fog reclaimed the space. Comforting fog. Enclosing. Secretive.

Tap, tap. Tap, tap.

The sound of a walking cane on the cobblestones edged closer; the confident steps of a gentleman. The wait was over! Each tap pulsed through the air. The mist itself trembled with excitement.

But would he turn this way?

A tall, top-hatted figure paused at the end of the street, a blurred silhouette barely visible through swirling layers of gloom. He struck a match. Faint drifts of acrid pipe smoke perforated the fog as he started along the adjoining street.

So close.

He paused mid-step, tilted his head as if listening to something on the breeze, then spun on his heel and strolled closer, along the lane.

Tap, tap. Tap, Tap. Closer.

Come closer.

The fog swirled around him, so thick that the smoke from his pipe appeared to melt seamlessly into it.

Tap, Tap. The smell of tobacco was now recognisable over the smell of the drains along the road.

Closer.

The sound of humming grew louder with each footstep.

Stop humming.

There was silence. The gentleman coughed, removed his pipe and tapped it.

Yes!

A glint of silver slashed the fog. Thuds repeated, in quick succession. The pipe dropped, bouncing on the cobblestones and into the gutter. The etched brass fittings faintly gleamed under the lamplight. He turned, wide-eyed, in a silent scream.

Another flash.

He fell to his knees and slumped to the ground. A dark pool of blood formed under his body, flowing away in rivulets between the cobblestones. His top hat was collected and placed beside the body, a single red rose tucked into its band. Fingers curled around the pipe and lifted it from the gutter.

Mine.

Sir John walked along the gloomy laneway towards his front door. He'd avoided the commotion in the next street. The stabbing pain in his head had escalated beyond any he had previously experienced.

A trill whistled in the distance. Sir John flinched and clasped his gloved hands over his ears to muffle the sound. Noises were unbearable when the migraines consumed him. He stumbled, catching the wrought iron fencing in front of his house. He leaned against the metal bars - a welcome place to rest as he struggled to gather his strength and wits to fight off the next wave of pain.

Cook would be abed and it was Millie's night off; no one would answer the doorbell. Blood dripped from his left hand, leaving its mark on the top step, as he fumbled with the key in the front door.

Lamplight reflected in glaring patches, unable to penetrate the grey fog. Millie could scarcely see ten feet ahead. She had finished her evening's business, replaced her red gloves and adjusted them as she strode home.

The hour was late. A chill crept through her bones. She tugged at the collar of her visite and held it tight against the bitter wind.

As Millie turned the corner, footsteps echoed in the fog around her. She searched the mist. Nothing...

No, wait.

The outline of a tall figure materialised out of the fog, tracing the path she had taken. The figure passed under the street lamp. Light glinted off his hat and buttons.

"Good evening, Constable Roberts." Millie tugged her gloves tighter.

"Good evening, Miss Millie." The Constable tipped his hat and smiled.

"Sorry to startle you. I thought you might want an escort home at this time of night."

"That is kind of you, Constable, but I can look after myself." She smiled back.

The Constable nodded, but continued to walk beside her.

A clacking din echoed along the street, as they reached her front gate. Roberts spun on his heel toward the noise. Millie heard it too: the sound of the Constabulary's wooden ratchet summoning nearby officers. Roberts made his apologies and sprinted toward the noise, disappearing into the boundless fog.

The morning newspapers heralded:

"Double Toff Killing: Murderer Escalates!"

Sir John struggled to focus on the words. He skimmed the article, discarded the newspaper on his desk, and pinched the bridge of his nose. Never had he felt so incapacitated the morning after a migraine.

The breakfast platter rattled on his desk. Papers rustled next to it as Millie nudged them to one side. Her gaze lingered over them. Sir John raised an eyebrow.

"I'll double the powders today, Sir." She reached into her apron pocket for a couple of sachets and placed them on the platter next to the teacup.

"Are you sure?" he asked.

Her lips curled in a slight smile. "Shall I post your letter, this afternoon?"

"What letter?" There were too many blanks in his memory over the past months. Was this another of them?

Millie picked up a letter from the jumble of documents, flipped it over and ran her thumb over the smooth paper where the traditional sealing wax would usually be. She sighed.

"To your brother?" she asked as she placed the envelope in her pocket.

Sir John cradled his head in his left hand and nodded gently.

"Sir, your hand?"

Sir John waved her away and tugged at the bandage, which was already beginning to unravel. A patch of blood had seeped through the dressing.

"I must have cut it last night. I think I tripped on the steps on the way in. The darned migraine started earlier than usual. I only just got home in time." He grimaced.

Millie cleared the breakfast dishes, tucked the newspaper under her arm and crept toward the door.

"I'll get Cook to make a strong pot of tea," she whispered.

Sir John nodded and waited until the library door clicked shut behind her. A desk drawer scraped open. He lifted the lid of the wooden box within.

"Sir John is not well," announced Millie as she scanned the kitchen. There was a distinct lack of kitchen staff.

Cook sat at the kitchen table, polishing the silverware. The kettle gurgled on the stovetop. She glanced up as Millie entered the kitchen.

"Where's Elizabeth?" asked Millie.

"She's gone to market," replied Cook as she placed the bone-handled knife at the end of the row of utensils on the table.

"I do hope luncheon won't be late."

"Oh, she'll be back by eleven-thirty to help," said Cook, "or I'll have her guts for garters."

Perfect.

"Have you seen your Constable today?" Millie slid the tray onto the kitchen table. Did you tell him about Sir John's new trinkets?

"Oh yes," Cook replied. "There was Lord

Hamilton Smith's tobacco box on the mantelpiece in the library, Lord Colville's signet ring in Sir John's desk drawer, the gold fob watch belonging to Lord Gilbertson that was in Sir John's pocket, the silver-handled knife that slew Sir Robert..." She counted off each item on her pudgy fingers. "Oh, and Lord Barrington's pipe with the etched brass fittings. He could not believe Sir John would be so foolish as to collect such trinkets."

Millie smiled as Cook finished her list. All were accounted for.

Well done, Cook. Millie glanced at the tea tray and raised an eyebrow. Humans are so easy to persuade. Millie centred the teacup on its saucer. Your Constable must be so happy you supplied him with all the clues he needs to convict the suspect.

"He was," Cook retrieved the newspaper.

I had better finish up, then. Millie circled the kitchen table and paused by Cook's chair.

"He is coming to arrest Sir John, directly--"

Millie gripped the back of a kitchen chair. Forget!

Cook stopped mid-sentence, and stared blankly at the stove where the kettle sat. Small spurts of water began to bubble from its spout.

I could kill for a cup of tea right now. Millie licked her lips.

"So could I," Cook replied.

Millie grinned, her teeth sharp and shiny. She grabbed Cook's throat, before she could react. Cook's grip on the newspaper slackened. It slipped and fluttered to the floor.

Cook clawed Millie's arm and kicked frantically, struggling to free herself and mouthing words never heard.

Millie's grip tightened as she manoeuvred sideways, so she could stare her prey directly in the eyes. Cook's pupils dilated; her terror was palpable. Millie's tongue traced the edge of her teeth. She breathed in deeply, savouring the fear.

Millie leaned closer, unfurled a pointed talon and nicked the now paling skin of her quarry, close to the jawline. A drop of blood beaded and trickled down the neck.

She inhaled deeply. The sweet smell rose with the body's heat. Slowly and deliberately, she pressed her teeth against her prey's throat, piercing the layers of skin, and into the artery. A rush of warm liquid burst into her mouth. Muscles relaxed. Her head buzzed.

Ecstasy.

This is the best part.

Her prey ceased its struggle. Millie's shoulders slumped. She loosened her embrace and rocked back on her haunches. If she'd had a heart, it would have raced with excitement.

The kettle screamed for attention.

Millie swallowed. There was no time to allow herself to be lost in the moment. She rose to her feet, brushed her blonde hair from her face and delicately wiped the corners of her mouth.

Sufficient.

Her hands trembled as she leaned on the back of

the chair. She'd lost control - given in to the hunger - and so close to home, with the Constabulary alerted and on its way. Fool! She had to work quickly.

Millie grasped one of the silver handled knives and sliced Cook's pale throat, destroying any vestige of puncture wounds. She stepped away and examined her clothes; there was insufficient blood left to soil her clothing. She'd drunk too deeply. She hoped the miscalculation wouldn't be noticed on close investigation. There should be no doubt Sir John was responsible.

The kettle bubbled. Splashes of water sizzled on the hotplate.

Millie smiled, picked up the newspaper and glanced at the headlines. Her smiled faded.

Two bodies? She bit her lip. She had only dispatched one soul last night. Yet the description of the fifth murder was similar.

A knife left behind? Millie searched her memory. She had cut her preys' throats to hide the tell-tale bite marks and had been careful not to leave any items behind. All clues should point to Sir John.

Her hand trembled. Millie swallowed. Perhaps she had drunk too much? She reached absent-mindedly for a cleaning cloth and glanced at the silver handled knife in her hand. Her muscles tensed. It looked similar to the one Cook had described earlier.

Millie discarded the unused cloth and set the knife near the body. A matching clue would tie it all together - and please the Constable.

Your Constable must be so happy. The thought echoed in her mind. Cook had replied to her thoughts, not her words. Millie pulled Cook's shawl back onto her shoulders. It had been so easy to persuade her to follow her instructions, to inform the Constable of her 'findings'.

Millie glanced at the ceiling. Sir John sat in the library above her. Had her thoughts influenced him to murderous desires of his own?

Her hand tightened around the handle of the boiling kettle; she placed it on the bench and straightened her shoulders. She had not slipped up.

Millie climbed the narrow stairs to the hallway and checked the library door. The hair she'd placed over the doorknob hadn't moved. Sir John had not yet stirred. Everything was going to plan.

She retrieved the library door key from her apron pocket and locked the door. Sir John needed to be contained, for now. It would not do for him to rouse early.

The maid, Elizabeth, should return from the markets by half-past. She was never late, lest she earn the wrath of Cook. It would take Constable Roberts twenty minutes to arrive from the Station.

Millie glanced at the clock. It was five past. The timing must be perfect. She stood by the telephone, straightened her skirts, watched the hands on the clock, and waited. Five more minutes. She just needed patience - and to stick to the plan:

Elizabeth would return and find Cook's body. She would answer the door to Constable Roberts. He would gallantly brave the newly discovered scene of carnage. The incriminating knife and other trinkets would be uncovered. Sir John would be confronted with evidence, unable to defend himself.

Millie smiled; she would be suitably shocked, and faint on cue - as any member of the fairer sex might in the situation. By the time it seemed felicitous to rouse herself, Sir John would be bundled into a Black Maria, Cook's body would be on the way to the Morgue, and Elizabeth would have handed in her notice.

His brother, Andrew Worthington, would visit before the end of the week. Sir John's letter would confirm the transfer of the house deed to her ownership. There would be no contention. She could persuade Sir Andrew, if required.

Millie ran her fingers along the smooth, polished wood of the main-stair banister. Soon it would be hers. She licked her lips. It would all be hers.

She fingered the locket at her throat and glanced up the servants' staircase. She would climb them - one last time - to retrieve her trunk and, in the solitude, would reclaim its contents, replacing Sir John's possessions with her own. After a hundred years of collecting, each item had a story; each item knew its place. And this was their new home.

It was a brilliant plan. She smiled and checked the clock again. It was time.

Millie straightened her shoulders and lifted the telephone receiver. It crackled in her ear.

"Police Station, please."

There was a knock on the door. Millie jumped. A dark shadow flitted across the glass in the front door. Millie glanced at the clock and frowned. The Constable was early. Her jaw muscles tensed.

Another knock; the door rattled. Millie stepped forward and opened the door.

"Good morning, Miss." Constable Roberts removed his custodial helmet and stepped into the hallway. "I hope I'm in time."

Millie hunched her shoulders; the damsel in distress always worked with men in uniform.

"Oh, Constable!" Her voice trembled. "Thank goodness you came. I'm so scared. I locked myself in my room until you came." She sniffed.

The clock chimed half past. Where was that girl? Cook's body needed to be discovered before Sir John woke. Millie dug her fingernails into her palm. Perhaps she could influence the Constable as she had done Sir John and Cook? She stared at him and concentrated: You need to check the kitchen.

The Constable shut the front door and glanced along the hallway.

Not the hall, you fool. The kitchen!

Footsteps thudded on the kitchen steps.

Ah, finally! Stupid girl. She'd sack her for her tardiness when this was all over. Millie turned, preparing herself for an attack of hysteria.

"Elizabeth, you know you are not allowed above stairs--"

A man in a dark suit, and carrying a silver-handled walking cane, emerged at the top of the stairs. Millie halted mid-step.

"Where's Elizabeth?" she asked.

"Was that her name?" The man removed his bowler with a grey-gloved hand and shook his head.

Millie glared at the Constable. You were supposed to come alone, you stupid man.

Constable Roberts raised an eyebrow. "This is Professor Green. He's Special Consultant in the Toff Murders investigation." He turned to Millie. "This is Millie Mulgrave, the maid. It was she who tipped us off."

"You've come to arrest Sir John?" Millie eyed the Professor. Why had he not yet said anything about Cook? Surely, he had seen the body in the kitchen? Just, stick to the plan...

"Where is Sir John?" asked the Professor.

Millie fidgeted with the library door key in her pocket and cursed silently; she hadn't had time to unlock the library door.

Footsteps echoed along the hallway behind her.

"Sir John?" asked the Constable.

Millie's fingers tensed and curled around the key. She turned slowly. Sir John was dressed impeccably, his eyes sharp; there was no sign of his previous malaise. How did he get out?

"Good afternoon, Sir John," said Constable Roberts. "This is Professor Green."

The Professor nodded in greeting. "I think you should come with me, Sir." He spun on his heel and tramped back down the steps.

"How are you feeling today, Sir?" asked the Constable.

"Better, now you're here, Constable," replied Sir John.

Millie's fingers relaxed. Her plan was back on track. Now, to attend to the body.

They followed Professor Green down the worn, narrow steps to the kitchen.

The room was as she had left it: Cook's body was sprawled over a kitchen chair, her arms dangled over its back top rail. Her head slumped back at an awkward angle to display her pale neck - sliced open along the carotid. A bloody kitchen knife sat near the body.

Sir John's eyes widened. The Constable swore. The Professor picked up a discarded cleaning cloth next to a rumpled canvas bag on the floor, and placed it next to the folded newspaper on the table.

Millie bit her lip; it would be unseemly to smile at such a gruesome spectacle. It wasn't as she had planned, but the result was the same. Sir John would soon be arrested for the murder and his 'mementos' would be discovered, linking him to the Toff murder spree.

"Oh, poor Cook. Not her too." Millie feigned a

swoon. "And I would've been next! Oh, Constable, you must arrest him now."

Metal rattled. Silver flashed. Handcuffs snapped around Millie's wrists and clicked shut. They burned, sizzling Millie's flesh. Millie winced, reeled backwards and hissed, as the smell of burned garlic filled her nostrils.

Sir John chuckled and handed the Constable a small wooden box with a folded piece of paper on top. "It's all in there." He tapped the paper. "And a list of dates."

"What have you done with Elizabeth?" he asked her.

"Nothing." Millie glared at the cuffs: Silver! She hissed and twisted her hands, struggling to free herself from the searing metal. "He is the one you want." She could feel the sharp points of her own teeth on her lips.

Sir John scowled and flinched, but stood his ground. "What are you?"

"You fiend!" Constable Roberts stepped back and crossed himself.

"He killed those Toffs!" she spat in Sir John's direction. "I have proof."

Constable Roberts kept his distance. "Sir John has explained how you drugged him."

"And fabricated evidence," said Sir John. "I've known for some time."

"No!" Her talons flailed in his direction as she lunged forward. "You cannot defend yourself. I have proof!"

Chains rattled and thudded on the floor. Millie's foot caught. She stumbled and crashed into the pantry door, forcing it open.

She landed on a lifeless body; she didn't need to see the blood-caked thatch of orange hair to identify it. She recognised the smell of cheap rose water and soot. It was Elizabeth. Millie screwed up her nose. It also smelled of stale blood. This was not a fresh kill. It had been here for hours. How had she not noticed?

Millie rolled off the body, crushing small balls under her weight. Fresh garlic filled the alcove.

She howled in pain as the smell clawed at her eyes and burned her nostrils. She scrabbled back out of the pantry. The pantry floor was scattered with cloves of garlic. Bunches hung from the back of the door.

Chains clanked and fell around her body. They squeezed tight under her chin. The silver burned. The smell of garlic made her ill. Her stomach churned, threatening to disgorge its contents. She squirmed, trying to distance herself from the garlic-coated links. The Professor grinned as he pulled the chains tighter.

Millie gagged and coughed on the stench.

"Don't be a fool," she growled at the Constable. "This kill is not mine!"

"Don't waste your words on him," said the Professor. "You belong to me now."

"She's not only a murdering daemon, Constable, but also a thief," said Sir John. "About that foul neck is an antique gold locket, with a circular cut ruby. It was my mother's. I should like it back."

"No!" Millie hissed and kicked at the chains. It was her locket; the only link to her family.

The Professor gripped the silver chain in one hand and lashed out his walking cane with the other, striking her across the face. The silver handle dipped and hooked between the buttons of her blouse. The material ripped easily, allowing her locket to slip free. He then twisted the walking cane, caught the gold chain and yanked the locket.

Sir John stepped closer, scooped up the locket and glared directly into her eyes. She knew that look. He was a kindred spirit.

The corner of his lip lifted into a crooked smile. His voice was eerily calm as he whispered, barely loud enough for her to hear: "I always get my way."

She lunged at him, close enough to smell his sweat - of tobacco, sandalwood, and fear.

"At least I only kill to feed," she whispered in his ear, through clenched teeth.

The Professor jerked on the chain, wrenching her away from Sir John, searing the garlic-soaked links deeper into her skin.

"My condolences for such a terrible tragedy in your household," said the Professor. "Thank you for your assistance, Sir John." He glanced over the bodies. "You have done a great service for The Empire." He thrust a hessian bag over Millie's head and wound the chain around its base. With each struggle, the chains tightened.

"Consider yourself lucky, Sir," said the Professor. "These killers like to keep mementos of their victims."

The gold locket glowed in the gaslight. The ruby glinted as it spun on the end of its chain. Sir John leaned back in his chair and surveyed his polished dark oak desk. A cut-crystal glass of the finest brandy sat on a silver tray, next to the evening's newspaper.

He traced the carved scrollwork down the side of the desk and curled his fingers around a rosette carved into the final curled flourish, and pressed the raised centre.

A whirring sound emanated from deep inside the desk. A rhythmic ratcheting joined in. A wooden drawer popped open with a faint click.

Sir John retrieved an ornately-embossed silver cigar box from the drawer and placed it on the desk. He leaned forward and held his breath. The lid opened silently. He assessed the contents: a silver filigree amethyst brooch, a delicate gold and emerald ring, several locks of hair. He could name each one.

Sir John slipped his fingers into his waistcoat pocket and retrieved his treasures. He licked his lips as he tied the lock of fiery orange hair with a purple ribbon and placed it in the box. He laid Millie's ruby and gold locket next to it, gently closed the lid and replaced it in the hidden drawer.

He poured himself a brandy, picked up the

newspaper and skipped over the headlines proclaiming Toff Killer Caught, and opened the advertisement section.

Wanted: Cook and House Maid.
References essential.
Please enquire Sir John Harcorte.

B . A . R . B .

Rob Francis

IT WAS AN ABSURD HOUR TO be abroad.

Archibald Leary stood at the corner of Charterhouse Square and Carthusian Street and stared into the mist. The trees lining the square cast dark grey shadows into the chartreuse world, but no God-fearing folk walked the avenues. A fragment of conversation drifted across the gaslit evening, then was gone. The city was subdued, waiting. The bells of St. Thomas's tolled the hour, their call muffled by the drifting miasma. It was eleven o'clock.

Where was the man, Pridd?

Leary sighed and tugged at the lapels of his frock coat, feeling the chill of the moist air through the broadcloth. He hadn't wanted to come, but Pridd had been in quite a state when he came banging on the door of Leary's Bayswater home. He'd agreed partly to get him off the doorstep and out of sight of the neighbours. Partly that, but also to be out of the house and away from poor Lily. He couldn't stand to sit by her bed, watching her cough her life away. It made him feel helpless, and the frustration that followed burned him clean through evening after evening. It could happen any time now, perhaps only a few more weeks, perhaps even sooner than that. He didn't want to think about it. He *couldn't* think about it. Better to be here, in the wretched fog.

He fished a cigar from his coat pocket and struck a match, taking his time to get it well lit. He didn't often smoke outdoors; the vapours of the city made the act less pleasant than in his study or the reading room at the Guild of Civil Engineers. As he pocketed the matches he felt the reassuring weight of the Beaumont-Adams, the pistol wrapped in a handkerchief and secreted beneath his pocketbook. He'd never had cause to use it, but its presence was a comfort at times like these.

Footsteps rapped on the pavement, and the shifting shadows along Carthusian Street resolved themselves into the small ferret-like shape of Noah Pridd, foreman of the Health and Sanitation Corporation's sewer repair and maintenance team. Despite being at least thirty, Pridd wore a flat cap on his head, like a boy. He doffed it and wrung it in his hands when he saw Leary waiting.

"Mr. Leary, sir!"

Leary nodded his acknowledgement, but did not extend his hand.

"Pridd. Why this hour, man?"

"Well, less... that is, fewer *solids* going into the sewer at this time of night, sir, as it were. And as I said at your gaff – your *house*, sir, well, I didn't think it could wait until the morning."

Leary frowned to concede the point. "Very well. Lead on then, Pridd. Let us see this collapsed wall and what can be done about it."

Pridd led the way, hurrying along in little nervous steps while Leary followed behind, cigar clamped between his teeth. Along the square and through Rutland Place, then down a narrow fetid alley to Glasshouse Yard and the stout red brick structure that housed the entrance to the Goswell Street line of the city's new sewerage system.

They stopped outside the iron gate, its black paint still shining and unblemished. Pridd fumbled in his pocket for a long moment to retrieve the key, and then they were through and into the small dark space that held stairs leading down into blackness. Both men were wearing Wellington boots, Leary's well scrubbed by his manservant, Pridd's already caked in filth. Two copper oil lamps sat forlornly on the floor by the stairs. Pridd fussed around with them, taking an eternity to light the wicks with matches and make sure both were secure before handing one to Leary. Then they descended the concrete steps into the underground tunnel.

Leary had been here a few years before, when overseeing the line's construction. But it had been some time since he had entered a working sewer, and the smell made him gag a little as he stepped from the final stair into the small stream of water and refuse that ran through the circular brick passageway. Pridd had been right; at this time there was little street water flowing through the channel, though this did leave the occasional stinking pile of human or animal waste standing on the floor.

"How far?" grunted Leary, trying to speak whilst holding his breath.

"Half the length of Goswell, as it were sir. Not too far at *all*." Pridd moved off, seemingly unaffected by the stench. Leary followed, stepping carefully to avoid slipping on the detritus that lined the bricks. Water dripped overhead, and Leary cursed as the drops pattered on his bowler. He would have to have it cleaned again.

"When did you discover this, Pridd? Checking for maintenance by yourself, were you?"

"Yes sir, in a manner of speaking, sir." Pridd didn't turn to address Leary but kept facing forward, his voice echoing around the chamber. "Since my Annie passed away, well sir, all I have left is my work. Sometimes I visit the older passages of an evening, just to check on them. Found this last night, sir."

"Ah." Leary made a show of studying the workmanship of the brickwork to hide his awkwardness as they walked, though Pridd didn't seem to notice. "I didn't know Mrs. Pridd had died. I'm sorry for your loss." He thought of Lily, lying in bed, coughing blood onto her pillow.

"We've only worked together for a half-dozen years, sir. Not all that long really."

"Indeed." Leary scratched at his whiskers; he was starting to sweat under his heavy coat. "Last night, you say? But why not come to me this morning. If it couldn't wait—"

"Knew you'd be *busy*, an important man such as yourself, sir. Hurried round as soon as I finished my shift; asked around for your home address instead of the office."

"I see." Leary cursed as more water landed on his hat.

They reached the collapsed wall. The gap was smaller than Leary had feared, a thin broken-toothed maw in the brickwork that a man must stoop to enter. The missing bricks were scattered before it in the sewer bed, half-submerged in the trickling stream of water and filth.

Leary reached out a hand to grasp Pridd's shoulder.

"It looks like the wall fell *inwards*. From the angle of repose, that should not be possible."

Pridd nodded. "Yes sir. It seems that the wall was displaced by some outside force, sir."

Leary shone his lantern into the darkness behind the wall to reveal damp stone and something yellow, glistening in the lamplight.

"You've looked inside?"

"Yes sir. When this section of tunnel was built, we excavated around the site of the old Carthusian monastery. There were *graves*, looked to be some old plague pits. We ran the tunnel alongside an old wall of the estate. I would say, sir, that wall has finally toppled, and brought ours down too. Inside looks to be an old underground chamber from the monastery. *This way*, sir." Pridd ducked through the gap without waiting to see if Leary intended to follow.

Leary removed his hat and stepped through. The lanterns illuminated a small room of slick granite blocks, the walls lined with alcoves holding brown-yellow bones and rotted robes.

"Monks." Leary turned his light on a grimy skull atop a pile of mouldy grey cloth. "This is a crypt, Pridd."

"A *special* crypt, sir. Look."

Leary swung his lamp around.

Pridd stood before a towering figure, a bizarre composite of bones of all shapes and sizes. A faded cloak stitched with golden thread enveloped the figure, and above the cloak a huge skull was fixed, its appearance similar to that of a cat's that Leary had once seen in the window of a taxidermist. A band of iron topped the skull like a makeshift crown, and the entire thing sat upon a tall chair of black wood, perhaps oak.

"Jesus wept!" said Leary. "A king upon his throne? Who is it supposed to be? Did they mean to recreate Christ here in their burial chamber? A monarch? Or...something else?" Now that Leary looked at the idol, it didn't seem very holy. Quite the opposite, in fact. And that monstrous skull....

Pridd gestured to the ground, where he had wiped the dirt away with the sole of his boot. "There are letters, sir."

Leary crossed the small room, peering warily at

the idol on its throne. There was something about it...somehow it seemed more *real* than the rest of the room. Now that he had seen it, it was hard to look away.

The flagstone before the king was cracked, but four carved letters could still be seen: BARB.

"What does it mean?" Leary was sweating heavily now. If the place wasn't so filthy, he would have removed his coat.

Pridd spoke quietly, almost reverently. "I have examined the broken stone for other letters most carefully sir, and believe that once it might have said 'Barbas.' Does the name mean anything to you, sir? No?" Pridd took a pocket watch from his coat and checked the time. "I looked it up. Barbas was a demon, a great commander of Hell. An engineer, in fact. Given the power to cause and cure disease. Perhaps not surprising that some chose to appeal to his mercy, when plague was rife and they felt abandoned by God. And Barbas, it seems, could shift between the forms of lion and man. That skull, sir...."

"Madness," whispered Leary. "Devil worship, indeed. I should speak to the archbishop, tell him what we've found."

"It is almost midnight," said Pridd. He pointed to the feline skull that dominated the figure. "Watch the eyes."

"The eyes? What—." And then he saw it. For a moment the empty sockets flickered as if housing faint green flame. Then the fire grew into a lambent flare that illuminated the chamber in a sickly glow, before fading again to shadows and lamplight. Leary felt a great hollowness inside.

"What does it mean?" Leary almost reached out to touch the effigy, but instead clenched his fist tight at his side.

"It means he is waiting."

"This thing? Waiting? Waiting for what?"

"For us." Pridd turned to Leary, eyes wide and fevered.

"Us? Are you insane, man? I've had quite enough of this!" Leary turned, but Pridd grabbed his arm.

"Wait, sir. He would value your service, sir, a man such as yourself. And imagine, the *favours* he could bestow. Not just on you, sir, but your poor wife..."

Leary hesitated. He imagined how it might be, if any of the nonsense Pridd was spouting were true. Lily restored to her old self, happy again. A place on the Sanitary Commission and a chair at the Guild for himself; enough power and authority to create whatever he wished, to shape the city itself. A formidable legacy. Money. Children, even. A family.

"No." Leary shook his head. "Even if it weren't nonsense, the price would be too great. This is ridiculous, Pridd. Gather yourself!" He looked again at the demon. "Madness."

Pridd punched him hard in the side. Leary lurched, stumbling to the wall, his lamp smashing on the floor and sending streams of burning oil about his feet. He turned to Pridd but his legs gave beneath him, and he saw the knife in the other man's hand shining in the firelight, half the blade dark with blood. He dug in his pocket for the revolver.

"If you won't follow, sir, you can *serve* in other ways, yes."

Leary dragged the gun free as he slumped against the wall. Pridd's eyes widened and he turned to run. Leary aimed and squeezed the trigger, but the shot missed, the bullet sparking against the wall.

He cursed. Pridd was gone, through the hole into the sewer. The light beyond the gap winked out, leaving Leary alone with the flicker of burning oil from the floor. After a few moments, that too dwindled and died. The darkness was absolute.

Leary sat against the wall and tried to breathe, while numbness crept from his side into his legs and gut. He kept the gun pointed to where he had last seen Pridd for a long moment, but then lowered it to the floor. He could see nothing. If Pridd returned, there would be little he could do.

"Damn," he muttered. "I'm dying."

Yes.

The voice came from nowhere, the word firing straight into Leary's mind without passing his ears. He raised the gun again, though he was not sure why.

You are dying, like all who walk upon the earth. But your life does not have to end now. Not if you choose otherwise.

The green light returned, a luminescent glow from the demon's eyes that outlined the room and the corpses it held. The broken wall was a black slash beyond which nothing existed. The demon bathed in the light, taller now that Leary was on the floor. He seemed regal amongst the decay surrounding him.

Leary raised the revolver and fired, the shot resounding painfully loud in the confined space. It punched a hole in the brow of the skull, but it did not fall. The iron circlet remained fixed in place.

I cannot be hurt, my friend.

"This is lunacy," said Leary. "I'm dying. I dream."

A shame that you will not follow. You have so much more potential than Mr. Pridd. I am sure you would have brought many souls to my salvation.

"I die. Lily and I will be together soon enough." He lay on the slick floor, feeling the wet coolness of the stones against his cheek. Closed his eyes against the putrid green of the crypt.

I'm afraid not. Poor Lily. Even now she worries that you have not returned home. Soon your manservant will confirm your absence. Lily will conclude that you have run away, at last. Found another to love and fled abroad. She will climb to the top floor of your home, and leap to the street below. It will take her several days to die.

"No! You can't possibly know that."

And as a suicide, she will be denied the afterlife that you have chosen for yourself, faithful servant of the Lord that you are. A pity.

Leary couldn't feel his legs. His breath was coming hard. Not long now. His heart began to stutter in panic.

Time is running out, Archibald Leary. Your heart

B . A . R . B .

will stop beating in a few moments. Even now, Pridd approaches the chamber in the darkness, though he will be too late to witness your passing. He will remove your body and find me another who will follow. Though I would rather have you.

From somewhere came the sound of footsteps, a faint wet scraping of boots on brick. Leary tightened his grip on the gun.

Now.

Leary stepped from the sewer into a dawn like none he had ever seen. The night fog was gone, and all that was left behind was dappled in silver dew that made the grim city beautiful. His clothes were filthy, but that did not matter. He walked through the sunlit streets feeling light as a sparrow. Leary stopped at the corner of Charterhouse Square and Carthusian Street, where he had met Pridd the night before, and lit a cigar. It tasted wonderful. He blew the smoke out on the morning air and sucked in a deep breath.

He would return this evening to mask the entrance to the crypt, install a hidden door amongst the brickwork. It would take him some time, but he knew how to do it. No one would check these tunnels for weeks, especially now that Pridd was gone. He would tell the Corporation that Pridd had become unstable, that he had come banging at Leary's door after work, agitated, and then had not shown to a meeting Leary had arranged that night.

9 8

No one would find him in the crypt. They would assume he had absconded, or thrown himself into the Thames. He had no family. No one would care enough to look.

He walked to Farringdon Road casually, enjoying the stroll. A Hansom cab was idling, the horse in its nosebag, the driver half asleep. Leary gave his address and they were off, rushing across the city as it awoke. As they flew Leary imagined all the things he could build to improve the city, to leave an indelible mark upon it.

The front door opened as he approached, and an astonished Lily stood in the hall, her eyes wide and tearful. "My God!" She ran out to him and gathered him up, a force of strength and joy like an untamed river. Her hair was shining black, her eyes green and bright as summer grass. She looked twenty years younger. "It's a miracle!"

Leary held her tight and laughed fiercely, both of them howling in delight in the morning light while a few passersby stared.

"Where were you last night, Archie?"

Leary smiled at her. "Praying for your recovery, my love."

She smiled back. "Well, it worked! A true miracle! I've never heard of anything like it. Come! I've such an appetite for breakfast, and to share it with my husband after so long..." She took his hand and led him into the house.

Leary looked back at the street. On the opposite pavement stood Pridd, a ragged hole where his right eye had been before Leary put a bullet through it.

Pedestrians walked by him, unseeing. Pridd cocked his head, questioningly.

Leary nodded, slowly. Then he closed the door and went in search of his wife, and breakfast.

THE RE-POSSESSED

JAMES DORR

I T WAS OUR IMMORTAL BARD WHO stated, through the lips of his Danish Prince, that there are more things in heaven and earth than may be even dreamt of in our philosophies. Of this I have no doubt. Nor would I now question so much either the words of that American poet, E. A. Poe, concerning Life and Death, that "who shall say where the one ends, and where the other begins?"

I had myself a few years past, perhaps twenty some years after that same Mr. Poe's death in 1849, been on a mission for the sake of an aunt of mine to go into London to make certain arrangements. And as it happened, I and the gentleman who I was dealing with, a Daniel Higdon, having to wait on some assistant or other of his to determine some matter concerning the churchyard, fell into conversing.

"I see," said Higdon, an elderly man yet large in stature and, judging from his voice, still quite enough filled with vigor, "that you are a squire, a gentleman by your dress?"

I suppressed a chuckle then, I must allow, in that his own dress — the worn, black frock coat; the black, crepe-hung top hat — left no doubt to anyone what it was *he* was. So, instead, I nodded.

"You must understand, sir," Higdon went on, "the reason I ask, that I will deal only with gentlemen these days. I mean with *true* gentlemen, those that will keep their words and not renege on agreements afterward. I mean no impertinence; rather, I say this because of a happening some years ago that, had it turned otherwise, might have left me in ruin. And yet, as it fell out, it, may have been worse for me in the long run, in terms of peace of mind."

Well, I thought, this was, despite his denial, certainly at least *some* sort of an impertinence, yet this Higdon was one I had sought out because of a reputation for honesty — scrupulous honesty — which is always a consideration in arrangements of the sort we discussed. So for my aunt's sake, for sake of her bereavement, I bade him go on.

"I have been," Higdon said, "an undertaker for nigh these fifty years, going back even before the Warburton Act of '32, that which permitted the bodies of those died in paupers' hospitals, provided no relative should state objection and that they be, afterward, interred in hallowed ground, to be used by surgeons for their instruction. For mind you, sir, there was need enough for that — especially here in our own King's College — for how is a doctor to help preserve life if he does not know, first, the workings of that which the soul inhabits?

"But I get ahead of myself on this. The thing was, in those days, the profession I follow was different from these days, and sometimes attended with danger to boot. Gangs of criminals sometimes calling themselves 'resurrectionists' — they 'raised the dead,' you see — sometimes called 'sack-em-ups' for their method of carrying off their prey, hovered near churchyards awaiting burials, so, at night, they might reclaim the corpses to sell to anatomists. It was a trade, as mine, but one opposed to mine in that, you understand, it is my duty to see the deceased at peace. Not cut apart on some lecturer's table."

I shuddered, I think. I had heard of these things, of course, but many years ago. How indeed — I realized what he was getting at — there were sometimes even what one might call practically pitched battles between these resurrectionists and the men paid by undertakers like Higdon to stand guard by new graves. By graves with "inhabitants" still "fresh" enough to be useful to surgeons.

Higdon nodded. "You do understand, then, that this was at some expense, paid from the pockets of men like me — we ourselves sometimes joining those that we hired — to see the graves of at least the wealthier, those whose patrons might then reimburse us as part of our fee, warded from those who would thus desecrate them. And, as we have discussed already, there are other fees, coffins, winding-sheets, tips for the sexton, not to mention the labor we do ourselves for the deceased, to make them presentable for their funerals.

"Now, sir, are you squeamish?"

I shook my head, no. I did not think that I was. Yet I did not *know*, not yet, what this tale would be. How it would end up.

Higdon smiled. "Good," he said. "Now I must say I was just starting out in this trade on my own, having formerly been an employee of others, and it was all important to me that I should establish a good reputation. You understand that, sir, not just in the work I did, of highest quality and, yet, discretion too — ours, for reason, is called 'the dismal trade' — but also as a man versed in the business side. Honesty, after all, cuts both ways, does it not? And thus I jumped at an early commission, this from a wealthy man, a man of business, whose young wife had just passed on, one who was younger than he by a score of years. One who was beautiful, lively, charming, from all that I heard of her, and much in love with *him* — that is important, that she *did* love him well. Though, as I learned soon, he did not deserve her.

"For he was *no* gentleman for all his riches, this John Andercost. Yes, I may state his name — it does not matter. At least not any more. He disappeared. Some say he went mad first, shortly after this story I tell you, leaving no descendants one knows of.

"As for his deceased wife, Calantha Andercost... ."

Higdon paused then and reached into his frock

coat, drawing forth a flask. Passing it to me, the air being chilly I took a small tot as well, as he continued. "This John Andercost had many business friends, clients and the like, which could mean future referrals for me and my services should what I did for *him* prove to be wholly satisfactory. So I spared no expense, having steadfastly agreed with him as to the particulars. There was to be a laying out, for instance. A viewing. Which meant I must hire a woman to wash the corpse. There must be also a casket of the best — not some temporary affair, mind you, but one to go into the earth with her. These things all add up, you know.

"And then the sexton's costs. Warders for the grave — the year this took place still being no later than 1830, and sack-em-ups roving the streets in profusion. Gravediggers' fees. Ice to keep the corpse fresh before the viewing.

"And it was all worth it. To me. To him, I *thought* — I, of course, had also by then seen the young deceased's beauty, her worthiness of his care. Of all we did for her. And, for the viewing, several came afterward, friends of this Andercost, to compliment me on the skill of my work. On my demeanor, my comforting words, my sense of propriety, remaining at all times well in the background, yet available at the gravesite to assist any who needed assistance. A handkerchief. Nosegays. Yet always discreetly.

"And so, a week later, I had my bill sent to him — *and he refused it.*

"I thought then it must be grief. That or some problem, perhaps, with the families, in settling estates perhaps. These were things that could always happen. And so I waited — one must be discreet, of course — to give him time to gain back his composure.

"And yet, a week later, when I sent my bill again, once more it was returned.

"And then I started to hear the rumors. Rumors that I hoped were certainly false, but that, if true, could destroy my hoped for success for the future. These were not rumors that my work or conduct had in any way been unsatisfactory — indeed I had witnesses to the contrary, anyone who had attended the viewing, or been to the gravesite, even now still guarded, as it would be for a week to come until that which was in would be far enough gone so as to be of no further interest to those who might steal it — but, rather, that in a *business* sense I had been made a gull of. That John Andercost had never had any *intention* of paying.

"And so I allowed just one week more to pass — it still *could* have been grief — before I dismissed my men at the churchyard and, making some pretext, made my approach to my client in person. It was, after all, an important matter: If it were borne out that Andercost cheated me, and got away with it, what chance would I have with even more clever, wealthier clients who might take example from it in the future? In short, Andercost's friends — those that I counted on. Those that, in one or two instances, had already passed hints in my direction that, in time, my services might be desired.

"Thus, receipts in hand, I confronted John

Andercost — and once more was rebuffed. 'Let this be,' he said, 'a lesson in business. That one does not get as wealthy as I by paying expenses when one can avoid 'em. I had to see to my dead wife's burial, and all that went with it, because those I do business with expected it — you, of all people, should know about proper form — but now it's over. It's finished, you understand?'

"No, I did not. I played on his guilt — I *tried* to play on it. His guilt and his grief both. 'But sir,' I protested, 'you did love your wife? I know — I've been told — that she certainly loved *you*. How would she feel if somehow she knew that you had refused to pay for her burying? That her good memory meant so little to you... ?'

"Andercost laughed — he was, sir, *no* gentleman. He even *leered* then. I blush to tell it: 'Warm,' he said to me. 'Warm for her bed again, and me between the sheets. She was insatiable, Higdon, a young woman — and, yes, she did love *me*. But, as for me, well, I loved her beauty, her slender form on my arm when we dined out or went to the theatre with business acquaintances — she had her uses then — but she is gone now, and that is an end to it.'

"Again I protested. I tried to protest. 'Still, Mr. Andercost,' I began, but again he rebuffed me.

"'Still, Higdon,' he mocked me, looming now over me — I am a large enough man, as you can see, but he was larger yet — holding his stick aloft as if to strike me, 'there's no need at all for me to throw good money after bad, is there? The funeral is over. What's done has been done. What's in the ground lies there. If you raise a squawk, let me remind you I have enough money — because I *don't* spend money unnecessarily — to overcome any action you might attempt. So I'll put it to you as a businessman to a fellow businessman: What do you think you can *do* about it, re-possess my wife's corpse? Sell her yourself, perhaps, to the sack-em-ups?'"

Once again Higdon paused, drawing his flask out. Passing it to me when he'd had a swallow."God help me, I thought on that, after I'd left him. Of digging up Calantha Andercost's corpse *myself* to get at least a part of my costs back, except, as I've said, it would have been far enough 'turned' by then that I doubted I could have found a taker. So, instead, I wandered — it was afternoon by then, *late* afternoon — walking my own grief out. Not caring too much where I might be going. Until, by chance, I happened to find myself near the dockside.

"And here I must tell you that, when I had been an employee of others, I often took on poorer sorts of clients. Some of them near here, where I had wandered now, and so, by chance, I met with an acquaintance. This was a Negro-man, a Haitian sailor who had seized his freedom during the time of Henri Christophe's rebellion there and never gone back, living in London somewhere in the East End when he was not at sea. And, as you see that I am a large man, this man, who I knew only as Georges-Michel, was even larger. Larger and stronger than even John Andercost.

"So I told him what brought me there, wandering, thinking perhaps — I do not know for sure

— that, with night nearly fallen, we might accost this Andercost in his home. Maybe, disguised, to take from him my money. I *was* not thinking well.

"But my friend calmed me — I call him my friend now. He bought a drink for me. We discussed my troubles, how what was really needed was that Andercost not only *not* get away with non-payment of his bill, but that it be done in a manner that could be plainly seen to be completely just. And, more than even that, if rumors of it should later get out, it might serve as a warning to others who might try to be less than honest in dealing with men like me — men who, after all, did perform a most *necessary* service.

"Thus Georges-Michel said to me, 'I understand, *mon ami.* This *Jean* Andercost, he is a bad man, yes?'

"I answered that he was, adding to that, though, perhaps because I feared what Georges-Michel might do — still thinking, you see, that we might yet assault him — 'They say his wife loved him...'

"'And yet it is she, the wife, who this *cochon* insults. She who has been sullied thus in one's memory. You see, it is simple, yes?'

"I did not see. No. Yet I followed him into Limehouse to where he was staying to retrieve his sea bag, then, taking a carriage, to my own establishment. Then, changing my clothes, at his insistence we went to the churchyard where Calantha Andercost had been interred and, setting our canvas sheet down at the grave's side — this to receive the dirt, you see, so it could be put back when we were done with our work — proceeded swiftly with short wooden spades, a kind that makes little noise, by shaded lantern-light to play at sack-em-ups.

"Except we did not just break off the coffin end when we had reached it, to hook the corpse out and up as sack-em-up men do, always in haste you see — after all, one does not wish to be caught at it — but rather climbed down into the grave ourselves and pried the whole lid off.

"'My friend,' Georges-Michel whispered, 'you *have* spoke truly. I see she *is* beautiful, or at least that she was. You can see here, though, how some of the rot has already taken her — to be expected, of course, in this length of time. How the grave beetles have burrowed *here* and *here*. And yet, still, some *shadow* of her beauty.'

"I nodded, as I recall, then at his order I scrambled back out to act as a lookout while Georges-Michel worked. I passed down his sea bag. While Georges-Michel spoke on of what he was doing.

"'The *ti bon ange* — what we call where I come from the "little good angel-soul" — it is the thing that is all important. These powders I use now, they will tempt it back. These words that I will say. You see, *mon ami*, insulted so by the one she so loved, this soul, it cannot rest. So there is time yet... .'

"'Is time,' I echoed him. Well I remember still even the slightest detail of that dark night. 'But time for what, Georges-Michel?'

"'Ah!' Georges-Michel whispered. Sprinkling more powders, he scrambled up himself out of the grave. 'For this, *mon ami*,' he said.

"And at that I shrank back. I nearly ran from

there, I will confess it now, except that my friend, Georges-Michel, grasped me by the arm. Because another form, that of a woman, had just climbed out, too, from that yawning, open grave. A woman half-decomposed, one entire side all blackened with it, yet recognizable. One with long, curled, blonde hair, on half its head anyway. Half its face still intact.

"'*Le corps cadavre*,' Georges-Michel whispered. 'In Haiti, where I was raised ... but wait! The moment comes.

"'*Calantha!*' he shouted.

"The corpse looked up now, its dull, glassy eyes opening wide. It turned then to gaze at *him*. At Georges-Michel who held something out to it.

"'It is the shouting of the *name* that joins them together, the soul and the body. The *ti bon ange* and the *corps cadavre*. That makes it remember. That and what I feed it now, that which is used by *bokors* on the island I dare not return to. And yet can be found, if one looks hard enough, even here in your London.'

"He turned again to the corpse, speaking in more of a normal voice now, while I, responding to motions his hands made, crept behind them to fill the grave back up. 'Calantha, tell me this. How do you feel this night?'

"The corpse grinned at us both first without speaking, a terrible grin, as, with crumbling hands, it adjusted its grave-clothes. Flicking the worms off as it pirouetted, then turned back to Georges-Michel.

"'Warm,' it answered.

"Georges-Michel nodded. Whispering to me

he said, 'She can no longer be a *gentlewoman*. That much has been stripped from her, forever lost now. But she *will* remember that which is important. A woman, she knows her needs.'

"She gave a moan then that I will not forget, never until I die. That of an animal — a sound *inhuman*. As if of some beast in rut. While I, trembling, finished the refilling, scooping the last of the earth back onto the grave. Folding the canvas up, the shovels inside it, into a bundle. Blowing the lanterns out, save for the one we would use while walking home. Finally speaking:

"'What now, Georges-Michel?' I asked.

"Smiling, he answered, taking the corpse-woman's arm on his as he led us out to the street, 'In simple justice, my friend, I should say that it is our duty to restore this poor woman to her husband.'"

THE VELVET RIBBON

JAY SEATE

1890

K
ATHERINE DID SOMETHING SHE WOULD NOT
normally have done. Toast a corpse with a
glass of champagne. But this was a special
occasion. She sipped from her glass as she stood at
her bay window. Between the cliffs, the ocean crept
onto the small strip of sandy shore like a watery
eyelid closing over the sand then receding again
into the darkening abyss.

She turned and looked at the body, and was
tempted to seek out Frederick's warm, moist places
before coolness and rigor became its master. His
and her playful antics had been amusing. "I'll miss
you, you know," she whispered to the body splayed
upon the floor of her boudoir.

Katherine sat down in front of her beautiful

vanity. Its mirror was large enough to lose oneself in self-examination. Events had not changed the face that looked back at her. If anything, her passionate rosy glow had deepened. She ran her palm over the smooth lacquered surface before opening the upper left-hand drawer. From it she took the sheet of Frederick's stationary that he had rolled and tied with a red velvet ribbon. It had been delivered this very morning. She slipped off the ribbon and read it one more time.

My Darling Katherine,

You are the queen of my heart. I will venture my soul to win you.

I have decided to act. I will come for you after I am done with the Baron.

Soon, my love.

F

Poor Frederick. Katherine was everything he'd ever wanted and would never have. She peered out from her bedroom window once more and watched the dying light extend and soften the shadows from the cliffs. It swept across the cold ocean while the waves pounded upon the ominous rocks with incessant rage, hungry to reclaim them. The scene could illicit a feeling of fading beauty, or even desolation after sunset, but tonight she felt anticipation. She looked out over the dark Atlantic which now appeared to be the edge of eternity in its sinister, vast blackness. But for Katherine, there was no room for darkness as a solitary star to wish upon popped out from a space between the clouds. No darkness on this night now that her admirer had fulfilled the promise revealed in his note.

She turned her attention to the winding road that ran across the coastline above the cliffs as she pondered over what she would tell the authorities. As the clouds rolled in and captured the star with damp fingers driven by the sea, the earth below darkened even more as she thought back over the events of the last hour.

Frederick's carriage had pulled up in front of the house. She ran down the stairs to greet him. She threw open the massive oak door and watched him climb from the carriage and approach. He was tall and straight, and his footsteps were deliberate as he plodded up the walkway. It seemed like forever until Frederick reached the top step, prolonging her anticipation. A cold dampness intruded, carried along with the ocean breeze that coursed up Katherine's legs beneath her dress and made her tingle in a way she hadn't in ages. Her heart was beating fast as she asked, "Is it done?"

"Yes, Katherine. It's done."

Her eyes gave away intelligence and revealed a careful mind which summed up situations quickly. She could see the truth of his words. She took hold of Frederick's arm and drew him into the foyer. "Then we must celebrate. It is the beginning after all."

"Yes, I guess we must."

She felt a mean and filthy joy, but joy nonetheless. She looked into Frederick's hooded eyes and thought she saw a flicker of regret. "No guilt," she said as much to herself as to him. "It had to be done." Then she smiled. "How would you have me this evening on our first night of freedom?"

"I'd have you in all manner of ways, as you've promised, once the deed was done."

"Then let's make haste to fulfill those promises." Katherine pulled him further into the house and kissed his lips passionately."

"Don't you want to know what happened?"

"No. Only that it is done and over, and no one will ever know. As far as I'm concerned, I would as soon never hear of the Baron again, although I must. There will surely be an inquest." Katherine kissed Frederick again then stepped back. "Enough of dour thoughts. It's time for you to take what's been promised."

Katherine knew her image was intoxicating and it always seemed to set Frederick aflame. How else could he have agreed to do such a thing? He'd always gazed at her as if she was some incredible treasure he'd stumbled upon, but his look was now colored by lust. "You're right, dear Katherine. It's time to begin our lives and our fortune together."

"Quite so. And it will be my pleasure to satisfy you." She held her hands out to Frederick. "Come to me, my love, and let the wrath of God take the Baron and his distasteful ways."

Frederick smothered Katherine's face with kisses. His hands sought the rest of her as though she were some exotic feast to be consumed. He squeezed her with an urgent hunger, trying to take in all of her at once.

Wouldn't the Baron be amused at this indulgent scene, Katherine thought. She was in a world no longer veiled by the shadow of her beastly, controlling husband.

"Sweet mother of heaven," Frederick gasped as he fondled Katherine. "Tell me this is only the beginning of our splendor?"

"It can only be so if we're not seen together for an acceptable period. But for now, to the bedroom," Katherine breathed.

"It wouldn't be prudent for me to spend the night," Frederick cautioned. "Not yet."

"I'm not thinking of all night. You must be on your way very soon. Yet we deserve a few moments of repose. I want us to have a comfortable place to express our love, dear Cupid, so you may release one of your arrows." She led him up the stairs and into the boudoir. She pointed to the champagne bottle on a sideboard and said coquettishly, "As soon as you've had your way with me, we'll toast the future."

Frederick adored Mrs. Morrison with his eyes. "Dear God, Katherine, I should have done what I did today long ago. So much time wasted." Like a true gentleman, he took her hands and kissed the center of each palm as if neither murder nor licentiousness had preceded this gesture. "I've waited so long for this sweet surrender. Parting, even for a while a while will bring such sorrow, my love," he told Katherine, anticipating a lusty consummation of their desire.

"True words. I will feel the pain as well." Katherine pulled free, reached under her pillow, and came away with a small derringer pistol her husband had given her for protection. She pointed it at Frederick's chest.

Frederick looked at her. His expression abruptly changed from rapture to vertiginous disorientation. "What's this?"

"I care for you with all that passes for my heart," Katherine said, "and I will truly miss you, but I can't inherit all of this merely to give it to another man. You can understand, can't you, my darling?"

Then she shot him.

With disbelieving eyes, Frederick pitched and fell facedown on the floor. One of his hands reached out toward Katherine's foot as if it might be the life raft that would save him. She stepped back and stood next to Frederick for several minutes until he moved no more.

She dropped the pistol on the floor, stepped over Frederick's body and took the glass of champagne to her bedroom window. Her pleasing reflection appeared in the glass. She'd managed to have her husband done away with and had dispatched her lover all on the same evening, two encumbrances removed for the price of one. Some things should not be experienced in a lifetime and these acts certainly qualified, but what choice had she been given—to run off with Frederick and leave the Baron's riches to some trollop?

One final time, she observed the body of the man to whom she had bestowed the hope of her charms, a poor infatuated man caught in her web, now fallen into the abyss. The side of his dead face was as pale as a dinner candle, but still he was a handsome specimen. His wound would make an ugly spot on the imported rug, but some compromises couldn't be avoided. Her dalliance with Frederick had warmed her. Her lips were swollen and puffy from Frederick's insistent kisses. Her mouth still held the taste of her dead lover. The memory of their capricious behavior brought a slight upturn to the corners of her mouth.

In a house no longer filled with her indulgent desperation, what had she expected to feel? Sadness at Frederick's passing? Euphoria at the Baron's demise, knowing she was no longer bound to the wheel of her inhibited past? She puzzled over the paradox, but only briefly, and settled on instant nostalgia for the way Frederick had wanted her. She froze the moment in her mind, preserving the rush without following the impulse toward permanence. The nostalgia would carry her to the promise of randy times to come for there was a world of possibilities to explore.

Katherine rolled up Frederick's missive and slipped the ribbon around its girth. Her plan was simple: A man other than her husband had shown interest in her. None could blame a slight, impulsive flirtation, given the Baron's overbearing demeanor and nasty disposition. At least that's how she would make it sound.

She'd shown the Baron the letter and warned him of Frederick's intentions, but he hadn't taken the lovesick Romeo's remarks seriously, she would tell the authorities. He had treated with scorn the notion that someone would pursue her. Frederick came to the house and announced he'd killed the Baron. He'd begged Katherine to go away with him. When she rebuffed his entreaties, he attacked her. She fought her way to her bedroom where she found the means to defend herself and shot him down.

It would be a scandal to be sure, but she would be good at acting horrified at the acts of the flirtatious Frederick.

After all the unpleasantness, Katherine intended to have a string of lovers, to surrender to the lure of adventure. Her pretty face and trim figure promised to be a portal into the future which contained other young, rambunctious men who would be as covetous of her affection as was Frederick. She wondered how long her period of mourning need last before pursuing a suitable replacement. She only hoped the next was as eager as he, but there would be great delight in the exploration.

Further, she planned to write about her dalliances. It was high time the world was exposed to the antics men and women might be inclined to undertake in their private chambers away from prying eyes. And she'd always had a way with words.

Katherine thought her story through one more time. "Everything done and buttoned down," her late husband might have said. In a moment, she would dress a bit more modestly, even chastely, and take Frederick's carriage to the nearest house with the story of his attack. She would cry as she told of him chasing her up the stairs into her bedroom where she had saved herself from his beastly advances with her tiny weapon.

Just then, she heard the oak door open in the foyer. She had not seen the need to secure it. At first, she heard nothing more than the waves and cliffs carrying on their perpetual quarrel. Then the sound of footfalls. Could someone have heard the shot? A seismic shift of attitude from breezy to bloodcurdling struck Katherine's marrow. She ran to the top of the winding stairway. Her next breath caught in her throat as if a large hand had closed around her windpipe.

Starting up the stairs toward her was the Baron. He was as pale as the corpse of Frederick, even a bit bluish perhaps, or was his coloring due to the rising moon? And he was, *God in heaven*, speckled with moist soil from what must have been a hasty burial.

"You're alive," Katherine called down breathlessly to her husband while remaining at the top of the stairs, trying to think quickly, not sure what he knew or didn't know. "Thank God you're alive."

The Baron climbed solemnly without speaking, each step thumping up the wooden stairs, bringing him closer to his wife.

"I've just been attacked," she hurriedly said. "I fought him off and was saved by your pistol." Her situation was too shocking to give a good, spontaneous performance. She forced her tear ducts into action. "If only you had arrived sooner. What did he do to you, darling?"

Finally, the Baron spoke in the deep, gruff voice that had often given Katherine the shivers, but never more so than on this occasion as he approached ever nearer. "Why would you think he did anything to me, dear wife?"

"Well, because...you're covered in mud and there's blood on your scalp."

"Very observant. It's not the blow to my head, but the suffocation of the earth that did the trick."

"What are you talking about? You're here and, thank God, you have survived."

"But I didn't survive. Frederick told me everything before he whacked me and made his feeble attempt to hurriedly bury me along the ramparts overlooking the ocean so I might hear its siren's call for eternity." The Baron continued his slow, deliberate climb, closer and closer to his beloved. A grimace painted his face, frozen into a death mask, his mouth moving only enough to form words. Rich men always felt confident speaking, even dead ones.

Katherine's mouth formed an oval. No words of explanation came to mind. No attempt at playacting would suffice. Her only thought was to retreat, pick up the pistol, and use it again to make sure this man, or this wraith, was truly dead. She turned on her heel in retreat, but ran into an object blocking her path.

The object was none other than Frederick. He stood on the threshold of Katherine's bedroom door.

"No more escapes, my sweet," he said to her as some of his voice seeped through the newly acquired hole in his chest.

"I didn't want to hurt you, Frederick. I was selfish. I wasn't thinking clearly. I—"

Frederick grabbed hold of her flailing arms and swung her around to face the Baron, who had reached the upper landing. "Too late, dearest," the hole in his chest whispered. He pulled her head back against his shoulder by her hair. "Happy new beginnings, Katherine," his lips thinly whispered.

"You're not real!"

"I'm afraid we're very real," the revenants said in unison.

Katherine had not noticed till that moment the hunting knife the Baron held at his side. "Yes, my dear," he breathed. "A toast to new beginnings on behalf of your cuckolded husband." His dead fingers tightened around the knife's handle. His frozen scowl was the most horrible sight Katherine had ever witnessed, or could ever have imagined.

Her next set of emotions were sudden, unexpected, and alien to all of the others—shock and despair not unlike the unsuspecting wave hurling itself to destruction against immovable rock. The emotions were accompanied by a gush of warm blood. Everything happened too fast to think about pain. She noticed her white blouse had turned crimson, the color of her most daring shade of lip paint, the color of Frederick's red velvet ribbon that encircled his words of resolve, words that had sealed the fate of all three.

For Katherine there would be no more champagne, for eternity might very well be spent in the grasp of two corpses who were very disappointed in her.

Agony In Red

Jen Ponce

W AS IT POSSIBLE TO BE SUFFOCATED by crinoline and petticoats, bustles and collars? I believed it was, because here I was at my husband's table, unable to breathe. Across from me, oblivious to my slow asphyxiation, Mr. Wold chewed his food with gusto, his attention buried in the newspaper. I wasn't certain what was worse: the smacking sounds he made or the manner in which he masticated—mouth agape so that crumbs escaped and landed in his beard. There was a piece of greasy pheasant there now, the oil gleaming in the candlelight.

For fifteen years I'd been sitting across from him, watching him chew, watching him ignore me, watching him stuff himself with food I helped prepare and all I could do was think about the interminable years of the same stretching before me. Hell wasn't filled with sinners and murderers; it was filled with men like Mr. Wold and women like me who have to suffer them.

He wiped his mouth, folded his paper, and adjusted his stout body in his seat as was his habit. Next, he would smile at me as if I were three and he'd like to pat me on the head. "Delicious as usual, Mrs. Wold."

The formality stuck in my throat and my words came out strangled. His smile didn't change.

"I shall see the children at half past seven, before they go to bed. See to it that they are quiet until then."

I had a fork in my hand, the silver heavy and cold. The tines weren't sharp but if I used enough force I could plunge it into the jelly of his eyeball and elicit a scream from him that would cut through that endless, dark monotony of my life.

"Evelyn?" His smile slipped, returned, as if he were unsure of what to do with whatever he saw on my face.

"Of course," I managed, still musing upon the utensil in my hand. I would hang for it, but even that eventuality was better than the invariability of tomorrow and the day after that and the day after that and ...

Perhaps it would have saved him, saved me, if he'd asked how I was, if he'd bothered to look past his own concerns to see me, really see me as an equal rather than his wife, his property. But he rose from his chair and gave me a perfunctory kiss upon my brow as was his habit, before leaving me to the remains of our meal.

I stared down at my plate, at my hand still holding the fork, and wished with all my heart I could walk out the door and away from my husband, my children, my house, my own womanhood, each a link in the chain that enslaved me.

If only I'd been born a man. Had I a cock, I would be free, for even the poorest man in Cheapside had more rights than I.

The candle flickered, disturbed by a dark breeze, the flame crackling and lengthening before going out utterly. One followed the next until I sat in shadows. Behind me, the window creaked as it opened.

What would I find if I turned to look? An empty street? A sweeper, away to his work? A monster with a horror-grin? I twisted in my seat.

The window was ajar, this was true, but no monster stared back at me. Across the way, a gas lamp flickered and the grandfather steam-clock piped six behind me, the notes once loud to my ears but now faded, like a memory I couldn't quite catch.

I shivered at the algid air caressing my arms and rose at once to shut it out. Sara, our maid, had cleaned windows today and she must have forgotten to latch this one. My mouth was open to call her when I saw movement across the way. A figure stood just outside the circle of yellow thrown by the gaslight, a manteau of shadows cloaking her face from view. Her face, because I saw the bell of her dress peep out from the umbra.

Come.

The mellifluous sound was only the suggestion of a word, but it filled and filled me with its promise. Gooseflesh rose upon my skin in its wake, the tiny prickles of discomfort the only thing keeping me from rushing out the front door to her. What was this strange compulsion I had to join her curbside, to let her take me wherever she wished to go?

I shut the window and locked it, panting, and pressed my forehead against the cool glass to watch the woman watch me.

Come.

How was it I could still hear the word when it could no longer carry itself to me upon the breeze? Something not unlike fear stirred in my belly and sped my heart as I stared out at the sentinel beyond. In truth, she was probably no more than a night flower come to do her work at one of the houses on my street, who happened to stop and stare into my window. Except I didn't believe that she was here for anyone else but me.

"Mistress?"

I startled, my hand flying to my décolletage. "Sara! Don't sneak up on me like that."

"I didn't, mistress, I swear it! I called your name five times and you didn't answer me, not once!" My maid's lustrous brown eyes stared at me in wide-eyed horror, as if she'd never before seen me gaze out of a window.

"Well, I'm sorry I worried you." I took a shallow breath, then another, not wanting to faint because

I'd forgotten, for a moment, how to exist as a bird in a cage of whalebone and satin. I smoothed my hands down my dress to settle my nerves and moved toward the table, away from the curious apparition outside. It had been cleared. "What—?"

"I brought the automaton to clean it up, mistress, all the while talking with you, but you didn't make a sound at all. I finally came over to touch you and it's then you heard me."

"I didn't ... I wasn't ..." The grandfather clock by the fireplace read five 'til seven. "That cannot be."

Sara checked over her shoulder and then nodded fiercely. "A whole hour, mistress." She stepped a bit closer, nerves drawing her skin tight across her cheekbones. Her former masters had abused her, she'd told me, and she'd never gotten over the fear of it. "My ma used to tell me there were creatures, dark, soulless things they, what come to us in times of sorrow and despair and feed on us. They steal time, she said, and told me to "ware beautiful strangers." She eyed me, trying to decide if I would hit her for sharing her ma's wisdom. Her slight nod suggested she trusted me. "Who were you looking at out there, mistress?"

I glanced at the window, beyond the glass, casting about the shadows for sign of the woman but she was gone as if she'd never been. "No one."

When I turned back, Sara crossed herself. "I hope that's true, mistress. But in case it's not, you'd best get on your knees tonight and pray."

Pray, said she. It wasn't prayer that I needed, but I nodded just the same.

After parading my children in front of Mr. Wold so that he could play at being their father, I put them to bed with the help of Sara, then sent that one to her rest early. Mr. Wold went out, as usual, but instead of going straight up to bed as was my wont, I went into the garden instead. I picked my way down the paving-stone path without so much as a candle to guide my way and stood beside the garden house to contemplate the black sky. As I stilled, the crickets began their songs again, and in the old oak tree by the back gate, a robin sang its piping tune.

It had worked before, this night-gazing, when prayer had failed me. Staring up at the stars calmed and centered me so that I could put on a cheerful smile for the children and remember the affection I had for my husband. Tonight, though, I didn't feel calmed but restless, and I again felt the urge to walk away from all my obligations. If only I had hope that I would find a better life somewhere else, but there was little prospect for me wherever I went. My choices were limited: scullery maid, governess, cook, or whore.

I was safe here, well-fed, well-clothed, and my husband, while inattentive, did not beat me with fists or force me in bed. It always could have been worse, and yet I yearned to be a person in my own right, someone who controlled her own agency, who made her own decisions and then flew or fell because of them.

A rustle of leaves behind me stilled my wandering

thoughts and narrowed them down to that one noise.

A footstep.

There was someone in the garden with me.

I expected fear but instead a wash of calm stole over me so that I was unafraid. Calm, yes, and something more, something that teased to life the tiny ember of rebellion I'd harbored deep within my soul for so long. Whoever it was behind me, I would embrace them. Murderer or monster, I would clasp them to my breast and thank them for shattering the monotony of my existence.

"Turn around."

A woman's voice, lilting and sensuous in a way mine could never be.

"Who are you?" I asked without moving, wanting to hear her voice one more time before I saw her.

"Freedom."

I turned my head, my shoulders, my feet, revealing her by increments: her dress, a dark blue watered silk; her arms, bare of gloves and so pale; her face... my breath caught in my throat. Her face was all sharp angles, her cheekbones blades, her lips a slash of red across the face of a corpse. She was beautiful and she was a monster. She was both of these things at once, and I could not absorb it. I averted my eyes, fixing them on her shoulder so that I might be able to concentrate on our conversation and ask my next question. "Freedom?"

"It is what my kind can offer to yours, if we deem you worthy." Without seeming to move at all, she came closer to me and I knew then that her footfall had been deliberate. Had she wanted to sneak up on me I wouldn't have heard her at all. "It is what our kind yearn for, is it not?"

My kind, our kind. I made the mistake of raising my eyes from her shoulder and her gaze snared mine.

"Don't forget to breathe, my dear."

And as if her words were magic, I took as deep a gasp of air as I could manage.

"Our kind," she continued, "trapped in gilded cages, eating only when our masters feed us, singing for them when they ask." She touched my cheek with her bone cold fingers. "Don't you wish for more?"

"Every day," I whispered.

She moved around me, widdershins, trailing her fingers along my arm, my shoulders, leaving behind sparks of the spell she wove.

"My kind," she said, the icy words dancing along my skin, "feed on your kind. We live in the shadows, yes, but not because we fear you, oh no. It's to keep our little cows placid until it's time to slaughter them."

She smiled then and showed her ancient and yellowed teeth with their fine points like needles. So very many needles.

She picked up my arm, numb from shock or fear I did not know, and flicked open the tiny buttons that did up my glove. No one but Mr. Wold had ever taken off my gloves in such a manner, certainly not Sara or Nancy, my maid as a girl in my father's house. With each button undone, so too I came undone, until I was but a mess of need and terror. The air on my heated skin burned with its chill but I could no more pull away from her than I could fly, and so I watched as she peeled the material away to expose the tender flesh of my wrist, my palm, and my fingers.

"This vein here"—she dragged a nail across my bracelet lines—"can be sliced this way or"—the nail went from my palm to my inner elbow, a touch so intimate I thought I must pull away or be guilty of the direst sin—"that. Both will cause you to spill your blood, but one will most certainly see you to your death."

Ensorcelled by the spell she worked with her words, I saw my blood spilling from my arm, great fountains of it, so much that it soaked the ground at my feet and rose up to drown me. I staggered backward, gasping, yanking my arm free of her grip. "You must leave, I must go in, you must go away now, I must ..." I panted, rubbing my arm and its intact skin, reassuring myself that I was still intact and unharmed.

"Oh, I don't think I will go anywhere. You called me here, after all, with your maudlin self-pity and your yearning and your despair. Do you believe I would leave you now without collecting what is mine by right?" Slashes of umber and indigo made her face appear skeletal, like death herself had come to escort me to the hereafter.

It was in that moment that I knew I would not be leaving the garden alive.

"Please," I said. The rest of the words congealed in my throat. Please don't. Please don't kill me. Don't harm me. Don't spill my blood upon the ground and leave me here for my family to find. In the distance, the chug of a steam-powered carriage made me furiously hopeful and then despairing when I realized no matter how loudly I screamed, they would not hear me.

"If you insist." She was upon me faster than a snake and struck me with her mouth as a serpent would do. Pain exploded from my wrist outward, her nails scratching me as they held me still for her needle teeth. I opened my mouth to scream, but I couldn't. I tried to pull my arm away, but the agony was too great. She had bitten me to the bone, she would tear off my arm, I would bleed to death in silence in the middle of the garden, all the details of my grisly murder would be passed from mouth to mouth before noon tomorrow.

My knees gave out and I sank down in front of her, a supplicant begging for the priest's blessing, only no priest, she. Her eyes rolled up to look at me and every joint, every muscle in my body felt as though they were rolled in glass and set on fire. "Please," I tried again, but darkness stole over me, the shadows she wore enveloped me, the sounds of the night faded, and I knew no more.

When I woke, London, too, was waking around me. Worker sounds, house sounds, pipes belching steam and gears grinding, though muffled. When I woke, I was buried in dirt that pressed against my face oppressively, insistently. I didn't dare scream, so I shifted, moved, clawed at my grave, striving toward the air. Had I not been panicking, perhaps I would have noticed my chest did not rise and fall, nor did my heart beat in my breast. These things I would discover later, when my predictable, boring life shattered into a thousand, glittery pieces.

Night air struck my left hand first, then my right, then I pulled myself free with a triumph unnoticed by any living creature but a crow that cawed at me reprovingly. A dog barked furiously in the distance, the sound burgeoning on hysteria and a man shouted back. I pulled myself free of my grave and flopped upon my back, exhausted.

Memories flooded back, of the woman, of her attack. I raised the appendage she had savaged. It was unblemished, unbroken, without a single scratch or bruise. My memory of the night before was not hazy with time; I remembered the pain of her teeth sinking into my flesh, the tearing of her nails as she held me, helpless. She had bitten me, but where was the wound?

The night sky was no longer blue-black and I was no longer in my garden.

A quick glance around me told me I was correct. No garden house, no oak, no stone fence surrounding the yard. If not my garden, then where was I? And why had she moved me? How? Too many questions and I didn't have time to find the answers. I needed to get back home before Sara noticed my absence and worked up a fuss. On my feet, I searched for a landmark or something to tell me where I was.

A great factory loomed over me on my left, its chimneys belching black smoke into the sky. The windows of the lower level glowed red from the great furnaces used to create the steam. Men yelled orders, acquiescence, and crude jokes to one another inside, their voices faint. Somewhere in the Steam District, then. That didn't narrow things down much.

A row of shops, shuttered and huddled together like frightened children stretched to my right. "Bartleby's Steam Driven Prams" read one sign and "Suits, Soaps, and Sundries" another. Farther down, a mechanical horse rattled, steam belching out of its ears while workers loaded the cart behind it with casks.

I did not recognize anything.

A smell caught my attention. A delectable smell, one that made my stomach growl in a manner most unseemly. I lifted my chin and sniffed like a dog. A host of scents filled my nose, scents for which I did not have a name. The most prominent, the one that piqued my interest most was the rich, warm, living copper that smelled like food. And I was so hungry. I got to my feet and followed my nose, uncaring for the moment that I was out at night without my husband, without any idea of where I was. The only thing that mattered was the mouth-watering aroma that led me to a young man sitting with his eyes shut, his head leaning against a crumbling brick wall. His eye was bruised, his throat red, and it was obvious his shirt was newly torn despite it being a filthy rag that had seen better days. The rip bisected his sleeve, and a bright red slash of color cut across his skin.

Why did I yearn to taste his blood? Why did it smell so good?

There was no one else around us. Of that I made sure, though I didn't know why...yet. I crept closer and knelt in front of him. "Sir?"

No answer but a brief flutter of his lashes.

A single drop of red slid down his arm to plop on the cobbles at his feet. I heard it move over his skin, the sound of fingers on velvet, heard it wetly hit the ground and splatter, and when it did, the spicy fragrance redolent of roasted deer cooked slowly over an open fire filled my nose.

I checked my surroundings again, and then leaned in closer, closer, to press my nose against his abused neck and breathe him in.

Pain erupted in my mouth, my jaws snapped open, and then I bit him, and oh, dear Lord in Heaven, he tasted so good. Light filled me. Heat. I soared, I was transported, the blood—his blood—sliding down my throat with every suck. His pulse weakened, the blood became sluggish and just as suddenly as it began, it ended. The second his heart stopped, the blood died with it and I threw myself away from him, gagging.

He slid backward, his blood smearing on the brick, and then his head hit the cobbles with a sick thudding sound. One of his pale hands flopped to the side, his fingers slack.

He was dead.

What had I done?

I wiped at my mouth with my hands, one gloved, one not, trying to rub away the evidence of my sin. I killed the young man, bit him like a savage beast, and I had enjoyed it.

"No," I whispered. "No!" Louder. I heard a man react some distance away and I knew I had to flee, but where?

I picked up my skirts and ran pell-mell in the opposite direction, down streets I did not recognize, past night flowers and nefarious sorts, always running, not stopping for them to question me or take hold. I ran until I smelled the Thames, its reek so pungent I gagged.

The sky had lightened more, which scared me for reasons I could not fathom. Surely I should be glad for the sun, but I panicked and ran down shadowed lanes, searching for somewhere to hide. I allowed myself to be scared, unable to quell the fear that rose in me at being caught out when morning became a reality. Later, when I was calm I would evaluate it. Now, I had to find a place where I could shelter.

A small girl walked out of a rotted and broken door, smelling of grease and sweat and dirt. I waited only until she was out of sight before stepping through the door she'd come out of. Somewhere above me, I heard a woman in agony or passion, I could not discern which and did not wish to investigate. I found a small closet off the kitchen and hid in the dark corner, pulling bags of potatoes and turnips about me. Only when I was safe did I think of what I'd done. A madwoman. A murderess. I would hang for it, just as I had so cavalierly considered a better fate than marriage earlier this night.

What a fool, I.

I did not wish to die at the end of a rope, hanged before my neighbors for all to jeer at me and my sins. Death should be a private affair and yet we made it public... *I* had made it public, killing that young man, that boy. Perhaps hanging was exactly what I deserved.

Despite the dim light, I could see myself clearly, could see the jars of jam, vegetables, and fruits quite clearly. I could also see my remaining glove, blood-soaked and dirty. I peeled the offending garment off, shivering at the memory of that woman in the garden taking the other. Before I could help myself, I pressed my nose into the fabric to smell the blood.

So good.

Good?

I thrust the glove away in revulsion, shoving it to the bottom of a sack of parsnips. Good? How could I think the scent of blood, good?

As the kitchen came to life, I fell into a deep but troubled slumber and did not awaken until nightfall. I was not sure how I knew the sun had set, but I rose invigorated, feeling strong and sure of myself.

The sounds of the house were more pronounced now, sounds of rutting, of whispering, of transactions being made. I found I could hear them all with ease. The boiler gurgling, the pipes hissing with steam. Even the poorer homes had steam heat, but it was usually piped in from a community boiler. That this place had its own meant the owners of the establishment had money.

I rose from my hiding spot and eased open the closet door. The kitchen was warm and yeasty, meaty too, the scent of burnt vegetables overlaying it all. I intended to go out the door and make my way back home, but I was arrested by the steady sound of all those heartbeats throbbing in my ears. How was it I'd never before noticed that beautiful sound? The sound of life, of heat, of...*food*.

"No, I won't," I whispered to myself, but it was too late; my body had a mind of its own, and my feet propelled me to the main room, what one might, with a generous dollop of imagination, call a salon. There were women there in such a state of dishabille that I could not warrant it. I'd never seen another woman's breasts before and yet here were three women, all bare from their waists up. One was being fondled by a man in a purple waistcoat fairly bulging at the seams. Another was bobbing her head over a skinny gentleman's crotch, and I felt heat rush to my cheeks when I divined exactly what act she was performing with such vigorousness.

The third woman was kissing a man I knew very well indeed.

"Mr. Greenleaf?"

My husband's solicitor jerked his head back, his

lips a red smear from the woman's coralline salve. "Mrs. Wold? Whatever are you doing here?"

"I could ask you the same question, sir. For isn't your wife eight months into her confinement?" The idea that Mrs. Greenleaf was home, more than likely alone and uncomfortable, while her husband frolicked with whores made me unaccountably angry. "What man does that to a gentlewoman?"

"I say, Mrs. Wold, I don't think it is any of your concern." He pushed at the night flower's hands, which kept fiddling with his buttons and popping them open until the great expanse of his hairy belly was exposed. "Stop it, girl, or I shall knock you senseless."

One moment, I was upset, the next I was biting into the wattled flesh of his neck while around me women screamed. Men screamed too, when I turned on them, and I took each one out until their bodies lay twitching upon the floor. The girls huddled in the corner, shivering, eyes lowered, which was good, because I wasn't sure I could keep my hunger at bay if they ventured close.

I was halfway up the stairs when the first man came out of a room, his pants hastily donned, his hair askew. "What the Devil is going on down there?"

I had him before the last word left his mouth. Then I had his fellow in the next room.

I killed them all, all ten of them, and drank until my belly was painfully full. I felt a bit drunk, actually, as if the alcohol my victims had imbibed was now affecting me. I leaned on the railing and caught sight of the women below. "I'm sorry." The words were too quiet so I spoke them again with more force. "I don't know what came over me." It had been too easy to kill the men, too easy to drink them down and feel the ecstasy of their deaths.

An older woman, fully dressed, peeled herself away from her fellows. "Are you planning on doing to us what you did to them?"

"No. Not at all. It's just...I think you must stay away from me in case..."

She nodded, clearly wary of me even as she mounted the bottom step. "Will you leave peacefully?"

I gazed down at my dress, a sorry mess of blood and other things about which I did not wish to think. "I will. But do you have something more suitable for me to wear?"

"I have a dress that might fit you, missus, if you let me pass." At my nod, she marched up the stairs like a general going to war, back straight, eyes filled with steel. For all her bravado, she hesitated when she was but a few steps away. "You promise you won't harm me?"

"I give you my word." Saying that made me feel powerful, and I realized what little control I had over my life to think that giving my word to a whore would make me feel in command of my own fate. I stepped back so she could pass and did not follow her too closely so as not to frighten her. We went into her tiny room, done up as neat as she could make it with what means she had. A small, cheap vase of dried flowers stood on the nightstand by a tiny window that looked out on a brick wall opposite. Her bed was made up with a quilt of blues and greens and yellows and when she opened the trunk at the foot of it, I felt bad for asking for a dress. She had very little and here I was going to take from her that which was very dear. "Please, I don't wish to pauper you. An apron to cover this mess would suit me fine."

"An apron won't cover shit, if I may be so bold. You're a right mess, you are." She dug out a blue frock, a bit worn and out-of-fashion, an old dress from the beginning of the century, when looking like a Greek column was all the rage. "This was my ma's. I kept it for no good reason and you can have it with my blessing." Her eyes were hard as she studied me. "You'll have to lose the corset, of course, and most of your underthings. These dresses don't look good with a bunch of nonsense underneath them." We stood staring at each other for a brief moment, and then she sighed. "Turn around. I'll help you out of that lot."

A lady's maid she was not, but she stripped me down efficiently enough, and helped me into the new gown. Without my stays, petticoats, and bustle, I felt quite under-dressed.

"Feels good, don't it? You can breathe proper and move without too much bother." She held up my gown with a discerning eye. "Good material, this. I can clean it up and sell it. For my trouble," she added, giving me a look that said I'd best not argue. I did not, though I admired her mettle at daring to stand up to the monster who had just murdered almost a dozen men. "Go on, now. Get out of here and go about your gory work."

I nodded and went down the stairs, marveling at how easy it was to do so. I could also take deep lungfuls of air, a treat I had not expected to enjoy so much. Certainly, I did not sleep in my corset, but I was in it most of the day from the time I woke until bedtime. It was novel being out in public without it.

"Do any of you know how I can get to Gloucester Street from here?"

Two blond heads leaned toward each other, their owner's conferring. One of them stepped forward and dropped a messy curtsy. "If it pleases you, mum, I could take you." Her eyes narrowed with canniness. "For a sov."

I would have to raid my husband's study for it, but this time of night he would be abed or out on the town. Of course, I had no idea what he was doing since I had gone missing. Perhaps he was up worrying about me or searching for me. I made a mental note to be cautious when going back home. "I do not have the money on me. I would have to get it from my home, if you don't mind waiting for it when we arrive."

"That'll do, mum. Come with me."

The other blond woman clung to her for a moment, their whispers furious, before my guide broke away and led me out the door and into the night.

My mind was on home, not my surroundings. If my guide had wanted to lead me to my doom, she could have quite easily, distracted as I was by all the possibilities that awaited me on Gloucester. Would my husband be overjoyed at my return or mortified at my state of dress?

Would I be happy to see him, or would I rip out his throat?

When I slowed, my guide gestured impatiently. "Come on, now. I ain't got call to be in this part of town and the peelers will run me off for sure. That'll cost me money, you know."

I didn't know, but I sped to follow her, unwilling to cause her trouble on my account. When we neared my home I stopped, gazing at its imposing edifice as if for the first time. Ordinary, boring, without a single thing to distinguish it from other houses nearby.

There weren't any lamps lit so everyone must have been in bed. So much for the notion that Mr. Wold had stayed up worrying over my disappearance. "I have to go inside to get your money. You can stay here or in the foyer." I didn't wait for her response, just went up to the door and twisted the ringer, the sound shrill in the night. It didn't take long for an answer.

Mrs. Burton, our housekeeper, opened the door, clutching her robe. When she saw me she paled. "Mistress Wold! Wherever have you been? The master's been worried sick, he has."

"I'm sorry for any trouble I've caused, Mrs. Burton," I said automatically, not feeling any such thing. "I need to pay this young woman for her trouble. Will you fetch a sovereign from the household accounts?"

She dropped a hasty curtsy, cast a dubious glance at the blond prostitute, and disappeared. When she returned, she clutched the coin in her hand. "Here you are and away with you before someone sees you." She slammed the door in the woman's face and turned to me. "Two weeks you've been gone, Mistress. We thought you'd been absconded with or murdered!" She hugged me, then held me at arm's length. "Whatever is this?"

"I borrowed it after mine was ruined. Two weeks?" How had that much time passed without my knowledge? Where had I been? What had been done to me during that time? "Tell me, Mrs. Burton, where is my husband?"

Her face colored and she busied herself with brushing nonexistent dirt from my gown. "Out, Mistress."

Out.

I'd been gone two weeks and he'd already given up finding me? "How many nights has he been out since I went missing?"

She licked her lips and straightened the vase on the small hall table and pinched off a dead flower and—

"Mrs. Burton!"

She jumped. "Every night, Mistress. But it was because he didn't know what to do with himself with you gone missing."

I sent her back to bed and stalked to my husband's study, violating the inviolable with my womanly presence. I searched through the desk he insisted no one touch but him and found a ledger that gave a true accounting of our affairs, unlike the household ledger I used to keep the household running.

He had a mistress near Hyde Park and paid a sum of twenty pounds per annum to keep her. He spent another ten pounds a year at brothels, several of them, all of which he labeled by name and ranked in order of his preferences.

Five children I'd given him, and this was how he comported himself.

I poured myself a tumbler of brandy and drank it down, then poured another, propping my feet on the desk to wait for my errant husband to return. What would I do to him?

What wouldn't I do?

What of the children? I did not wish them to suffer; however, I felt no yearning toward being their dear, sweet mother any longer. My sister and her husband would take them in and if not then Mr. Wold's family would keep them. Perhaps it was heartless of me, but that particular softness of feeling I normally had when I thought of my children was gone, eaten away, perhaps, by whatever evil had consumed me after the bite of the woman in the garden.

A soft whoosh of sound behind me, the smell of dried flowers and musty funeral parlors filled my nose, and I knew who it was before I turned.

"Why are you back in your cage?" she asked me.

She no longer looked like a woman, though she wore the same dress as she had that night in the garden. This creature was sallow, skeletal, and most definitely dead. "I set you free."

"I came home to settle my accounts." My fingers brushed the rough leather of my husband's book of perfidy. "What am I?"

She whispered about the room, flitting, moving too fast for me to track her, and I only knew where she was when she stilled. A long, bony finger tipped a book off a shelf. "I would have thought you'd figure it out by now, my dear." Her movements were smooth and hypnotic, just as they'd been that night. The book fell open in her palm and then she walked it over to me, moving slowly this time so that I might see her. "We are vampires, and we exist by feeding on the essence of living creatures. We are dead, and our souls are damned by He who dwells in Heaven. We kill, not because we must, but because we enjoy it." She laid the book in front of me on the desk. "I have but one kindness that ever I shall grant you and it is only a piece of advice: Do not do what you plan this night. Leave here and never return."

"Why ever not? Why did you make me so if you did not want me to succumb to this blood lust?"

"Because someday you'll regret it." She was gone in but an instant and I was left with her scent lingering in the room like an unpleasant memory.

My mind was filled with more questions than before her appearance and my heart with bitter anger. Why had she made me so and called it freedom? Was being bound to the Earth and damned freedom? In her crazed mind, perhaps. The part of me that had yearned for marriage, for a husband and children, railed against her injustice. A darker part rejoiced in remembrance of the brothel and the taste of the poor woman's death on my tongue.

The ring at the door made me sit upright. My husband, then, home from his pursuits. I had but little time to decide to heed the woman's advice or stay and let nature take its course.

In the hall, Mrs. Burton happily announced my return to Mr. Wold. His silence was telling. When he finally spoke, he said, "Where is she?"

"I do not know, to be sure, Master. Upstairs with the children would be my guess. What mother wouldn't go straightaway to her young ones?"

I swung the door open. "Here, Mrs. Burton. Not so motherly am I this night."

The housekeeper's eyes went wide at my tone and beat a hasty retreat. Then it was just me and my husband. His cravat was in his hand, his vest askew, his hair rumpled. He had just tumbled from a woman's bed; I could smell her on him as easily as I could discern the scent of his blood. His essence. That upon which I fed.

"What ... where ... I say," he stuttered, discomfited beyond words

"Did you miss me, Mr. Wold?" I asked, coming at him on quiet feet. His eyes took in my dress, on my clearly silhouetted nakedness beneath, and a beefy-red embarrassment stained his cheeks.

"Where have you been? The children have been beside themselves at the loss of you."

"I could ask you the same question, but I already know. What is her name? And what sorts of nasty diseases did you carry home to me, your wife?"

His chin rose, and his face took on that piggy stubbornness I recognized from his arguments with his blue-stocking sister. "I do not have to explain myself to you, Evelyn."

His use of my name made my eyebrows rise in surprise. He never used my name, had always insisted on the chilliest of formalities because he thought it made us seem more genteel. "That's quite all right, Harold," I mocked in return, "because I do not care to know it."

"Where were you? I demand an answer this instant!"

He was drunk; I smelled it now on his breath and saw it in the way he swayed in place. It would have scared me, once, though he had never put his hands on me. Drunk men were unpredictable and men, in general, had little to fear from the law if they harmed the women in their lives. No, he had never put his hands on me, but the threat had always been there. He liked to read aloud articles in the paper about this man or that who beat his wife or humiliated her in public. He liked to rejoice in any violence toward the blue stockings. He once put his fist in the wall because I had burned his supper, though he later apologized and told me not to be a ninny for crying about it because, "at least I didn't hit you, now did I?"

"Well? Cat got your tongue?"

I was on him before I could stop myself, pushing him hard against the wall, the radiator banging his calves with a clang. "You do not deserve an answer, Harold, not a single word."

"Get off me! I will put my hand to you, woman!"

My fingernails bit into his fleshy neck and cut off his air for a second. Or two. I didn't count but when I released him he was gasping and frightened. It was right there in the exposed whites of his eyes as he stared at me. "I was gone and now I'm back." Blood, I thought, inhaling his fear-sweat with a pleased smile. "I was given the gift of freedom, you see, and I was told that meant I must leave you and the children, never to return."

He tried to grab me, but I spun him around and pinned him back against the wall. His cry of pain when his shins now barked against the metal made me smile. "I could have left without anyone the wiser. In fact, I believe you would have been happier without me." I released his arm. When he spun around to attempt another assault, I held up my finger and he stilled. "Good boy." His breathing was loud in the quiet hall. "But why should you get to live when all my days I dwelt here as one half-dead?"

I smiled and he recoiled. I smiled broader.

"I will ruin you. Drag your name and reputation through the mud until not even a common whore would deign to help you. If you don't go upstairs right now and take off that disgusting dress, you're done. I'll divorce you and you'll never see your children again."

I sidled closer, my eyes on his. "Is that the worst

thing you can think of to do to me? Rob me of your venerable presence? Do you think that is what will keep me with you?"

"No respectable woman would—"

"Shut up." I wanted to drain him the way I had those other men, but I didn't want to touch him even one more time. No, he had never hurt me or hit me, but he was guilty of treating me like a child, a thing, someone less than and for that he deserved my enmity. I had not yet decided if that earned him his death. "I am no longer a woman. I am a corpse, a monster and with but a bite I could end you." I showed him my smile again, the one that held promises of things best left to his imagination.

"The Church will abjure you."

I stared at him long and long, looking for any sign that he cared for me, for me and not his reputation. Had I still a heart, his disgust and fear would have broken it. "Am I not anything to you at all? After all these years, I warrant nothing more than your antipathy?"

"You deserve no kindness, for it is obvious you have turned your back on all good sense."

The red anger threatened to take over my actions, urged me to rip out his throat and leave him bleeding on the floor. "You don't deserve my mercy but I'm giving it to you anyway. For our children's sakes, I will not murder you where you stand. I will leave, but know this, Harold, I'll be watching. And if you take one step toward your mistress or another bawdy house again, I will come back, and you will not survive it. Treat our children with respect. Be their father, not just their dispassionate master. Do your duty to them and you will never have to see me again."

He was silent, chest heaving.

I poked him, hard, hard enough to make him squeal. "Understand?"

He nodded hastily, and I left him without a backward glance, no chance of becoming a pillar of salt, I. Left him, my children, and my old life. I flagged the first steam carriage I found and let them carry me away from the cage that had held me too long.

I was a monster, this was true, but I was free, and I would cherish it for as long as I walked upon the Earth.

A Visitor At Sultana's Castle

Lori Tiron-Pandit

"WHO'S AT THE DOOR? WHO'S KNOCKING?"
"It's nobody, Madam. Just the rain."

It has been raining for twenty-three days, and the water has seeped into everything. But this castle, which the locals call *Lone Aerie*, rests safely on its cliff and remains an impenetrable fortress. We are not afraid. Except of disease, which we have all been expecting. I am no doctor, but the coffins unearthed by the torrents and brought down on the town's main streets are not harbingers of good news.

It seems that an old, abandoned cemetery on the coast has been flooded, and the caskets have made their way out of the mud and are travelling on water to new destinations, like ancient boats carrying their decomposing passengers to places they had never hoped to see again.

Everyone in town is hiding inside their houses, barricaded, unwilling to face the disaster that is the outside: the putrid smell of the mold blooming on wood and brick, the rotting, sticky mud growing on walls and front steps, the caskets and their inhabitants, aligned up and down the streets, where they have been washed up in the deluge. And the water keeps rising. We all know we're doomed.

Sultana has been urging me to write everything down each day and I do, to please her, although I don't put much trust in my memory, or my hand.

I feel despondent, of course, being caught in this devastation without hope of returning home anytime soon. But I can't forget that I am the Sultana's guest at her extravagant seaside castle, and this is nothing less than a magnificent thing.

The irony is that I have come here for the fresh air. My doctor told my poor, well-meaning father that I needed a sojourn by the sea to recuperate and strengthen my weak lungs. He recommended the salty air of the Black Sea, and this is how I ended up in Bazcik. I probably never should have left home, but since I'm here, I do fully intend to make the best of it.

And truth be told, I knew something was about to happen. I knew I'd have to face death—my little gift can be useful like that. So I will not protest too much. I am delighted to be on my own and to be living in this beautiful house with the old and peculiar Sultana.

She's happy to have me around. My gift intrigues her and she hopes I can communicate to some of the ghosts that live in here.

"Who's knocking at the door?" the Sultana asks again. This time there is a distinct noise coming from the front door. The maid goes to check the entrance and though the scream that reaches us is not loud, the whimper that accompanies it terrifies and leaves us paralyzed for several moments.

The coffin that the water pushed straight into the castle's door looks unlike others I've seen. The moment I lay eyes on it I know there is something unusual: it looks very old and rather small, and it seems to be made of solid metal, as if trying to keep its contents secured for eternity. It doesn't have a dent in it and it is still, after its long journey, safely and inexorably shut.

The Sultana shivers when I tell her who's at the door.

"A good time for you to use your gift," she tries to persuade me. But I am not sure. Sometimes it works, but many times I try in vain. I worry she will be disappointed.

In the morning, the groundskeeper and several of his men carry the coffin into the empty aviary, at the edge of the garden, until the authorities can come to remove it from the property.

It is a foggy, misty day, with low clouds. We haven't seen the sun in some twenty-four days—so long that it seems like a distant dream. The light is dense and gray underneath the glass walls. But it is not pouring anymore.

The aviary was abandoned years ago, when the old Sultana's husband died and this castle, a vacation retreat during their marriage, became her last sanctuary. The Sultana adored Lone Aerie. She told me how this piece of land by the sea had been ripped from inside of her and planted in the earth. After her death, she wanted her heart to be buried here, where it belonged.

As I examine the coffin up close, I can see that the lid is secured shut with a type of mortar that is breaking off in pieces. I show it to the groundskeeper.

"I don't think that is a good idea, Miss." He didn't look like he wanted to get any closer to the object than he had to. Even the young men who had carried it had now moved several feet back, toward the door. "I don't think we should open it. What good can come of it? And in any case," the groundskeeper continued, "I don't think Madam would approve. She is not fond of death."

The Sultana had been married young to the ruling prince of the small Balkan principality that she could never make her home, as hard as she tried. She converted to their religion, took to wearing their traditional clothes, unlike any other woman of her rank, learned their language and even wrote a volume of poetry professing her dedication and love for her new country. She gave birth to five daughters and three sons, and only two of her daughters survived to adulthood. Her subjects felt her sorrow, but she didn't find a place in their hearts until her husband died and she left the capital, isolating and removing herself from power. Only then they lovingly called her their Sultana, because of the Turkish-inspired architecture of her small castle.

I leave the coffin alone for now and go back to the house, but not before making note of the engravings on the lid: a snake holding something in its mouth. It needs to be cleaned so I can take a better look, and the groundskeeper agrees to humor me.

Sultana is waiting for me in her suite, out on the balcony facing the sea. The cup of coffee on the table in front of her looks cold and untouched. Like sparkling diamonds, droplets of mist cover the wool shawl she's wrapped around herself.

She still looks beautiful: cheeks smooth and flushed, dark eyebrows over light gray, almost entirely depigmented eyes, her most striking feature.

"Is anybody knocking? Who's there?"

"It's just the wind, Madam."

Her eyesight is poor, and as she can see less and less each day, the Sultana gains a hearing acuity of almost supernatural proportions.

"It is only me, Madam. Julia. How are you this morning?

She nods lightly and then leans back on the chair.

"What do you think of this view, Julia?" she asks pointing at the sea with a faint flutter of her hand.

"Isn't it sublime? This view has had my heart from the first moment I laid eyes on it," she says without turning toward me. "This view told me I belonged here. I belonged to it, from that first day."

She tightens the shawl around her.

"I shall tell you, since I have a feeling you would surely understand," she continues in her low, raspy voice. "I have never spoken a word of this to anyone, for fear they'd think I was barking mad, but I heard a voice calling my name on the day I first stepped on this estate. It sounded like it was coming from the sea, so it might have been only my impressionable nature. In any case, the voice told me to stay. *Stay. Stay*, it repeated over and over, with every gust of wind and every crashing wave. *Stay*. It was more of an order than a request."

In my room, as I sit at my desk, my hand goes for the pen and starts writing.

Stay. Stay! My home is your home. You are never to leave again.

"This is it?" asks the city sergeant when showed the small casket in the conservatory. "Well, Miss, I am afraid to inform you we will not be able to take this off your hands. I am surprised that you haven't noticed already, but the coffin has the castle's insignia on it. It belongs here. It was probably washed up from the estate's chapel. An unfortunate circumstance, to be sure, but you'll have to deal with this yourselves."

The sergeant is a young gentleman of a pleasant demeanor who seems genuinely troubled by the prospect of letting me deal with the ghastly situation.

"Will you be able to take care of this, Miss, on your own?" he asks before leaving. "I am aware that her ladyship is not in condition to watch over the affairs of the estate and the steward left his position some years ago and was never replaced. Everybody in town loves the Sultana, as you must know, but at this time of difficulty for us all, there aren't enough people available to help."

"It's perfectly all right, Sir," I reassure him. "We have the means to take care of this on our own, if we must. And, as a matter of fact, I have been asked to inform you that the Sultana is more than willing to lend a hand to the townsfolk, wherever she may be of assistance. She has no use at this time for the Tea Pavilion, for example, which is on high ground, safe from the waters, and it can be used by the town as a hospital or other facility, as necessary."

The sergeant nods. "I'd recommend that you don't open that coffin," he says, "and better leave it here untouched until you can take it back to the chapel. This is a most serious matter and I beg you to treat it as such. We fear disease and people have started speaking of curses of the dead, who were not supposed to see the light of day again, they say."

His voice trembles as he says these last words, and I wonder if it is because he too is disturbed by the possibility of the dead harboring desires of revenge or because he thinks it is too absurd to even mention.

I am supposed to meet the Sultana in the library for afternoon coffee, and as I wait for her to come, my hand starts writing.

I am here and my fate shall be undone. The punishment was underserved and cruel, I want it known.

"Who's knocking at the door? Anyone there?" The Sultana is standing right behind me.

"No, Madam, it was only the city sergeant who just left. He cannot help us at the moment, but he does appear to be a trustworthy and goodhearted man. I quite enjoyed taking with him."

"Yes, very good. Very good."

She sits on the chair by the large French window that can open into the front terrace.

It is already dark outside, but the Sultana looks out the window intently, as if she can distinguish a spellbinding scene happening right outside, in the pummeling rain.

"So it wasn't her?"

"Who, Madam? Have you been expecting someone?"

She doesn't answer and continues to watch the phantasmagorical scene outside, while her hands fidget in her lap with a small book and a handkerchief.

My hand starts writing again.

You must come and you must listen. I am not guilty. It was not me.

The groundskeeper is unnecessarily boorish, I think, when he follows me back to the conservatory to investigate the casket once more.

The clouds have been looming for twenty-five days. My eyes hurt. The sea, the sand, the land, its buildings and its people have all taken an ash-gray pallor. In the defunct aviary, large and empty cages, hung from above or supported on tall steel pedestals from below, fill the air with their loss and longing.

The groundskeeper watches me as I copy the heraldic symbols on the casket in my notebook: the dragon is biting its tail and surrounds two angular shapes that look like sharp teeth.

The Sultana, who is expecting me in the library with news, already knows.

"She has returned to torment us in death. The murderous countess. The witch."

Not a witch. Not a witch! Not a witch! The words form quickly under my pen.

"Countess Thobary. She was my husband's great grandaunt," the countess continues. "She lived here, in this castle. And she brought death with her."

The Sultana sits in her chair by the window and imitates the pitter-patter of rain with her fingertips on the book on the table. It is pouring again, so heavily that it doesn't look like drops but pillars of water descending from the skies, ready to crush us under their weight.

The book the Sultana hands me is a history of the Bazcik castle. It talks about the monstrous countess who sold her soul for eternal youth and power. She enjoyed hunting, partying lavishly, and killing young girls so she could have it all forever. Instead of aging, she become younger as years passed. When her husband came back from the war, he didn't recognize her; she was only a child.

He left and never came back after that, his bones scattered on the battlefield while she reigned unstoppable in Bazcik. Until the king appointed one of the neighboring magistrates to investigate the matter, after the townspeople complained about the depraved lifestyle on her estate. The countess was condemned as a witch when her unspeakable crimes were brought to light.

Twenty-seven girls were found dead, according to all accounts at the time. She was jailed in a walled-in underground room of her own castle until her death, which came a long ten years later. All in town celebrated.

They hated me. I was not loved. I was not loved! The paper under my hand is filling with an ornate handwriting that is not my own.

"Nobody must know whose coffin this is," the city sergeant says, drinking the first glass of cognac in one gulp. "This may be an ancient story, but no one has forgotten. Spirits are fragile right now. Any word of this and we'll have an uprising on our hands, I can promise you that."

Only in the night, sometimes, the rain becomes almost invisible and forgettable. The darkness covers it and takes away its power of seduction, because the night is mightier than any other horror to ever descend upon humanity.

The sergeant sits on the chair stiffly, hat on his knees, more warmth coming from his eyes and smile than this house has felt in years.

"Another glass?"

"If you don't mind, with pleasure."

He takes small sips from this one and uncrosses his legs, putting the hat on the table.

"She is still our most terrifying local ghost: Countess Thobary, the monster that mothers use to scare their children so they don't go out at night. They say that after her death, she returned to her home to retrieve her favorite doll. She will come to play with the children's toys at night, if they don't behave."

I have done nothing. They hated me. They lie.

I pour a glass for myself too this time.

"Do you believe the story?" I ask him. "Does it still stand, today, the case against her?"

He looks for answers inside the empty glass in his hand, then lifts it. "Would you mind?"

I fill both our glasses.

"I'm certain we can find out, if we search the archives. Is that something you'd like me to do?"

He seems eager. I give him a nod.

It's been twenty-six days of unabated rain. The ground is soaked like a sponge; unable to take in any more, it spits the water back out in bubbles. There is no beach to speak of anymore, the waves now digging into the castle's rock foundation. From the balcony, it feels like we are stranded on a ship, in the middle of a merciless ocean.

"I hear knocking," the Sultana insists. "She's at the door! She's come for us!"

"It's only the sergeant, Madam. We have been expecting him."

He is excited by the results of his investigations.

"It certainly looks like the trial could have been only set up to take her land and title. She was a single woman with too much power. After the trial and sentencing, her fortune was split between her accusers: the king, the magistrate, her relatives, even the townspeople, who were awarded the use of the castle's beaches. Everyone had something to gain."

The sergeant accepts joyfully the glass of liquor I offer.

"After all this time, we might be able to clear her name! Did you know something about this? How did you suspect?" he asks.

"I had an inkling," I respond.

Good girl, my hand writes. I cringe.

The Sultana rejoices: finally, the dark history of her beloved home can be put to rest.

"I always felt like her curse had enveloped this castle in a dark cloud. It marked my life and the lives of everyone who lived here. But now we're free."

Forever, my hand writes.

"Yes, you have to do it," I tell him. "The Sultana ordered."

It takes the groundskeeper and his men half of the morning to force the heavy casket lid open. They all move away when it swings up, as if expecting the angry spirit of the dead to fly out at them with fury.

Inside the casket is another, smaller coffin. This one is wooden, not metal, with a small, oval window on top. For the dead to look out. None of the men want to get close enough to see inside. They make the sign of the cross and look at me with disapproval.

The window is covered in grime, impenetrable. I wipe it clean with my handkerchief until the face inside appears clear: her hair is still shiny and curled around her face, her dry skin stretched out delicately over her bones, teeth grinning in victory. It is the beautifully preserved body of a little girl. In her hands, she clasps a doll wrapped in silk rags.

She lied to me. Have I set her free?

I ask the groundskeeper to close the exterior coffin again. The lid falls like thunder, and the whole aviary trembles.

We've had twenty-seven days of unforgiving rain. I don't know if we can hope for sun anymore.

EIRA ALBA AND THE
SEPTUM SCIENTISTS

ALICE E KEYES

"ARE YOU A PHYSICUS?" asked a voice from the shadow.

On this dank November night, the full moon created eerie halos around the clouds. I held the gray wool cape tightly at the neck while the wind whipped up the leaves around the hem of my skirts. The doors to the most prestigious scientific society headquarters beckoned me from the top of the stairs. I had an invite to participate in tonight's salon of fellow scientists.

The voice added to the nerves bubbling and to my fear that I was under qualified to be here. The street was empty of carriages and signs of life except for the stranger and me.

He stepped out of the shadow.

"You look at the door of the Vivus Scientific Societatis and appear as if you will enter. I, therefore, think that you are a physicus. Though someone of your beauty has little need for such trivial conversations about evolutio and materia."

"Excuse me, sir. I don't mean to be rude. My appearance has little to do with my ability to contribute to discussions about science."

I walked up the steps and twirled the bell knob. The light sound it made was in contrast to the massive black door heavily adorned with iron scrollwork.

Had the stranger left? I glanced to see. Was he to join the salon? I wondered at his use of the Latin term for a scientist. It was odd in this era of enlightenment.

The street was empty, and I twirled the bell again. Without the stranger's presence, the feeling of being utterly alone engulfed me. Was I too early, too late, or had I misread the date on the invite? A blush of embarrassment heated my cheeks, already red from the crisp autumn air.

I let go of my grip on the cape and went to pull out the invite when the door opened.

The butler stood looking down his nose at me and then said, "Miss, produce your invite."

The moment I pulled the heavy cream paper from beneath my cape, he accepted its authenticity and instructed me. "This way, Miss."

We walked up a flight of steps, down a long

hallway, took a jog to the right, and down another hallway. He opened a door, and the light blinded me.

"Your cape, Miss."

I gave him my cape and entered the room.

The room was full of the familiar faces of professors and science lecturers, or should I have said scientia lecturers. I'd heard something from all of them, except for the woman who was now walking toward me. She did not give scientific lectures, but she was well known within the Oxford and London enlightenment community.

She drew to a halt right in front of me. I was intimidated yet, drawn to her. Inexplicably, being in her presence gave me the comforting feeling of a warm bowl of mock turtle soup.

"Miss Eira Alba, I am so pleased that you have joined us this evening." Her voice soothed me like I taken a dose of laudanum and eaten an apple at the same time. It was an odd sensation especially considering that her voice was high pitched.

"I am elated to be joining the salon this evening." My desire was to prove myself worthy of a regular invite and eventually membership.

"This is my house and my salon. I will introduce myself because these men are not capable of such manners. My name is Madame Hermina Malum. You will call me Hermina."

I extended my hand. "I'm pleased to meet you." My hand was ignored which I assumed indicated that I was here on a trial bases.

The butler walked in with a decanter of ruby red liquid and the scientists moved toward the sideboard. Hermina walked through the men and took two glasses that held barely an inch of the drink. She walked back and handed one to me. Then in seemingly synchronized movements, the group was seated though no one had taken a sip.

"Professor Biant, please tells us the discussion topic this evening," said Hermina, taking a seat and gesturing for me to sit on the settee next to her.

"Yes, Hermina. This evening we are delving into bioscience. And, in particular, what is *Alive*; be it the flowing of blood or the spark of electricity." His eyebrows raised to punctuate the word *alive* which was used as a noun instead of an adjective for the rest of the evening.

"If that is the topic of conversation, it will be brief because the only one in this room with any essence of life is the exquisite creature who entered last."

I hadn't noticed the one man who wasn't seated and who I couldn't associate with a lecture or class I'd attended. He smiled at me and drank from his glass without taking his eyes from me. The intensity of his stare sent a shudder of defenselessness through me as if I were prey and the wolf's tooth had started to pierce the vein in my throat.

"Yes, Mr. Maddox. We should welcome our newest member. She is indeed a welcome and lovely addition." He held up his glass. "I'm Professor Edwyn." He took a sip.

"No," said Hermina and Professor Edwyn sank into his seat like an admonished child. "We will not spend our time with needless introductions. I'm sure she is acquainted with all of you, save Mr. Maddox. Now, she knows his name. Thank you, Professor Edwyn." She downed her glass of red liquid and held it out. The butler swiftly refilled it. Professor Edwyn also held up his empty glass though it was ignored. "Eira, would you please start us with your thoughts about *Alive?*"

The substance in the glass didn't smell of wine. I hesitated to even raise it to my lips, and now I had to speak, so I lowered it slowly to my lap to give myself a moment to compose my thoughts. I then spoke with conviction.

"*Alive* in plants is the moment the roots are able to nurture the plant. *Alive* in animals is when they are able to imbibe nourishment—" Before I continued about what was *alive* in a human, the scientists started to argue.

I sat and listened, picking up bits of the several discussions. My initial discourse was part of every conversation. It was a thrill. In a moment of pride, I brought the glass to my lips and took a sip. The distasteful syrup was thick on my tongue and I had an urge to spit it out. I had to be accepted as a full member, so I brought the glass back to my mouth, downing it like a shot of medicine.

Professor Gareth who was to my right said, "*Alive* exists up to the very moment of death. It is a condition which cannot be about the ability to nourish, but about a *force* within the being."

I had to speak to his thought and found my voice through the red vile syrup clinging to my throat. "I disagree, Professor Gareth. The carrot plucked from the ground is dead. It is only alive while it is in the nourishing ground. Therefore, an animal without the ability to nourish itself is dead."

"Is the animal dead between meals?"

"Don't be ridiculous, Gareth," said Mr. Maddox who now hovered over Professor Gareth and me. "You understand the essence of what Eira means. You are alive, though you are not eating at this very moment."

"Then, perhaps, it is better to say that when the tree has sap flowing it is alive and when an animal has blood pulsing in its veins, it has life," said Professor Biant who joined our discussion.

"Blood is the body's nourishment," I said.

"Though I understand your argument, Eira, I disagree. *Alive* is an electrical spark. Carrots and trees are as alive as a rock," said Mr. Maddox.

The conversation continued for four hours, delving into the nuances of what *alive* constituted. The red syrup was being sipped by all but me. Thankfully the butler, after I had downed the liquid, took my glass and did not return with more.

My mind is laden and I ached to record all the differing opinions and how they'd evolved and expanded upon my original definition of *alive*. I still held onto the core idea of nourishment as the condition for something to be alive. In an odd irony, I felt flush with life, though I'd not imbibed a morsel since my afternoon meal. Most salons I'd heard about included some kind of food, along with a variety of drink. Thick, red, salty syrup wasn't mentioned by the friend I asked about salon etiquette and refreshment.

When the clock chimed the midnight hour, the men approached Hermina, thanked her for the evening, and left. This orchestrated behavior mimicked the earlier part of the evening when they all retrieved a glass and sat.

When I stood, hesitating as to the proper etiquette, Hermina took control. She escorted me to the front door where the butler stood with my cape. He whispered something in her ear.

She stepped out onto the stoop, and the butler closed the door. He handed me my cape. I wrapped the cape around me and pulled up the hood. I stood waiting with the butler for Hermina's return.

"It is on the verge of raining." she took a moment and scanned me from head to toe. "Though I'm all for a woman's independence and walking. A wet wool cape is disgusting and not a good image for a member of the Vivus Scientific Society. My carriage will take you. We will say our goodbyes at the back door."

I followed her carefully through the downstairs hallway. Every door was closed, and no lit scones were along the way. "Thank you, I appreciate it, especially at this late hour."

"If it is the hour that bothers you, then you should have arranged a carriage."

Instantly from her tone and the feeling of comfort that left me, I knew I had said something wrong though I wasn't sure what. I knew walking the neighborhood of Rives was not the wisest decision a woman could make, especially since my dwellings were closer to the Asim district than the Rives district.

I was so hungry that I couldn't think of a feasible excuse and I wanted to correct my previous mistake. This is what came to mind as she stared at me like I was a silly child. "Of course, it's that I forgot that it's the new moon and many streets lack good lighting. I wish to get home quickly because I was too busy to eat my afternoon meal. I'll be better prepared next time."

"One should never skip afternoon tea. It is not good for one's constitution." The warm soup feeling enveloped me once again. She waited as the butler passed us and opened the door.

"The carriage is ready," said the butler.

"I shall send the invites to the next salon when I know you are ready to participate," said Hermina.

"Thank you, Hermina. It was a lovely evening."

The door slammed behind me when I was barely past the threshold. A thunderclap echoed the sound of the door, and a small squeal of fright escaped me as I picked my way along the path to the carriage. It was horse drawn and thankfully enclosed. Most of the scientists at the university had steam carriages, which is what I assumed Hermina would have.

The driver held the door open for me.

Two thoughts perplexed me as I rode off and the rain started to pelt the roof. One, how did the driver manage to have us on our way before I set myself on the seat? It felt like a mere second between him closing the door and speeding off. The second thought was of Hermina's last words to me. How would she know that I was ready to participate? And, would there be other salons in the meantime that I would miss?

Usually, after a block, the rocking of a horse drawn carriage always lulled me to sleep. Tonight, however, even though it was past midnight, I was all nerves. I reached over, opened the curtain, and regarded the buildings. We were traveling quickly. I hoped the driver would slow down because the turn for my street would be soon. The buildings didn't look familiar, and I assumed it was because I rarely rode in a carriage to travel within the city.

As each moment passed, I anticipated the turn. It didn't come. Then, the buildings changed to houses with grand yards. I couldn't believe it. We were heading out of the city. This neighborhood would end abruptly when we entered the Tenebris Forest.

I opened the window and stuck my head out of it. "Sir, we are heading the wrong way. Please turn around," I screamed against the wind pushing my voice back to me.

The driver didn't turn his head and instead of slowing, he snapped the reins. The jolt of the horses increasing their speed threw me back into my seat.

Moments passed, and I must collect my thoughts. I searched around me. Lifting my seat, I found several long handled umbrellas. I grabbed one and thumped on the ceiling with the handle, hoping it would get the driver to slow or hopefully to stop.

I waited a minute and thumped again. Thankfully,

the carriage slowed and then we turned, though not completely around. We bumped along like we were going over roots. I put down the umbrella and grabbed the edge of the seat to hold myself to it.

The carriage stopped and the door opened.

"Miss, we have arrived," said the driver.

His calm demeanor unnerved me. I stared at him a moment, not moving. "We have not arrived. This is not my home. Please take me back to the city."

Another man appeared at the door of the cab. "Miss Alba. We have been waiting for your arrival." His head extended to help me out of the carriage.

"Sir, I'm not leaving this carriage until it arrives at my home," I said shakily. Thinking I could use it defensively, I grabbed the umbrella and held it to my chest.

"The rain has stopped. Put down the umbrella and come with me."

I stared at the seat across from me and held onto the umbrella a bit tighter. He grabbed the umbrella and started to tug.

In a small voice and holding back tears, I said. "No, I wish to go home now."

The umbrella was yanked out of my hands. I screamed. Then, in a swift movement my head slammed against his back, my ears rang, and I was over his shoulder being carried. I passed out.

A sharp smell pricked my nose. I opened my eyes with a violent shake of my head.

"That's it, darling, there you are." The silky voice calmed me and wakened all of my nerves.

"Why?" I asked. My voice sounded weak. Deep within me, I screamed that I needed to be strong and to think like a scientist and not a girl.

"Why? A scientist who asks *why* is not unusual. Hermina said you were unusual." His face moved away and from my prone spot, I saw the ceiling, which was painted with a scene of men in Greek costumes having a picnic. "Sit up, my lovely."

The independent woman part of me didn't want to obey his command, none the less, I sat up.

He sat behind a table littered with papers. "I questioned her as to why she would want a female scientist as part of her colony. Why would a queen want a princess? I fear she'll regret creating a potential rival within her group. Especially, a beauty who is versed in the sciences."

I tried to understand what he said. Was he speaking about Hermina? Her words about being *ready* to join the salon came to mind. The non-scientific world of queens and princesses didn't fit in contexts with the Vivus Scientific Society. And, colony? I am a citizen of an empire. What utter nonsense his words meant in this modern world of independence!

Was I the beauty versed in sciences? The men at this evening's salon were famous for a myriad of scientific discoveries. Their faces as they formulated arguments crossed my mind.

A connection clicked into place.

I examined the painting on the ceiling. Staring back at me were seven pairs of eyes that had so playfully argued what it was to be *Alive*. The intense look of Mr. Maddox was almost mocking me. Professor Biant's look was flirting with me and poor Professor Edwyn look of once again being demeaned pulled at my heart.

I tore my gaze from the painting to the man. He admired the painting and then turned to his gaze to me and continued.

"They're quite a colony and I've enjoyed watching them through the centuries, trying to turn rocks into gems and lead into gold. As you know, their knowledge extends to more than making wealth, and they are always exploring the many facets of life." He smiled as if he'd been a fly on the wall of tonight's salon. "What do you know about them?"

"I've had some of them as professors, and I've gone to some of their lectures. They are all members of the Vivus Scientific Society. The society's only female member is Hermina Malum." I started to take in more of the room, which was lined with bookshelves from floor to ceiling. The antiquated leather style of the bindings made me think the books were old though well preserved. I said, "Is this your library?" It was the only thing that came to mind while I worked through the meaning of his words.

"Yes, take a look if you wish." He gestured with a hand at a shelf near him. "It is a shame that women have become less a part of the University world in recent centuries."

I stood and looked at the books on the shelf behind the couch. The idea of getting close to him gave me a shudder of repulsion down my spine. He kept saying century like he'd experienced every single day of those many centuries.

"Though the inner colony never needed more than the seven of them to further their scientific pursuits, perhaps they felt the need of a new fresh mind to enliven their latest pursuits. And, then they convince Hermina to find a fresh mind. I could hear Professor Gareth begging for a female scientist," he added, laughing as if he'd made a joke.

Every word he said in his melodic tone had me searching for a concise thought.

I pulled a book off of the shelf, drawn to the beautiful, unblemished, azure blue binding. I opened it, found the title page, and ran my fingers along the string of Roman numerals. The page was bright white. The type was odd. I calculated that it was four hundred years old. It was like everything else in the room. A contradiction to what my senses were telling me.

Rattled, I started to ramble. "I'm more than willing to become part of their salon. I have let each of them know how interested I am in studying with them, and, to my embarrassment, I've begged that I might get to be, even at the smallest level, part of the Vivus Scientific Society to anyone who was a member. You can't imagine the thrill I felt when I was invited to the salon. I assumed it was one of them that took pity on me when I received an invitation. I'd never met Hermina Malum before tonight. Does she work on experiments with the others? I thought perhaps she was a sister to one of the gentlemen."

"A sister? No, indeed not. The sun will soon be up, and since you've been begging to be fully a part of the salon," he hesitated and didn't complete the thought. "And, Hermina says she too desires it. Let's get on with the initial part of the process."

"What process?" I asked while placing the book back in its spot.

The word *process* doesn't pass my lips.

He grabbed me around the waist. I release the book from my grasp. His other arm cradled my head, and his hand tilted my head back. The book makes a thunk noise as it hits the floor.

His nails dug into the tender flesh beneath my chin and his hand pinched my waist painfully. A shoe dangles from one of my feet that no longer touch the ground.

"Your skin is so beautiful and white like fresh snow. It is a shame to damage it." The soothing tone of his voice abated my need to flee. His exotic spicy smell intoxicated me. I lost all urge to struggle.

He sunk his teeth into my neck and sucked.

Paralysed in his arms, I thought of the life giving blood that was leaving me. And then, thoughts left my consciousness. I went limp. The painful grip on my waist ceased.

The nerves in my skin felt electrified, briefly,

and then died. The painting of the picnic dimmed and became black.

His voice resounded in the nothingness. "My beautiful child, I will put you where quiet life surrounds you. The first part of the process is all but done."

The first sensation beyond the nothing was cold. It was a cold of being buried in the icy depths of the ocean and a cold so deep within the marrow of bones that it started to feel like it was burning me from the inside.

I thought I screamed out in agony but I heard nothing.

I touched stone though I thought I'd clutched at my neck expecting to feel a gaping hole wet with blood. It was smooth and cold like a marble statue.

The burning cold ebbed, and I thought about my eyes. I couldn't sense the flesh of my eyelids, so I scrunched them. They were closed. I opened them.

Why was I here? What had that man done to me? What is this process? Who are the Vivus Scientific Society? Why had I wanted to be a part of them?

I stood.

Where am I? Why do I feel frightened but not fearful?

"Shush," I said. "Shush, Alba." My own voice was the sensation of eating a warm bowl of mock turtle soup. The unanswered questions left me.

I saw large trees everywhere and a dim glow peeking through at horizon level though I didn't know if it was morning light or the last light of a day. A glimpse of bright white shined through the dim brown and greens. I walked towards it. In the middle of the forest, there was a table with a white tablecloth, a cloche, and a card on it and a chair. A formal picnic waited for a guest.

The card was addressed to me. It read; 'The first part of the process is done. Welcome, new one,' signed, 'forever, Immortus.'

I lifted the cloche, and there was an apple, a perfect red apple. I picked it up and lifted it to my nose. It smelled heady of summer. I wanted to bite it.

"Prohibere, stop! Eira Alba! I know I'm too late to truly save you, but I beg you...*do not eat the apple.*"

A man I didn't recognize ran toward me. I set the apple back on the tray. Somewhere in the far reaches of my mind, I knew I should feel fear or empathy or something toward the man running at me.

I stood still, oddly calm, and waited for him to reach me.

He stopped before me, winded. I asked, "What do you mean too late? Who are you?"

"We spoke at the entrance to the salon. My name is James Venuste. I didn't want to frighten you and didn't want you to enter the house. Then, I decided I'd wait and make sure you made it home without incidence. I failed.

"When I heard the carriage leave from the back

of the house, I followed as best I could. But I couldn't catch up, and now, I'm too late. Though, I can rescue you in one small part. Do not go to them. Do not eat the apple. Be mine, and I will keep you safe from Hermina and her colony."

His accent eluded me, and he spoke so rapidly I had a hard time catching it all.

I touched my smooth stone-like neck. "You're not too late. I am unharmed, though I do not know how I got into these woods, nor anything about this apple." I held out the note and gestured to the apple. "It says I've gone through the first part of a process. Do you know what the process is? And, who am I to you that you would go through all this trouble to rescue me?"

He smiled and his ideally symmetrical face flushed. "Put down the card, walk away from the apple, and I'll try to answer your questions."

I put the card on the apple and covered it with the cloche. Once the apple was out of view, he sighed, took my arm and placed it in the crook of his. This gentlemanly gesture was not new to me, though his touch felt odd. His touch failed to give me even the slightest sensation.

I felt nothing.

We walked away from the table, I waited to speak and realized it was getting darker, not lighter. I'd woken at dusk. How many hours—or days—had I been in the forest?

"I am different. I lack—feeling. Who was the man who bit me?"

"You have received the bite of a Rex vampire. *You* are now a vampire. There's nothing I can do to undo the first part of the process."

Vampire. I knew he spoke the truth.

The smell of blood, not only from Mr. Venuste, but also from the birds, the rabbits, and even the insects penetrated at my nose. Each creature had an individual blood scent and the blood pulsed at different rates.

The scent and sound of blood woke an overwhelming lust.

Mr. Maddox was wrong. One is dead except in the act of nourishment.

I was void of blood and desired to feed.

Sanity Slips Through Your Fingers

CC Adams

"Night is not something to endure until dawn. It is an element like wind or fire. Darkness is its own kingdom; it moves to its own laws, and many living things dwell in it."

– Patricia A. McKillip

West Norwood Cemetery, South London
20:18, 20/05/1843

*C*HUK!

Moments later, a shower of dirt flew out of the open grave, adding to the growing pile of earth graveside, along with a panting from deep inside the pit. Robin, seated further back on the grass in the sunset with his legs apart, rubbed a gnarled old hand across the back of his neck. Beside him, a grimy brass lamp filled with oil, and a half-empty flask of gin. It would have been a full flask, but he simply couldn't wait until the job was finished before his next little taste. Anyway, this evening's job would keep him in gin for a while.

He puffed air through his cheeks in resignation and took in his surroundings. The cemetery was quite new, construction finished only a few years earlier. In his estimation there couldn't have been more than forty tombstones: proud slabs of grey stone, each epitaph etched out with the finest of care. The stones appeared to stand in rank and file like soldiers, at the heart of an expanse of trim grass that rose or fell slightly, depending on which direction you followed the terrain in.

Chuk!

Somewhere in the distance, you could see the grey line that served as the back wall of the cemetery; a wall too tall to scale. Robin scoffed to himself. Lord knew he wasn't up for a brisk walk, let alone climbing. Digging halfway into the grave had been hard work, but it killed two birds with one stone, so to speak. One, it gave James an idea of what to do, and how. Two, it meant that Robin got his chance to not only rest but also take in the scenery. And it was beautiful. He cast a glance over his shoulder, looking in the direction of the cemetery gates up at the entrance. You could just make out the left-hand path from here (the path inside the gates split into a fork further in). And if you looked to the left, beyond the grounds, you could see the sun's hue melt from yellow to orange as it slid toward the horizon. Poetic, really.

Chuk!

More panting from inside the grave, bringing Robin's mind back to the present.

Easing onto his hands and knees, Robin pushed to his feet, hearing a joint in his knee pop. Lacing his fingers together, he pushed his palms out in front of his face and his elbows answered with a crack, his back muscles sighing with contentment.

"Don't you throw any dirt in my face, you hear?" he said, ambling past his own shovel and over to the graveside.

"Huh?"

Robin stopped at the edge of the pit and peered down. "I said don't throw any dirt in my face."

James, panting, propped himself up on the handle of the shovel as it stood upright in the earth at his feet. Sweat slicked his brow and plastered his shirt to his body. Behind him sat the silhouette of a coffin, shrouded in a heap of earth. Robin's gaze settled on the younger man's paunch, tenting the shirt. *You little fatty. I should have let you do all the bloody digging.*

"Is that enough?"

Robin nodded. "Sure, that'll do. See if you can open it now. If not, just take the shovel and scrape the rest of the earth off the lid," he said, miming the scraping action with the flat of his hand.

James turned away from his shovel and made his way to the coffin, with Robin noting the man's waist was as wide as his shoulders. James bent at one side of the coffin and heaved at the lid. Apart from a dusting of earth trickling over the coffin's side, it looked the same as when Robin first came to the pit's edge.

"That's why I said use the shovel if you can't do it."

So James shook his head in disgust. And picked up the shovel and again followed Robin's instructions, scraping away the earth on top of the coffin in one smooth motion, where it ran off the side in a whisper, leaving smooth dirt-stained wood behind. A scratch marred the near end of the coffin lid. No matter. They were going to cover the coffin back up later, so no one would know they were there.

"Go ahead and open it."

James leaned the shovel against one side of the pit and lifted the lid, which grated with the sound of heavy wood. The lid hung wide open, revealing the plush cream padding inside. Nothing more.

James spun round and looked up at Robin, his hand clasped to his forehead. For all his exertions earlier, *now* the young man's face flushed red, in stark contrast to the blond of his hair. "Oh, my God..."

Robin tried to process the sight below him. He came up empty.

"Are you telling me we dug up this dirt for nothing?"

Empty grave. Empty coffin. No body. Why would anyone bury a coffin without a body in it? Had there been some mistake at the mortuary? It seemed unlikely. Arms folded, Robin lifted a hand to his cheek, his palm rasping across stubble. *Whatever happened ... ?*

"Robin! Are you telling me we –"

"I'm *thinking,* lad!" he said sharply. He leaned over the edge of the hole a little, eyebrows raised. "Would you pipe down and let me think?"

James held his gaze with a sullen glare. The young man in a sweat-stained shirt, with his dirt-smeared face was a far cry from the fellow Robin once knew. The one who could be easily bought with fatty sweets, or a glass of port. Tension thrummed in Robin's chest and he turned aside under the guise of contemplation. *He's going to give me a damned good thrashing if I'm not careful. Even if we brawl, maybe I'll last a few punches ...* Robin shook his head, forcing himself to think clearly. The grave. The empty grave with the empty coffin. The Winwood family only lived streets away, so it followed that when Norman had died, this was where he would have been buried. It wasn't like the cemetery didn't have any room for him. It didn't make any sense. How could –

Footsteps whispered through grass some distance behind him, and he spun toward the sound.

Her dress black and heavy, the woman drew near, and although a veil of black crepe masked her features above a necklace of jet, her height and gait gave away her identity. She halted yards in front of Robin, trembling as she raised a pistol in both hands and aimed it at Robin's head. Robin's mouth went dry.

"How could you?" she asked, her voice breaking. Beyond the veil, an expression of wretched disgust. "How ... *could* you?"

"Lizzie ..." Robin took a moment, swallowed, and raised his hands in surrender. The woman ... had a *pistol* aimed at him, for Christ's sake! The last thing he wanted was to say the wrong thing. "Lizzie..." Still he came up empty, his thoughts fogged by alcohol and panic.

"Well? Did you find him?"

Robin let his gaze fall to Lizzie's feet. What could he possibly say now that would make things any better? At the periphery of his vision, he could see the revolver, wavering but still trained on him.

A sniffle. "Did you?" The voice was choked with tears. "Of course not, because *there was no bloody body!*"

Robin's head shot up as Lizzie stormed toward him, and now he could see the tears on her cheek, glistening, the gun barrel mere inches from his face.

"We had to hide the body from you! From YOU! Why wouldn't you let our father rest in peace? Why?"

He stood frozen.

Oh, God.

"You knew my father. You knew him, and this is how you *treat* him? You worthless ghoul. I ought to kill you right where you stand!"

"N-n-no, no," Robin stammered. "Don't kill me, you don't need to kill me."

"No?" She cast a sidelong glance in contemplation before turning back to him with a cold look. "Why not?"

Uhhhhhh... Robin opened his mouth to speak, and found he had nothing in the way of a meaningful answer.

A flash from the pistol's barrel along with the crack of a shot and Robin flinched, shying away. The sound was close enough that he swore he felt the bullet whip past his ear. His heart thudded in his chest, panic choking his airway. When he looked back, Lizzie was taking aim again. "I won't miss this time."

Robin backed away, losing his footing at the edge of the grave, pin-wheeling as he turned. James, listening in dread to the exchange on the grass was standing right below the falling man, and so broke Robin's fall at the expense of his ribs and neck. When both men looked up, Lizzie stood at the edge of the grave with the pistol oscillating between both of them.

"I guess I'm not surprised that it's you as well," she said. "As if one bloody idiot wasn't bad enough, now there are *two* of you?!" She glared at James, veil up, tears running. "I guess you're too stupid to think for yourself, to realise just how *wrong* this is!" Another bullet spat from her gun, ploughing into the earth at James' feet and sending up a clod of dirt. Not wasting any time, James dove into the coffin.

Leaving Robin standing alone.

"That's the right place for you!" She trained the

pistol on him. *"At least when you die, no one will ask where you're buried!"*

Robin leapt into the coffin just as another bullet buried itself in the earth behind him, landing heavily on top of James. The younger man, already injured from Robin's fall, yelped as Robin scrambled over top of him, reaching madly for the coffin lid.

"Ow, watch the neck!"

Robin pulled the lid shut, sealing them in darkness. Something small and heavy bit into the wood of the lid, the sound reverberating in the coffin and both men cried out in alarm.

Then silence.

"You listen here now, both of you." Lizzie's voice, muffled and distant from above them. "If I see either one of you again, I swear I'll bloody kill you."

James began to blubber, but Robin shushed him. While the coffin was big, it certainly wasn't big enough for two people. Robin lay facedown on James' chest, the heat and sweat from the younger man's body seeping into his own shirt. His face pressed against James' neck, where he could hear and feel him swallow and almost taste the tang of salt in his skin. Rapid shallow breathing punctuated the darkness.

"Robin," James whispered. "What are we going to do?"

What *would* they do? Robin closed his eyes and inhaled. From sitting in the fresh air of early evening to lying on top of a sweaty young man in a brand new coffin; you could smell lavender and charcoal as well as the elm wood.

What would they do?

As if in response, something heavy pattered on the coffin's roof, like rain. More came at a steady pace, landing here and there about the middle of the coffin.

Realisation dawned on Robin, sickening him as his eyes widened in the dark.

"She's burying us?" James' whisper held a note of pleading. "She's going to bury us?"

From underneath him, Robin felt James' hands drag along his torso before pushing at his shoulders, but Robin hugged the younger man's arms to his sides, restricting his movement. *"What are you doing?"* he hissed. *"She still has a pistol! Do you hear me? She still has a pistol!"*

Both men lay panting in the silence, as earth continued to rain on the coffin. Robin closed his eyes and took stock of his surroundings. At least James had remained still underneath him, apart from the rise and fall of his chest. The lid of the coffin, though arched, sat close along Robin's back, with his head and bottom feeling most of the discomfort. The trick, Robin decided, was not to let anxiety and panic set in, which surely wouldn't help you at all. At least for the time being, they were safe in here. So he waited, even as the rain of earth grew less frequent.

Grew more muffled.

Until silence returned.

James' chest still rising and falling against him, his stomach more so.

Robin licked his lips and felt James stir beneath him, ever so slightly. "I think we're okay."

A pause.

"Robin?" James' voice was thick with contempt, and Robin was reminded of the final moments before Lizzie's first shot. "How exactly are we okay?"

Hmph. "You can't hear, lad? She's not talking or shovelling. She's gone."

When James failed to answer, Robin assumed that the younger man didn't understand or was perhaps in shock – after all, in such a small space, he couldn't fail to hear. Maybe he couldn't accept there was a way out.

"Really. In that case, why don't you open the lid and get off me so I can get out."

Smart-mouth, he thought, his eyes rolling beneath their lids. Bracing his hands against James' shoulders, Robin pushed up against the lid of the coffin and felt the padded lining thin and grow harder against his back. Robin's heart began to beat faster and he pushed again, this time groaning and straining with the effort. And in return, the lid of the coffin opposed him, increasing the pressure on his back until he slumped forward on James' chest. His heart beat wildly. Bad enough he couldn't control his anxiety, but this close, James would know too. It didn't take a genius to figure it out.

"You've trapped us both?" James shouted. Within the confines of the coffin, normal speech was loud enough, but a shout was deafening. "You ignorant bastard, *you've trapped us both?!*"

"Don't you dare –"

"*Shut up, you old fool!* You fell on me, and even worse, you've gone and got us trapped in here! Where the bloody hell are we supposed to go from here? *There's no getting out of this thing!*"

"Didn't you hear me before?" Robin snapped, his voice trembling. "She had a pistol!"

"Yes, she did, and she was a lousy shot. You might have had a chance to wrest it from her if you were man enough, but you wanted to play the part of a gentleman. Look where it's gotten us, eh? Stuck in the bloody grave. Stuck in a grave reserved for you!"

"Who do you think you're talking to?"

"You, you bloody fool! That's why the coffin was empty, wasn't it? She knew you were coming? She set a trap for you!"

"You came too!"

"Yes, because you asked me to! So shut up! *Just shut up!*"

Robin obeyed, his mind racing. How could he have been so pathetic and foolish? From the last couple of graves he had broken into, he wasn't sure if he was being watched. Certainly, there were no visible precautions on the grounds against grave robbing: no locking of the gate, no nightly patrol, no groundskeeper at the entrance; at least, not as far as he knew. But obviously someone *had* seen him, and even worse, they had warned Lizzie. Unless it was Lizzie herself. So she confronted him, armed.

He didn't doubt that she would have shot him in anger. Was she cold-blooded enough to leave him and James here to suffocate? That was a different matter altogether. His stomach growled, but he ignored it. More than getting food, he needed to get out. They both did.

"You're heavy," James breathed, gurgling a little.

Guilt stabbed at Robin. He had he fallen on top of the man twice, and he was *still* lying on top of him. He braced his hands against either side of James' body and pushed up. Again, the roof of the coffin came into gentle but firm communion with his back, and Robin swore under his breath. This time, both men heaved against the lid until they fell limp with spent effort. How long had they been shut in here now? Robin had missed dinner (not that ham stew was his favourite, but it was better than living on scraps), and had no idea when he could get out and to his next meal. More to the point, he had no idea *how* he would get out. So he slumped his head in the crook of James' neck. The younger man didn't appear to be in the mood for talking, and who could blame him? Resigned to the fact there wasn't much else to do, Robin lay there, praying for sleep.

It came and went, bringing exhaustion.

Now in the presence of hunger.

And fear.

Mounting fear.

And if an old dog like Robin was starting to crack, what must young James be going through? Guilt scratched at Robin like a cornered cat: he really should make an effort for the lad. Heat from imminent tears pricked at his eyes.

With difficulty, Robin drew a hand up and cradled James head with it, as if to console him. Cool hair slid under his palm.

"That's it, lad, save your strength," he whispered.

No answer, apart from the sound of his own breathing.

No.

Eyes wide, Robin trailed his hand down to cup James' cheek, pressing a little when the man failed to stir.

Nothing.

Fingers trembling, he reached for James' earlobe and pinched, until he applied all the pressure he could.

The only response was the sound of his own breathing, fast and shallow.

Now his tears came.

Blood pounding in his ears.

No one would come for him.

No one had come so far, so why would they come now? No one would believe that the daughter of an old friend had buried him alive any more than him robbing the grave of the same friend. Down here in the darkness, no one would hear him through a coffin, let alone six feet of earth. Gin, his only solace, lay in a flask up top, along with his tools.

Air...

How much air did he have, would the air run out? Robin wasn't sure. Cramped though the space was, he didn't really have difficulty breathing ... yet. James, on the other hand would have done, since he had not only been injured by Robin falling on him twice, but also had to breathe with Robin's weight on him. Was any precious air used up? What would happen? Would you suffocate, starve or ... or go *mad*, as sanity slipped through your fingers like dry earth?

Hands fluttering like the wings of caged birds, Robin groped his way about the contours within the coffin: the floor, the walls, the floor, the walls, the ceiling. The floor, the walls, the arms, the James, the floor the walls the ceiling *the walls the James the floor the ceilingthefloorthewalls the floortheJames...*

Surging forward, Robin hugged James as tightly as he could, gibbering to himself, an earlobe pressed against his lips like a fatty sweet.

JamessweetJames

The notion now nestled in his subconscious like a worm in an apple, and Robin gasped with the force of it.

...sweetJames

Robin licked the earlobe, the skin cool on the tip of his tongue.

Tasting dirt and salt in the skin, he closed his lips around it, almost in a kiss. He licked harder at the tip of skin, sliding his teeth over it, and his jaw trembled in hesitation.

The first bite gave springy resistance until, tentatively, he bit down harder, scissoring the skin away--only to spit the morsel out. Self-preservation warring with revulsion.

"I'm sorry," he muttered. He hugged himself closer to the body beneath, his lips now presented with ragged skin instead of an earlobe. Viscous tissue. Young James lay so still, so ...

I'll ask first: please, may I? You won't say no, will you?

Another bite, this time grazing cartilage. Then swallowing.

May I?

More bites followed, crunching through cartilage and tearing at sinew and hair until a gaping hole remained at the side of the dead man's head. Eyes already tinged yellow from alcoholism grew wider – and *larger* – in the darkness, hunting for any scrap of light.

"Did I ... hurt you?" he whispered? *Did I?*

No answer. Somewhere in the darkness, the stink of faeces.

No? Good.

Hands running over the shirted body and pulling the fabric open. The head now lowering to cold and sour flesh.

I'll take just enough: no more. Teeth, digging into skin and muscle. Tissue that wouldn't give easily. Jaws worked with each bite, the head and neck working to tear away flesh that pulled taut, stretching like elastic. Another ragged mass, another edge of hunger dulled. One body continued to rot and decay and the one lying on top continued to gnaw at it, removing skin and ravaging it. Time, formless in the dark, blurred moments of sleep and waking, compressing days into a fraction of the time. With a meal of carrion seemingly minutes earlier, hands trembled and pushed at the padded walls of the coffin. Apart from a creak of elmwood, the coffin held its silence. Another push. Again, another creak. But even a damaged mind may understand the truly horrific.

No.

Fingernails digging through the fabric and into the wood as realisation set in. Head swivelling to and fro in the darkness, eyes searching. Eyes that now bulged past the eyelids, rendering them useless.

No, noooo, pleeeaaase, nooooo...

Trapped with dead flesh and human waste.

Memories of ham stew and ale sunk in the depths of madness and hunger. Those two very qualities crept through that starving form and perverted it, and where a human body would normally have died and decayed, this one continued to warp and *change*.

Scratching and pounding now and then at the walls of a wooden tomb.

Through days and weeks.

Months.

Skin fading to a greasy white, slowly but surely shedding hair from the arms and legs. Greying hair falling away from the scalp, strands at a time.

Bones lengthened as nails grew thick and hard.

Years later, when the pale fist finally punched through the wall of the coffin, daylight was the last thing on the creature's mind. Through a hole of splintered wood and further ahead in the earth came the scent of other wooden tombs; fresher.

One thought rose in the mud of that consciousness, grasping at the notion of glassy-eyed bodies.

Food.

Dead lips curved in a smile and the creature, bald now, gripped the side of the hole and ripped it wider. Clothing long-soiled and rotten tore away as the creature surged forward.

Foooooood.

The Book of Futures

Wendy Nikel

O N A SEASIDE CLIFF ON THE far edge of town, a single gaslamp sent Dr. Lucia Crosswire's thin shadow cowering into the tangled pines. Her heels crunched steadily along the winding cobblestones, and a well-fed rat darted across the path, screeching at the disturbance to its nocturnal traipsing.

Nighttime strolls along the outskirts of Clifton weren't generally advisable for an unaccompanied lady, but Lucia wasn't concerned. With her pistol securely in its strap upon her leather tool belt and her newly invented electroshock weapon at her other hip, she was confident that she'd come out ahead in any altercation. Besides, the townsfolk of Clifton were highly superstitious when it came to the reclusive monks of Mont Saint-Vogel. Rarely did young ne'er-do-wells trespass on the monastery's hallowed ground and certainly never after dusk.

Even the forest itself seemed to cower from the expansive hilltop monastery, its pines bending outward from the stone pillars and walls. Far above the arched entrance, an angel held a balance, rays askew. *Thou art weighed in the balances and art found wanting.*

Lucia pulled her cloak tightly to herself, her tools and instruments clanking in the many pockets.

A red cord hung beside the massive door. When Lucia tugged it, the iron cogs surrounding the doorframe shifted and clicked into place, a discordant clatter in the night's placid silence. After a still moment, a mournful bell tolled somewhere deep within the stone walls.

The door opened. A figure blocked the way, clad in a hooded gown of rough brown cloth that obscured his features and form. Its only adornment was a dull medallion, engraved with the image of a bird. *Be ye wise as serpents and harmless as doves.*

Preferring to err on the side of wisdom, Lucia rested her fingertips on the tiny clockwork mechanisms of her electroshock weapon. "Are you Brother Primicerius?"

"I am." The figure stepped backward, fading into the monastery's inky recesses. "Please, come in so that we may more discreetly address the events of late."

Lucia narrowed her eyes and gripped her device more tightly but didn't back away. She'd come this far based solely on a strangely whispered message emanating from a wind-up bird delivered to her investigative offices in the town far below. "Trouble. Please come. 10 o'clock tonight," it had repeated each time its key was wound. The only other clue to its origin had been the return address on its packaging, indicating that the sender was a Brother Primicerius at the Mont Saint-Vogel monastery.

Lucia stepped inside. The door closed with a dissonant *clank.*

"Forgive me the request of your presence at such an hour." The voice in the dark seemed to come from everywhere, nowhere, somewhere within Lucia's own head. A spark flared, a match lit, and the shadowy hood of Brother Primicerius hovered before her as if disembodied by the night. "The brothers of this sacred place have sworn a vow of seclusion from the outside world. Therefore, I felt it best to wait until the hours of rest for this meeting so that your presence here would not be a distraction. This way."

He turned, momentarily blocking the candle's light and plunging Lucia into cold darkness. Her heart thudded in her chest like the measured strokes of a pendulum, but she followed, matching him step for step. Around a corner, at the end of another long, silent corridor, a gentle light glowed from beneath a closed door.

"You must swear to me," Brother Primicerius said, "that never, though you suffer a thousand years of torture, will you reveal the contents of this room."

Though the people of Clifton often whispered and gossiped about the mysterious goings-on upon the hill, Lucia had never heard of anyone being tortured for this information, so she replied confidently, "I swear I will not reveal the secrets of your order."

Brother Primicerius nodded grimly. "My brother is the vicar in village below. He's assured me that he's confided in you in the past and that you are worthy of this great trust."

"Yes, he called upon me last spring to investigate some thefts at the cathedral. Has there been a burglary here?" Even as she said it, she knew it was unlikely, for who would climb all the way up this hill to steal from those who'd taken a vow of poverty?

The door had no handle, but Brother Primicerius pressed a series of springs on one side as deftly as an organist playing a chord, and after a moment of shifting and clicking within, the door slid to one side, revealing the chamber.

"A library?" Lucia gazed in awe at the rows after rows of books. Their spines stacked upon one another until they reached the top of the domed ceiling where an elaborate wrought-iron chandelier hung, dark and unmoving. This was the great secret of the monks of Mont Saint-Vogel? Books?

"These are not ordinary books," Brother Primicerius said as if reading her mind. He walked among the tomes, touching one and then another with awed reverence. "These books contain prophecies from the beginning of time, from every man who walked the earth and claimed to have some deeper insight into the future. It is our sacred duty to weigh each line, study each prediction, and determine which prophets were true, which visions are yet to come."

A library of prophecies... Lucia looked with new appreciation on the rows of shelves. "But what do you want of me?"

On a table in the center of the room stood a bronze case with intricate carvings on the lid. Brother Primicerius unlocked it. The case unfolded like the blooming of a mechanical flower, revealing a heavy black tome. In blood-red letters upon the cover was the title: *Liber Futures*.

"The *Book of Futures*," Lucia translated.

"In the holy book of Acts, we are told that Paul drove a demon out of a female slave whose owner had been earning a great deal of money through her fortune-telling. This book is whispered to contain all her predictions of the future."

"*Wars and rumors of wars...*" Lucia recited.

"That and so much more." He snapped shut the bronze case, enclosing the book once more. "It arrived at the monastery a fortnight ago. It is also my belief that this particular relic brought with it some sinister force."

"Sinister force?" Lucia's keen eyes darted about the room where each flicker of the candle and turn of her head made it seem as though shapes were moving among the bookshelves. Her voice came out louder than she intended, its tone barely concealing her skepticism. "Demons, you mean?"

"Perhaps the very one which the apostle drove from the slave girl."

"I don't know what you've heard of my investigations," Lucia said, taking a step toward the door, "but my expertise is in human crimes with human wrongdoers. The spirit world is entirely unknown to me."

The monk's hood bobbed in acknowledgement. "That is precisely why I summoned you. For our expertise is in the spirit world, yet none of our attempts—no prayers or chants or exorcisms—have had the slightest effect. My brothers have asked that I put aside my own convictions and consider the possibility, however small, that these crimes have a more...natural cause."

"And what are these crimes?" Lucia asked with some relief at her new understanding of the situation. How strange it must be to live like these monks in a society where demons are the first accused and human culprits only considered when no other explanation can be found.

"Each night," he said, "as the brothers take their rest, this library is locked. Its door, you may have gleaned, is unique. The combination is known solely to me, and I consider it my sacred duty to alter the code each Sabbath. Were any man to apply the wrong combination of levers, the mechanisms within would release a poison to kill him in an instant.

"As you can see, there are no other entrances to this chamber, yet every morning, the brothers discover that their books have been misplaced, picked up and set elsewhere. Also, each night, one book—one each night—is missing entirely, and the one from the previous day is returned, as though it had been there all along.

"To a demon this would be but a mischievous prank." He paused, deep in thought. "But if the culprit is, indeed, of flesh and blood, his motives may be far more devious. With the words these pages contain, you can see why we guard them so carefully, why their disappearance causes us such distress. If someone else were to be taking these pages and using them for their own purposes—"

"Yes, I see what you mean." Lucia wandered about the library, noting the orderliness of each table, the meticulous nature by which these monks arranged their books. She touched the cover of one, careful not to move it from its current position. "The books in this library—would they have monetary value? Perhaps to collectors?"

"Oh, yes. Even the books whose prophecies have been deemed false would still be deemed priceless for their rarity. Except, of course, the books on the history of Mont Saint-Vogel itself, there, on the northern wall."

Lucia studied the shelf indicated, reaching up to straighten an ancient leather-bound book that stuck out further than the rest: *An Accounting of the Property Deeds, Construction, and Dedication of the Most Blessed Monastery of Mont Saint-Vogel*, the thick spine declared.

"Were any of these record books stolen?" she asked.

"No, of course not. They're just tedious accounts of feast day celebrations. Ordinations, deaths, and burials. Money given to the poor or spent to procure the other books. They'd be of no value to man or demon. I've compiled a list of the books taken."

He held out a scrap of parchment upon which had been written a list in elaborate calligraphy of a dozen books, ranging in subject from the biblical prophet Samuel to a girl in an impoverished island country whose visions dated back only three years from the current day.

Lucia pocketed the list and circled about the room, peering into each darkened nook and tugging gently upon each shelf. She stopped suddenly. "Have you had any visitors to the monastery recently?"

"No."

"And when you received the *Book of Futures*, was it brought here, or did one of your monks fetch it from elsewhere?"

"It came from the Ottoman Empire, relayed via airship to the New Breckinridge port."

"Highly guarded?"

"On the contrary, sent as inconspicuously as possible. The bishop of New Breckinridge paid a boy three coins to deliver it, claiming it to be a particularly thick prayer book."

Lucia pulled a magnifying glass from a pocket in her cloak and snapped it open. She inspected the lock mechanisms of the door, which bore no sign of forced entry.

"Did anyone else in the town know of its arrival?"

"No, not a living soul."

"And what lies beyond the walls of this room?"

"The chapel and the dining hall, both locked."

"And below?" Lucia stomped her heeled boot on a tile, which held firm.

"The catacombs, I'd assume. Please, Dr. Crosswire, based on what you've seen, you must agree that this is an impossible crime. There could be no temporal explanation."

Lucia looked about the room. "It certainly is strange, but before I say for certain, I'd like to test one theory, and for that, I will need you to trust me with the combination to that door."

Five minutes later, Dr. Lucia Crosswire bid the monk a polite adieu and set off back down the winding path toward town.

Twenty minutes later, she emerged silently from the shadows of the pines and crept to the monastery's eastern side where the hooded monk had unlatched a window before saying his evening prayers and laying his head upon his small, unpadded cot.

The corridors were black and cold as a crypt, but Lucia found her way to the library by the light of her small, hand-cranked lantern. At the door, she carefully studied the set of springs and pressed the ones which Brother Primicerius had indicated. The door slid open with a wisp of cool air.

The library was illuminated by the golden glow of a single candle. Lucia tucked her lantern away and kept to the shadows, stepping carefully. When she reached the farthest corner where the entire length and width and breadth of the room could be seen without moving her head, she sat and settled in for a long night.

The candlelight reflected on the *Book of Future's* bronze case, warping and twisting the golden light into shapes both strange and hypnotic. It was unsettling, the way that it drew her eye, and she could see why the monks of this place were superstitious regarding it.

Lucia pulled a pair of spectacles from her cloak and placed them on the bridge of her nose. She flipped through a series of overlapping lenses. One revealed the temperature of the white-hot flame, gradually cooling to the purple edges of the room. Another showed gray and white, only displaying any shade of color when she glanced down at her own hand. In yet another, the air took on the appearance of blue waves, which rippled like a rock thrown in a pond at the slightest hint of sound.

Over and over, the cogs clicked as she cycled through the lenses. Each time, her gaze was drawn to the center of the room, where the bronze box sat still and unchanging, like a creature lying in wait.

If only there was one with the ability to show spirits—a lens that could tell her if there were mischievous imps hovering above the pages of the holy men's books or seeping out of the book's bronze box. If only she could forget Brother Primicerius's words about demons and vengeful spirits and ghosts.

Click.

Lucia held her breath, listening. She slid the auditory lens into place just as the noise came again.

Click.

The waves spread from the center of the room where the *Book of Futures* sat upon its wooden table. The table itself shook ever so slightly, and for a single heart-stopping moment, Lucia thought that Brother Primicerius had been right, that there was something sinister contained within that holy relic.

The next moment, it all became clear. A smile spread across Lucia's face.

"You'll be pleased to hear, Brother Primicerius, that I have solved your mystery. I discovered what has been happening to your books."

Lucia stood in the doorway of the library. The monk had come to retrieve her before the morning bells roused the others from their cots and to their daily meditations and work. The monk clasped his hands in what Lucia could only assume was a gesture of excitement, for as before, his face remained entirely hidden.

"You have? Please, tell me! What was it? Was it the spirit within the book? The one driven out by the apostle so long ago?"

"On the contrary," Lucia said, stepping to one side. "It was none but a small boy."

The child standing before them looked to be but twelve or thirteen with a slight frame, ragged clothing, and large, curious eyes that even now barely rested for a moment and darted about the library.

"A boy? Why, this was the same boy who delivered the book to the monastery!"

"Indeed. It seems that upon receiving the book, you and your fellow monks were so caught up in your acquisition that you didn't even notice the young intruder following upon your heels to the library. Once in here, he hid among the copious shadows, watching as you went about your work, enthralled by all he saw. When all of the monks retired for the evening, he found himself alone in the library."

"Good heavens! Has he been here this whole time? And what of his family? They must be worried sick!"

Lucia turned to the boy. "Go on. Tell him what you told me, Pierre."

The boy dropped his chin to his chest, as though suddenly recalling that he ought to feel remorse for his intrusion. "I've got no family, sir, nor a home. This library is the most amazing place I've seen in my life, and it was my curiosity kept me here. Was my curiosity made me take that book, sir, not evil spirits."

"Tell him which one you took first," Lucia prodded.

"It was a book about the history of this place. I tucked it in my shirt and kept it with me as I snuck out that night. I wanted to know what the monks were doing, that's all. I intended to drop it on the front stoop the next day, but then I found the map."

"Map? What map?"

Pierre proffered up the book, open to a sketch of the entire layout of the monastery.

"Good heavens," Brother Primicerius said. "I'd no idea that was in there."

"And look," Pierre said, "there's a hidden route to the library, up from the catacombs. Soon as I found that, well, I couldn't help myself, sir."

"You entered through the catacombs?" The monk quivered in his robe.

"I only wanted to see more of what you did here. The lock on the mausoleums was rusted, and from there, I used the map to find my way. I returned everything I borrowed, I swear. Please, you won't kill me, will you?"

"Kill you?" From deep within his cavernous hood came a thick sound like the grinding of gears. It took Lucia a moment to realize that the monk was laughing. "Of course, I won't kill you. In fact, seeing as you find our work so fascinating, I would love nothing more if you would join us, become one of our order and help us in our sacred task."

"Truly? I could?" The boy's head jerked upward, a hopeful smile brightening his dirty face.

"Truly. Why, I'd wager you already know more of our secrets than most the ordained brethren do!"

Dr. Lucia Crosswire strolled down the hill from the Mont Saint-Vogel monastery, grateful to be out in the open as the sun lightened the morning sky. Somewhere in the stone structure behind her, the morning bell gonged, calling the monks from their cots. Soon, Brother Primicerius would reveal that they had another among their number. Would he tell them all how it had come about, or would that be yet another secret?

An airship passed overhead, its horn bellowing like a behemoth, and Lucia wondered if any of the books within the library of Mont Saint-Vogel had foretold those mechanical marvels. In all the time spent within the mysterious room, it had never occurred to her once to search her own futures within the pages. Only now did the curiosity tingle the back of her neck, making her wonder what she'd have found.

But just as swiftly as the airship disappeared from view, obscured by the forest's pines, the desire vanished within her, overpowered by her good sense. The future, she decided, was one mystery best left unknown.

HARVESTERS

E. SENECA

I HAVE SCARCELY BEEN ABLE TO SLEEP since that day. All I can see behind my eyelids are those *creatures* looming around me, reaching for me, the fathomless black wells beneath their cowls.

It was said by a few that the Harvesters had always resided here; that the growth of the city had never truly driven them out; that we had done something to anger them, as if they were heathen forces of nature. I do not claim to know their origin, and indeed, I do not believe that anyone truly knows other than the Harvesters themselves. All I know is my own encounter with them, a horrible event that is seared into my memory forever more. As soon as evening falls, I do not dare set foot outside my lodgings; our sole advantage against these monsters is that they do not emerge while the sun is in our sky.

It happened one night on my way home. Like any other reasonable, ordinary gentleman, I had gone to enjoy a hot supper at my club and paid little heed to the hour, enjoying all the usual pleasures of good food, good company, and a good game of cards. The constraints of time, the ever-encroaching night and the presence that occupied it faded from my mind, so absorbed was I.

I only became aware of how late it was when the clock chimed seven and all around us, those at the other tables began to rise, to say their goodbyes, knocking back the remainder of their whiskey and sodas and abruptly sobering. Even if I wished to remain on my lonesome, I could not: the club would be closing shortly, as soon as all the patrons departed. It did little to soothe my disappointment, but I was aware that it was not by choice, not for any of us. Heaving a sigh, I joined the queue out, a dozen other gentlemen bearing nearly identical put-upon and worried expressions departing, their fretful thoughts visible in their eyes through the comforting haze of cigar smoke.

The streets outside were dark and thick with fog, swathing the row of hansom cabs and only somewhat dispelled by the burning gas lamp beside them. The horses' tack glinted dully in the light, and even in such gloom, the faces I could see were pale and drawn as they broke apart into groups. I looked at the sky, and despite the gloom, night had not yet fully fallen. My lodgings were not far; on foot, it would perhaps take me no more than half an hour. It would be more than enough time, when the monsters only began to appear when it was truly pitch black. Only the fog would be my enemy, if I made haste.

How foolish I was! I had so blithely, so carelessly believed that such an awful event could never happen to *me*, as if my arrogance made me immune to the dangers of the world. How I have repented that decision, how I have accepted that it was only my own lack of forethought that brought it upon me! The attacks were so sporadic, without rhyme or reason, that I thought the odds were surely in my favor. My gambler's heart—long gone now—had been so assured that I would arrive perfectly fine at home, absurdly confident. It was only half an hour; thirty minutes was no time at all, it had always passed so quickly on my previous walks.

Never did it pass more slowly than that night. I walked quickly, briskly, perhaps only slightly faster than my usual pace. The fog hung over me, thick and oppressive, weighing down on my shoulders and cold in my throat. Despite my coat, before I knew it, shivers were chasing each other down my spine, and the yellow gas-lamp glow from the lanterns seemed to barely drive away the darkness. As I passed beneath one, the next one seemed impossibly far away—I could not see the post, only the glass and the light, bobbing in the fog like a lighthouse beacon across an endless distance of fog.

It was then—rounding the first corner, I believe—that I realized how *silent* the streets were.

I could hear my own breath, strangely rapid, my blood rushing in my ears, but beyond that, nothing. All the usual night-time sounds that populated the heart of the city were absent; other than the hum of the lanterns and the distant rattle of a passing cab, there was nothing. None of the women, none of the constables, none of the enterprising pickpockets hoping to ambush an oblivious passerby; nothing. All was still. It seemed that I was the only living being in the entire city, small and alone in the fog. Even as I told myself rationally that I was within arm's reach of a building where people were safely barricaded, where life resided, concealed, it seemed impossible, unthinkable, distant.

When I tipped my head back, my breath faintly visible, the sky was similarly shrouded, impossible to make out, only a dark gray expanse beyond the fog. The sun was doubtless already below the horizon, but where was the moon? Could its silvery rays pierce the fog to reach the cobbles? Perhaps it was already there, but there was no way to see it.

I shook myself, suppressing the frisson of fear. Loitering was unwise; I had to make haste. There was no reason to linger out of doors.

The further I went, the colder I grew. The back of my neck began to prickle with the sensation that something somewhere was watching me—I glanced in every direction, continually checking over my shoulder, but within the small radius of my vision, I could see nothing but all-consuming, all-encompassing fog. I was—ostensibly—completely alone, surrounded by this horrible, crushing silence.

The fog itself seemed alive, coiling maliciously ever nearer to me the more I increased my pace, encroaching with the promise of suffocation, of death.

With each step I took, I knew I grew closer and closer to my destination, but it still seemed to be an insurmountable distance as the fear began to take hold of me. My hands, once warm, began to tremble slightly in my gloves; the street signs, barely legible mounted on the walls, bore names I knew yet seemed to display alien words. *Still?* I thought as I rounded a bend. *Still am I so far away?*

The wild idea crossed my mind to hail a cab if it passed me, but there was no jingle of harnesses, no grind of the wheels. All I heard was my heart pounding, faster and faster, the quaver spreading from my hands down my arms as if of its own will, ignoring all reason that it was barely cold out. The idea that I would make it safely home seemed pitiable, laughable, its likeliness fading with each step I took with my coat pulled tighter around me, my fingers curled so tightly they ached, my teeth longing to chatter. I had made it this far, I was only a block away—yet I could not stop the shudders of fear, could not stop myself from flinching at each sound: a droplet of water plummeting from the gable, a loose stone skittering away down the road from my foot, a stray cat's hiss and yowl, loud and near in the gloom.

That was when the *smell* reached me. It was the unmistakable, gut-churning scent of rotting meat, halting me in my tracks. Frantically I searched for the source, every instinct bidding me to retreat to the nearest lamppost rather than advance to the island of light around the next one, barely half a dozen steps before me. Light meant safety, some primal part of my brain thought wildly. I had to get to the light, not remain here in the side-street, in the corridor of semi-darkness where I could hardly see my hand in front of my face. Caught in the middle, I swayed, wracked by indecision—forward? Back? No, I couldn't retreat, I had to press ever onward!

I made it to the mouth of the street, heart in my throat, and as I neared the lamppost on the corner, the bitter ice of regret flooded my insides as it struck me—the smell was strengthening. Despite the fog, *their* shapes were clearly visible, patently obvious. There was no mistaking the five tall forms, the sickly, dirty yellow cowls; the way they stood in a ring around their victim, the gruesome scene I had seen in the papers, the same every time: some poor innocent pinned to the pavement through their extremities by long, bony needle-like claws, while their skin was flayed back to expose their organs, as emotionlessly and methodically as a surgical operation.

I had to run, I *knew* I had to run—but I was transfixed by the sight even as I was revolted by it, frozen to the spot even as my skin crawled. It must've been mere instants, but it felt like minutes—I don't think I breathed, for all I could do was stare. And right before my very eyes, one of them reached down and speared a wet, bloody gibbet—tore it free with a soft, wet noise and held it up for scrutiny: the purple, lumpish shape of a liver, dripping with blood and silhouetted eerily by the light. They chittered, a grotesque sound not unlike a beetle rattling its wings, then the liver vanished into one of the cowls.

I must have made an unconscious gasp of horror, for in unison they turned, and beneath their hoods there were only bottomless pits of darkness, and although they had no eyes that I could see, my stomach gave a lurch as they saw *me*. I was looking at Death—and it was faceless and horrible.

I turned on my heel and ran. I pelted over the cobbles faster than I ever dreamed I could run: blindly, thoughtlessly, heedless of where I was headed so long as it was *away* from those awful monsters. I could think of nothing else, the sole desire in the whole of my being to escape. I ran, the fog thick and cold and burning down my throat, and all I could see in my mind's eye was the hideous sight of their victim, innards splayed out for the world to see and left only an empty shell, naught but skin and bone—and myself in their place. My fear seemed to give me superhuman speed; my feet scarcely seemed to touch the ground, yet even as I ran, I had never felt more human and feeble. My pounding steps echoed with no other sound to comfort me that I was not alone in the company of monsters; my heart clawed the inside my chest with visceral force, as though it would burst forth and tumble to the pavement. Even as my legs began to ache I knew I couldn't stop, not until I reached safety.

I did not even dare look behind me—I could not

spare the precious energy, and I didn't need to look to know that they were in pursuit: I could hear the snap of their cloaks billowing, even if I could not hear any feet but my own, and I hoped desperately that they did not possess the ability to fly.

This hope was short-lived. In my periphery, suddenly I saw one of the flapping yellow cloaks appearing out of the fog, the faceless monstrosity rapidly gaining on me, gliding over the ground as if the forces of gravity held no dominion over it. My fear blossomed into panic, and I poured what energy and willpower I had into accelerating. I had to get away—frantically I searched the shadowy, looming shapes of the buildings around me for any shelter, any open doorway or window. Even a balcony would do! Something to clamber up, anything to put between myself and the advancing death—but I had not the faintest idea where I was, and all was barred, all wise and prudent souls safely behind their locked and shuttered entrances! No sane person would extend even a finger outside at this hour!

As I threw myself around the next corner, I felt that inexorable, inevitable, dreadful sensation: my strength beginning to wane. I could not maintain this flight for much longer, my pitifully weak human body possessing such pathetic limitations. But to stumble here was certain doom, it would be the end—fitting for such a fool as I, but oh, how I did not want to die! I could feel Fate closing in on me, feel them nearing as my body began to reach its limits. Hope began to shrivel in my breast, giving out its final gasp.

Then, on the horizon, appeared a flicker of salvation: a blazing lamp, yellow light muted and dulled by fog, not standing on its own but rather attached to a building—one that I recognized with a lurch was a police station. It was my only hope.

I summoned up my reserves and put on one final burst of speed, knowing this was my final chance, my sole remaining opportunity to continue drawing breath for the foreseeable future.

Of course, like all the other buildings, the doors and windows were barred, but that did not stop me from throwing myself at it, from hammering desperately at the door with all my remaining strength. I could not bring myself to feel any shame for the loudness of my voice as I begged frantically for aid. "Please! Somebody, open! Please—they're coming—help, please help!"

Above my own voice, I heard the snap of fabric, and then the next thing I knew, pain lanced into my shoulder blades and I found myself lifted off the ground and airborne, flying backwards to crash horribly into the pavement with such force that my vision swam, the breath gone from my lungs. I couldn't breathe, I couldn't move, and then the Harvesters were all around me, looming over me, the darkness beneath their cowls impenetrable.

I shrank, instinct compelling me to make myself as small as possible for all the good it would do. There was no escape, with so many of them, and there was only one thing left I could do. With my heart racing with the impending doom, I sucked in a great breath in preparation to scream—and tasted something sweet against my palate. It reminded me of honey, and a sudden numbness flooded my limbs. I could not longer feel my own extremities trembling—I tried to curl my fingers, but could only manage a twitch. A nerve toxin! My heart quailed within me. It all made sense now; they had no need to be swift when they possessed that, and I had long wondered why their victims were so silent at the point of death. Even dragging air into my lungs became a laborious task—but even as my body fought and struggled to move, I remained alert and aware. I was trapped, a prisoner in my own unresponsive mortal flesh.

Silhouetted by the harsh light of the lamps, every detail was visible but their faces—each tear and rip in their cloaks; the silent extension of those long, bony yellow claws, stained from all their previous victims. It was all I could do to rasp for breath, unable to flee or even cower with fear, all but motionless where I had been thrown, my own blood warm and leaking against my back. I could see the Harvester raise its claws, I could see the tiny pockmarks dotting the surface before they lowered to tear effortlessly through the buttons of my coat. Dimly I heard them bouncing on the road.

In that moment, unable to turn my neck sufficiently to even avert my gaze from the death clustered around me, I thought that perhaps that would be the last thing I ever concisely heard. What a foolish way to die!

And then came my salvation—a gunshot rang

out, shattering the stifling stillness of the night. My cries for help had been heard. I scarcely dared hope I would be saved, for the bullet struck the nearest Harvester with a colossal crunch, as if beneath the cloak was a hard exoskeleton. But the horrid monster cringed, uttering a high-pitched shriek of agony, and dark, viscous fluid began to seep into its cloak. The others hissed and turned away from me, raising their claws, only for a second shot to strike the wounded one's head with another splintering sound. As it staggered, its cowl—torn ragged by the bullet—slipped down.

I shall never forget that sight. It had no face, only a shiny, taut blue-black membrane, and it had no eyes nor mouth, only wet, glistening hemispheres and a jagged hole. It was only a glimpse that lasted perhaps no longer than an instant or two, but it filled me with the utmost revulsion. From what depths these creatures had emerged to walk the human world, I could not even begin to imagine.

There was another shot, then another, as if a second gun had joined the first, and the Harvesters ignored me in favor of huddling together and advancing towards their attackers, and the sliver of hope my breast began to flicker.

At that point, perhaps the numbing gas that they secreted reached my brain, or the overwhelming relief caught up to me, I do not know. All I knew was that my vision went dark as I fainted dead away.

How I wish I could say that my encounter with the Harvesters ended in triumph, but it did not. I escaped, but only narrowly, nothing short of miraculous. Certainly, they were driven away by the policemen and I was dragged to safety, and I am grateful. Certainly, I was told by the doctor who was examining me when I awoke that the strange anesthesia had worn off, and that it seemed I was physically sound.

Mentally, however, I knew that I was not, and have not been since. And there is little I can do.

The Harvesters haunt my every waking moment. I cannot purge their frightful shapes, their hideous visages, the sound of their cloaks rustling, the nightmarish vision of their forms clustered around me. At the first red ray of dying sun I flee to the safety of home; I bar the doors and windows each night; I attempt to sleep, but find myself unable to do so and ply myself with sleeping drafts should I wish to have any slumber at all. I cannot close my eyes in the dark without seeing those horrible faces behind my eyelids, cannot help but see them lurking in the gloom with their long claws dripping blood. For I know they are still out there, hunting, waiting for me.

ODESSA

LAWRENCE SALANI

EVERYTHING APPEARED PAINTED IN SHADES OF SEPIA. From the dirty, wooden floor on which he was lying, Lucian reached for the frayed curtain and pulled it to one side. Blinding light filled the dimly lit room, stunning him into wakefulness. He raised his hand and blocked the stark brightness from his gaunt, unshaven face. Realization overwhelmed him as recollections began inundating his still sluggish mind; how long had he been sleeping? He ran his fingers through his long black hair then fell back into the shadows, avoiding the stream of light and the harsh reality outside the window.

"Lucian." The soft, gentle call drifted through the gloom. "What time is it?"

"What does it matter," he answered forlornly as he glanced at the naked figure, entwined amongst the white sheets, lying on the bed. Sated and exhausted after another night of unbridled lust, he gazed around the shadowed stillness of the room. Time no longer existed. The past and future had merged, and only the present had any significance. Sunrise indicated the coming of another day and the sunset, well, the sunset bought the darkness.

She had come from the night.

Along the sidewalks or under the wan gas lighting of backstreet alleys and brothels, the endless parade of flesh offering ostensible pleasure became tiresome. Although money bought anything, sex had always been mechanical and quick, and not what he wanted. Good looking streetwalkers, who were never short of clients, were the worst. Plain, less attractive women tried harder to please, but, still, they never truly satisfied his desires and instead left him feeling empty and alone in a callous world where only Mammon ruled.

The name first came to him from a drunken stranger in a local alehouse. Alcohol fueled the man's loquaciousness, and as the night progressed Lucian listened to his drunken ravings with great interest. "They say Odessa will do anything. She's the best you'll ever find." Despite never having met Odessa, the man claimed anecdotal stories circulating throughout the district were true. At first skeptical, Lucian's burning desire overcame his fears. The name burrowed into his mind and began preying on his subconscious, filling him with dark yearning, until it hung suspended in the darkness of his thoughts like a specter floating on the warm city night breeze.

The girls along the streets would surely know of her. However, when he began asking questions, the few who did recognize the name were reticent to divulge anything and only gave him a curious look before turning away.

Sleazy lower class brothels also provided little information. "She doesn't work here," they told him when he questioned the girls.

Finding information about Odessa became difficult, so he began frequenting alehouses again. Strange, cold faces confronted his questions. "She moves around," they replied, "You'll be lucky locating her." Some had heard the name, but nobody actually knew the woman; his constant questioning came up against an impenetrable barrier which frustrated him all the more.

Unperturbed, Lucian began wandering empty streets away from the main centre of town. Fewer people frequented these areas, and the strangers he approached only gave him an awkward glance before walking by. Days slid by without success, but his determination to find fulfillment and sexual gratification knew no bounds.

Autumn was slowly turning into winter, and a biting chill filled the night air. Another fruitless night's search, and the orange glow of the occasional gas light along the cobbled roadways faded into early morning grayness. Twilight enfolded him as he sauntered along a deserted sidewalk. A sudden movement from within the gloom of a darkened shop front startled him. Quickly, he turned around, but the tingle that flowed through his body caused him to approach with caution. Gradually the odd movement became more noticeable and the indistinct outline of a man hiding in the shadows became discernible.

"Who's there?" asked Lucian tremulously.

From the darkness, a haggard figure emerged. "Can I bother you for a few coins?"

The voice was unexpectedly cultured but within the stranger's grey eyes there lurked a deep sadness beyond anything Lucian could fathom. Lucian drew out the few remaining coins in his pocket, but, when he stretched out his hand containing the money towards the derelict, a strange thought drifted through his mind. At first, it sounded like the wind moaning through the laneways and alleys of the surrounding buildings, but as the sound became tangible it formed the name "Odessa," and Lucian quickly drew back his hand before the man could take the coins.

"Odessa. Have you ever seen or heard of a girl called Odessa?"

A strange glow lit the man's face and his eyes opened wider. "Yes, I know of the girl."

"Where does she live?" asked Lucian, desperately clutching the money.

"Yes, I know the girl," he repeated sadly, "but, if I were you, I'd keep away from her."

"Her address, what's her address?" he asked, holding his handful of coins towards the old derelict.

The stranger looked at the outstretched hand with a gleam in his sad, grey eyes until the temptation became too much to resist. With resignation, he stammered out the address before snatching at the money. "Stay away from her, fool. Don't say I didn't warn you." His words faded into the gloom as he quickly turned towards a nearby alley.

The man's silhouette staggered briefly beneath the glow of a dirty gas light before being absorbed by thick shadows cast by the buildings that surrounded him. "Poor wretch," thought Lucian. "You meet them all around here."

Cold and miserable, Lucian shrugged and pulled his woolen coat closer to his body. Tomorrow he would try locating the girl, for now the time was late. In any case, the place was not close by, and he needed sleep before going to work in the morning. Tomorrow evening he would see if the address proved correct.

The following day dragged by. Thoughts of finding Odessa that evening constantly interrupted his concentration at work. Excitement filled him as his working day finally came to an end, for if all the tales about her were true he would certainly be in for a good time.

Twilight found Lucian trudging listlessly through the city streets. The terrace house was situated in a secluded area well away from the main centre of town. Although Lucian knew the neighborhood, he had difficulty in locating the address. Over the years the area had degenerated and had built up a bad reputation. Poverty and crime were rife, and, as the night grew darker, he became slightly reticent in continuing his search.

Small, dirty, and badly lit, the laneway he sought sent a flush of nervousness through his body. The ancient, shadowed buildings lining the footpath brooded malevolently in the darkness and cast an aura of foreboding over the barren roadway. Overcoming his fears, he crept along the night shrouded road until he stood before a dilapidated two story, brick residence. Doubts began filtering into his mind when he peered through the shadows at the darkened house before him; it appeared deserted. Suddenly, from a sash window on the lower floor of the building, a yellow light shone onto the roadway. A premonition caused him to procrastinate; however, he quickly cast aside his inhibitions and opened the rusting, ornate gate and walked along the stone path leading to the front door.

Red and blue colors coruscated magically from a small stained glass design that decorated the unpainted, wooden door. Nervously, he waited, contemplating if he should knock. When he did knock, the sound hung in the silent darkness as he waited for a reply. The tapping of footsteps and shuffling from behind the door drifted through the night. Then the sound of keys turning within the lock, the opening of the door, and finally, to his wondrous delight, after countless days of searching, Odessa appeared before him.

At first he felt intimidated by her presence, but the warm, sensual aura she exuded quickly dispelled his fears. The woman exceeded his expectations, and the price, although expensive, was well within reach. Her incredible hunger surpassed anything he had formally known, and the unimaginable pleasures he experienced left him contented and sated - he had never felt so alive. The afterglow was complete bliss.

Although he resolved never to return, visions of Odessa filled the days that followed. The memory was more than just an image within his mind; he could *feel* her. Her soft voice; her smooth, sensual touch; and her erotic smell were constantly there until his infatuation became a burning ember within his heart.

Only a week passed before he eventually succumbed to his intemperate desires. "I knew you would return," she said when she opened the door and welcomed him. "I have been waiting." After this, his visits became more frequent, for her willingness to accommodate to any of his sexual wishes exceeded anything he could have wanted.

During the weeks that followed, Lucian became distant and had a tendency to daydream. His appearance became haggard whilst his attitude turned taciturn and moody. Something was consuming the life from his body, but he seemed blissfully unaware of his degradation.

This degradation was not just physical but financial as well. His savings were gradually depleted until his rent payments began mounting and he began avoiding his landlord.

Although his factory job required a limited amount of skill, he constantly made mistakes. At first slight and unobserved, these mistakes grew until he began jeopardizing the safety of those around him. Surreptitious whispers among work colleagues, who began noticing his strange behavior, started circulating until he was eventually dismissed from his employment.

Without income, his expenses and debts began mounting. Overly generous, the landlord allowed him to stay longer than usual, but, eventually, he asked him to vacate the premises, for there were many wanting accommodation. Amidst all this his only thoughts were of Odessa.

"Odessa, I need you. I have given you all, and have no money left to give. I am in penury and have nowhere to turn."

"Money, what need have I of money? There is something greater you possess." The woman's eyes looked into his soul and saw the desire that lurked there. "The ecstasy I have shown you is but a fragment of what I can give. Let me show you what hides within the darkest recesses of your subconscious mind. What lies there will threaten your sanity and freeze your blood. Stupendous horror spawned before the advent of light within the unimaginable, timeless abyss. A slithering, entwining chaos that will fascinate with unimaginable awe as it devours your being."

The words were full of promise and power.

"Come; join us, the decision lies with you. Submit with blood. Feel the power surging within you; feel the fire flowing through your veins. Eventually, in death you will arise stronger and stand above the bovine cattle that surround you."

Lucian, at first, rejected her offer, but curiosity and avarice filled him with desire. Her promises seemed genuine, and, in his present condition, he had nowhere else to turn. Ah, what pleasure he would experience. And so, after reconsidering, he accepted, and a date was set for his immolation.

Unimaginable horror lay outside the thin curtain surrounding this mundane world. He worshiped dark, forbidden abominations that made him cringe in fear; but his rewards had eclipsed his wildest expectations. Stupendous wonders in nameless places left him spellbound until his mind could no longer accept reality, and only the world Odessa created for him existed.

Lucian sadly gazed at the figure lying on the bed and wondered how he had fallen to this nadir. Turning towards the window he looked outside again; the landscape beyond the grimy pane was incomprehensible. A leprous violet crept over a crimson sky. Scattered throughout the parched, red soil of the dilapidated town were dead and mutilated bodies writhing in agony. Silent and brooding, the air was palpable with death. The boundaries of what had formerly been reality were beginning to fade; was he looking outside or was he seeing what was left of his shattered self?

The rustle of bed sheets as the figure on the bed moved startled him from his pensive reflections. "Lucian, come love me again." The voice whispered seductively throughout the room, but Lucian's thoughts were fixed outside the window.

"Odessa, I may leave soon. This unbearable wretchedness fills me with pain. My life is in ruins, and my soul cries out for relief. I have given you everything, and now you want my very essence. Is there no limit to the horror to which I must succumb?" Lucian turned towards the figure on the bed, and the light from the window outlined his gaunt face and emaciated figure.

"Please, Lucian, close the curtain You know I dislike the light. Come back into my arms."

Lucian could not fathom the limit of this creature's lust. She had drained him and, still unsatisfied, demanded more. All that remained within him was a faint hope, clinging limply to his heart, for release from her ravaging lust.

"Lucian," she said turning her head, "I am with child. I bear your brood."

Astonished, Lucian stared at the face before him. The eyes were two long slits within which were two unnaturally black orbs. There was no nose or ears, and what resembled a mouth was a long gash. The head was hairless and smooth.

"Yes, Lucian, I bear your children."

The figure removed the sheets and crawled from the bed. It crept toward Lucian like a human spider on its four arms and two canine legs. She was completely hairless, and although the skin was soft, radiated warmth, and resembled human skin, it had a snake-like quality that moved as if it were alive. Lucian recalled the numerous occasions when she had crawled over him and her limbs had entwined his body; the ecstatic feeling had been more than he could endure.

Odessa squatted before him on her hind legs, her four breasts firm and erect, and opened her legs exposing her smooth, hairless labia. "Come back to bed. I need you."

Misery filled him. Lucian felt as if what had remained of his world had now collapsed around him. This new low surpassed his most wild imaginings. This woman would be the mother of his children. *What abominations would this creature spawn?*

"Lucian, you cannot leave now. The pact has been signed; there is no turning back."

"I must leave." Lucian turned towards the door not knowing where he would go. His only thought was to leave this wretched house and cleanse his body of the putrescent horror that crawled over his flesh.

When he opened the door, she did not prevent him from leaving. The fresh, clean outside air was like a new world, a new life. Without looking back, he hurried toward the tangle of rotting streets and desolate tenement buildings, and his figure became lost among the shadows. Time had slipped by quickly, and he knew she had been correct in saying that soon the appointed time would come. If he relaxed and fell asleep perhaps he could obliterate the past from his memory and find a way out. A dark alley in the distance looked deserted; a silent corner away from the congestion and noise, away from the squalor and crowds of people. The quiescence lulled him gently into a state of calm, and finally he slept.

Sleep was like a soothing balm as oblivion draped its black cloak over his wretched body. Odessa was a nightmare that had never happened. Reality faded, and his troubles disappeared into the darkness. But the peaceful embrace of slumber was short lived. A cold night breeze filled the streets. Shivering and alone, he awoke surrounded by the murky shadows within the lane, and the reality of his situation cascaded around him.

The sound of a rat scurrying amongst the festering rubbish within the alley caused the blood to drain from his face. Beneath the pile of waste in which the rat had hidden, something gleamed in the diffused light shining between the two buildings. At first, the object looked mundane and harmless, but the odd coruscation began to prey on his mind. He rose from his huddled position in the shadows and moved towards the light. A sliver of fear spiked through his body. It was a discarded blade lying in the middle of the lane way. The cold, thin steel beckoned menacingly in the wan light. Regret and doubt gnawed at his stomach. The appointed time was near.

Bitter and hard, winter dragged on listlessly. The

cold shadow of Death in the frosty breeze whispered through the city streets and laneways. Not even the usual streetwalkers were standing along the sidewalk. The last few coins Lucian possessed were enough for a warm drink and some comfort in a coffee house. He placed them in the pocket of the old coat he had found and continued trudging along the barren street.

A fine evening mist materialized, giving the naked trees along the roadway an ethereal look. Illumination from shop front windows lit the sidewalk with murky yellow haze. In the distance, a figure emerged from amidst the tangle of buildings and bedlam of murky street gas lights shining through the soft white mist. The grey silhouette drifted eerily towards him.

Pangs of hunger gnawed Lucian's stomach. "Can I trouble you for a few coppers to buy a meal?" he asked the stranger.

The man stopped suddenly then quickly turned his head to confront the voice. Modern and clean, his attire bore the mark of a gentleman.

"I may have something I can give you," said the stranger looking down at Lucian's miserable form. "But, wait! Do you know of a girl named Odessa?"

Many months had passed, and, suddenly, memories flooded through Lucian's mind with the mention of her name. "Why do you want this woman?" he asked the man.

"I have heard of the name and wish to meet her. I'll give you two florin coins if you know where I can find her."

Lucian looked at the money, and a spasm of pain racked his stomach. "Fool!" said Lucian bitterly as he snatched the money from the man's hand and told him the address.

The stranger disappeared into the last clouds of mist still clinging web like to the silent tenements lining the roadway. Odessa, the name awakened the darkest fears that lay embedded deep within his soul.

"Ah, Death, I welcome your cold kiss to rid me of this wretchedness, but what new horrors will you reveal? The thought of the anguish I must relive fills me with incredible dread." He looked at the money in his hand before stuffing the silver coins into his coat pocket. At least, tonight he could eat.

There were those who said that time is a stream, but to Lucian the days were a raging fire within his heart. The realization that each passing minute might be his last now dawned upon him, for visions of Odessa began appearing in dreams.

"Lucian, my love, the time draws near. The master beckons." The visions were more than dream, for her taste was upon his lips and the luxuriant musk like fragrance she emanated filled his senses. She stood before him, and beside her was something that could only be described as a shadow; an indiscernible black shape that emanated an aura of intense evil. "Soon, my love, we will be together." Her words sent a flood of anguish and bitter remorse flooding through his wretched form.

The darkness of the barren lane when he awoke from his nightmare was welcome relief. She had been taunting him, entering his thoughts as he slept, and playing with what was left of his shattered mind. How much more could he endure?

The night sky was a black, vacant void. The moon and stars had disappeared and a chill, as of the tomb, had overcome him. Uncomprehending, Lucian gazed at the silent abyss above, thinking it a dream, but eventually he realized black clouds were obscuring the stars, and the cold chill he felt indicated oncoming rain.

The first rumble of thunder bought with it a torrent of rain. When the storm hung directly overhead, he became wild eyed with fear and overcome by a frenzy of emotion. Clutching the wall, he raised himself from his crouching position and put his hands to his ears in an effort to muffle the sound then commenced screaming.

A flash of lightning lit the night, and the rumble of thunder that followed shook the very earth.

"They are coming!" he screamed, but no one listened to his maddened cries, for they were drowned out by another bolt of lightning followed by a thunderous roar. "They are coming to commensurate the pact!"

Lightning tore the night apart. Its sickly anodyne light lit the darkness and cast black, skeletal silhouettes of trees, which had been shredded by the merciless cold winter, along the grimy sidewalk.

Blackened windows gazed onto barren roads from morose grey and black stone buildings that surrounded him. Another flash of lightning eerily lit the cold, silent walls, followed by another loud clap of thunder.

Lucian began running. There was nowhere to run, but he didn't care. Aimlessly, he ran through the streets, screaming. Gaunt and haggard, his figure looked odd and spectral as the lightning flashed and thunder roared about him. Faces looked out from the surrounding tenements and shop windows, but they quickly sank back into the safety of their closed doors when they saw the crazed figure running along the road.

When the storm finally abated, Lucian slept, but unimaginable nightmares riddled his sleep. Again, Odessa appeared before him, and again he awoke to the comfort of knowing it had been a dream. But when the semblance of sleep once more enfolded him, a black shadowed form appeared.

"Lucian, I have bought your children for you to meet." The voice was soft and beguiling. It drifted through the darkness of the lonely laneway and echoed through the corridors of his mind.

Unimaginable, twisted shapes crept from the shadows; some were male others female. Their smooth skin glistened and moved in the pale diffused light shining into the laneway from the main road. Some sat on their hind legs exposing their engorged members while others crawled through the debris of the laneway on their six limbs. Those that stared at Lucian sent a shudder of unfathomable fear through him, for there was a spark of madness deep within the blackness of their eyes. He began to scream in an attempt to awaken from this nightmare, but there was no awaking from this dream and his screams only faded into the black shadows of the silent, cold tenements that surrounded him.

Odessa crept from the darkness and stood before him; her smooth, succulent form tempting with blasphemous pleasures. "Lucian, the appointed time has come." Her gaze fell upon the discarded blade lying amidst the decaying refuse scattered within the laneway; its edge gleaming in the darkness. "Either you do it yourself or the master will do it his way."

Lucian looked up at the stern, hard eyes that emanated from the shadowy form, and he knew *his* way would be slow and merciless. Then, with sorrow in his eyes the pitiful form crawled toward the gleaming blade.

GRETA SOMERSET

STEVE CARR

USING ALL OF HER STRENGTH, GRETA pushed on the lid of her coffin, lifting the dirt that lay on it. The boards cracked and splintered against the force of her exertion. Her long slender fingers, thin and cold as icicles, broke one by one as she shoved against the weight of the damp earth. Slowly, a fissure formed in the mound of dirt above her grave. She pushed her head up through the opening in the soil, then her shoulders, then her narrow waist. As the worms, grubs, and beetles that would have made her flesh their meal fell from her long red hair, adorned with blue ribbons, and linen nightgown, she crawled out of the grave. Fog blanketed Bow Cemetery. Its moss covered headstones were barely visible in the dark of night.

h his tongue. The horse began to trot. "Pardon my asking," he said, "but aren't you chilled?"

"Not at all," Greta said. "But I am famished."

"There are no bakeries or pubs open this time of night," he said.

"What about your horse?" she said.

"My horse?"

With her feet in a trough on Salisbury Lane, Greta washed the dried cemetery mud from her feet and the blood from her face and hands. Dawn began to break through the dense fog, casting a hazy blue light on the facades of the shops that lined the street. A middle aged man dressed in business attire walked by. He paused to stare at her, his face contorted into a display of shock and distaste.

"Madam, have you no shame, bathing in public?" he said.

"I've met with very unfortunate circumstances," Greta said. "I'm on my way home now, only two blocks away. If you would be so kind as to let me walk with you so that I can continue unmolested, I would be indebted."

He took a gold pocket watch from a vest pocket, then flipped open the ornately designed cover. "I have little time to spare to get to the accounting house where I work, but if we don't dawdle I can walk with you for a short distance."

Greta stepped out of the water, grabbed the gray knitted wool scarf draped on the edge of the trough and wrapped it around her neck. She grasped his arm, her bare feet slapping the pavement as they hurried along.

"You're a comely young woman and your speech indicates moderate good breeding," he said. "Have you no one that cares about you going about in such a manner?"

"I have only my maiden aunt who was unable to intervene on my behalf," she said.

He stopped and gazed at her pale face. "Intervene in what way?"

"To stop me from being put to death."

As if slapped, he jerked his head back. "Madam, your jesting isn't funny in the least."

"I have no intention of being funny," she said as she pulled down the ruffled neckline of her gown and showed him the rope burns that encircled her neck. "I was hanged only a few short days ago."

He pulled his arm from her grasp. "Have you escaped from Bedlam?"

Greta laughed. "I've spent time imprisoned there, but I am not an escapee. I was hanged for murdering the man who stole what little money my aunt and I had and left us to starve."

"This is unbelievable in every way," he said. "If you have died, why then have you returned?"

"To satisfy my hunger," she said as she pushed him against a wall. She bit into his neck and pulled away his Adam's apple. She chewed and swallowed it, then bit into him again.

Greta entered the dark, narrow alleyway just as the fog dissipated and sunlight bathed the street and buildings beyond the alley. At the end of the alley, she raised the iron knocker on a weather worn door and tapped the wood three times.

The rusted hinges creaked as the door slowly opened.

"It's me, Greta," she said as her aunt stared blindly out, her eyes turned white from age.

"Greta," the old woman screeched. "How is it you've returned from the grave?"

"What forces are acting on me I have no idea," Greta said. "I have returned to the living just as I left it, hungry. I am ravenous."

"This is your home," her aunt stammered. "Come in and warm yourself at the stove." She stepped aside and held the door open until she felt Greta pass by her. She closed the door.

Greta surveyed the room, straining to see in the dim light cast by a flickering wick in a kerosene lamp. Her aunt's rocking chair was inches away from the stove. The room smelled of burning coal and dust. Another chair and a small table sat in the middle of the room. A tattered curtain at the side of the room hid the bed. Her aunt tentatively walked across the room and sat in her rocking chair.

Greta knelt by the rocking chair and took her aunt's hand in hers. Her aunt flinched at the feel of Greta's icy cold skin. A gold watch dangled from around Greta's wrist. "My dearest aunt, you are so thin. Have you not been eating?"

"Tom Price brings bread, fruit, tea, and milk when he can," she said. She touched Greta's cheek. "Your hand, your face, are so cold."

Greta placed her aunt's hand on her breast above her heart. "My heart no longer beats, and blood no longer courses through my body to keep me warm. I am in no distress because of it. It is quite remarkable how quickly I have become accustomed to being dead."

"What will you do now?" her aunt said, trembling from a mixture of sadness and fear.

Greta let loose her aunt's hand, stood, then went to the cracked mirror hanging on the wall by the curtain. Her reflection startled her. In death she had retained her beauty. She had only been in the grave for a few days, but in those days she had not lost the flush of pink coloring on her porcelain cheeks, and her lips had retained their cherry hue. Only her blue eyes had changed. They were as vacant as her aunt's.

"I will find the judge who sent me to the gallows," she said.

Greta pushed aside the curtain and stepped out, wearing a simple gown of dark blue linen.

Tom Price placed a loaf of bread, a jug of milk and three apples on the table. "Your aunt just told me you've returned, though I saw you being hanged with my own eyes," he said, staring at her in disbelief.

"It was an injustice," she said. "I have returned to feed."

"Feed?" he said, his voice trembling.

Seated at the table, Greta's aunt gently placed her hand on his arm. "You have nothing to fear, Tom. The Lady Somerset that you knew when she lived at Claymore Abbey before the Claymore fortunes were lost is the same as she was."

"Except now I'm dead," Greta added with a bitter laugh.

Tom took a yellowed handkerchief from his back pocket and wiped the perspiration from his brow. "It's in all the papers that the carcass of a horse and the horse's owner were found hidden behind some shrubs near Bow Cemetery where you were buried," he said. "I cannot relay what was written concerning the gruesome state of their bodies." He shoved the handkerchief back into his pocket. "I served your parents when you were just a babe still in the cradle. I hope that has some meaning."

Greta walked to the table. "You've been a faithful caretaker to my aunt. You have nothing to fear from me. She handed him the watch. "This should bring a good price at a pawnbroker. It will more than pay for the food you bring."

Tom examined the watch. He had been in the watch shop when it was sold to a wealthy businessman. "Is this the watch of the dead man found not more than a few blocks from here?"

Greta patted Tom's hand. "Just be cautious who you sell it to, lest it lead the police back here." She broke the loaf of bread into two and quickly devoured one of the halves quickly. She put the bread on the table, then looked into Tom's astonished eyes. "I would prefer meat, but bread and fruit will do for now."

Tom crossed himself and mumbled a quick prayer.

Greta stepped out of a dark alley and wiped the blood from her mouth with her victim's lace handkerchief. She tossed it away and proceeded down the narrow, dimly lit sidewalk, keeping to the shadows and close to the brick buildings. The street and sidewalk were empty of other pedestrians. When the courthouse came into view through the dense fog, she stopped and saw Judge Paxton's carriage waiting for him in the glow of a streetlamp. The driver was standing in front of the two horses, adjusting their bridles and reins.

Greta stepped into the light and let out a scream of terror. "A woman's been attacked."

The driver spun around and after a moment spotted Greta. "Is she injured?" he said.

"Yes, her body is in the alley just a short way from here," Greta said. "Please come see what can be done for her."

Hesitantly, he looked around, then let go of the

reins and followed behind Greta as she ran to the alley. "In there," she said, pointing.

The driver pushed past her and went into the alley. Greta followed. A very short while later she emerged from the alley wearing the driver's gray inverness cape and John Bull top hat. She went back to the carriage, collected the reins and climbed up onto the driver's seat.

Judge Paxton came out of the building alone and slowly made his way down the long flight of stairs, tapping his cane on each step. When he got to the carriage, he said, "I'll get the door myself, James. It's been another late night, as usual. I'm hungry, and I'd like to get home to my roast mutton dinner as swiftly as possible." He stepped into the carriage and closed the door. Greta flicked the reins and the horses began to trot.

Greta finally pulled the carriage to a stop in front of Bow Cemetery. She hopped down from the seat.

Judge Paxton opened the door and got out just as she removed the coat and hat. He blinked hard several times. "What manner of evil is this? I watched them put the noose around your neck."

"The noose you callously and gleefully directed to be tied there," she said. "I went to my grave hungry, and now you will go to yours equally famished."

Before he could react, she leapt on him. She tore open his clothes as he struck her with his fists while screaming in pain as she bit into his ample flesh. She opened his body while he was still alive and feasted on his organs. He didn't stop struggling until she ripped his heart out and stuffed it in her mouth.

She didn't stop until all that was left was bone, hair and cartilage.

Greta stood at the end of her grave site for some time before she began digging through the dirt with her broken fingers. She dug the dirt out of her broken coffin and lay down, her hands across her breasts. She closed her eyes, and with her stomach full, never rose again.

THE HUNGER

ROSS SMELTZER

THE GRAVE WAS SHALLOW, NOT MUCH more than a rough cut in the sodden ground. It was filling fast with water and worms.

And it was empty.

"Put 'er in there a fortnight past, Inspector," the old gravedigger said, pointing to the grave. His words came out jumbled, a sludge of Cheapside grunts and grumbles. "Came round this patch this morning, to dump another one in, and I found 'er dug up an' gone. As if she dug 'erself out of the ground and went off for a stroll in the churchyard."

He paused awhile and spoke again: "I never learned her name, sir. She was a vagrant—that's what they said when they brought 'er to me. Found 'er dead of laudanum poisoning in the street, they said.

An' no family to claim 'er. Poor 'eart; it's enough to drive an old man to despair."

There were delicate pink flowers strewn around the grave. Some had been trampled into the wet earth. Footprints circled the area. I could make out indistinct toe prints in the flattened grass and mud. An odd detail. Even the wretchedest of the poor went about in shoes. It was a fool who let his naked skin touch London's squalid streets.

"That seems like a rather improbable scenario," I said laconically, my indifference palpable in every syllable. "I'd prefer not to resort to resurrection as a hypothesis just yet." I could disguise neither my boredom nor my hangover. I wanted to be anywhere else but in that old graveyard on Goulston Street.

"Do you think she'd been buried by mistake, inspector?" the gravedigger asked. He'd pressed on, still eager, oblivious. "Perhaps she'd been in a deep slumber and been put in the groun' in error. I've 'eard of stranger things in my profession. I do 'ope I didn't put 'er in the ground while she were alive. I wouldn't be able to live with meself if that were true."

"No doubt," I replied. "You can rest easy on that score, though. I think it most unlikely the woman was mistakenly interred. If she were, we would never know of it. She would have been in no position to extricate herself from her premature resting place." The gravedigger nodded dejectedly and stared into the pit he'd so recently dug. His face was gnarled, putting me to mind of a piece of old wood, like those that drift in the Thames, among the dead fish. His eyes were black and shiny, two buttons stuck deep in doughy skin.

"Third one this month," he added, talking to himself now, mumbling. The gravedigger rasped, his tongue flicking against the roof of his toothless mouth. His voice was wet, sticky as mud.

"Is that true?" I asked, my interest now piqued. I turned to Constable Smyth, who'd rudely wrenched me from the public house on Mary Street and brought me to the graveyard.

"Aye, sir," the tall and thickset man with the brushy silver mustache replied. A pink scar arched across his forehead. It began under his helmet and bisected his nose and upper lip. Rumor had it he'd earned it at Kambula, from a slashing Zulu *assegai*. "The gentleman is correct. This is, indeed, the third grave disturbed this month." He motioned to the gravedigger with his truncheon and said, "This poor chap has been most disturbed by the whole affair." His voice was cool, unruffled. He'd seen worse things in his time.

"Aye," the gravedigger said. "Most disturbed. The 'ole thing is regrettable. The dead want only their justly deserved peace an' quiet. An' 'ere they are, bein' dug up in the night! Most distressin', I'd say, inspector. Most distressin'. I 'ate to think of meself bein' taken from me eternal restin' place and dragged off in the dark...off to who knows what unhappy fate. They are cold—the dead. So very cold. Their 'earts that used to fill with love are still and silent. Their skin is soft, though. An' I hold their 'ands before I send 'em away. Then, I cover them in the black earth an' they are gone."

"How do you know they've been dragged from here?" I asked.

The constable pointed to the ground near the grave and said: "Inspector, you can see faint hollows in the ground consistent with a heavy body being dragged out of the grave and through the wet grass. The ruts and hoof prints one would expect to find if a cart had been used to transport the body from here are absent." He swung his bulging, heavily-muscled arms away from the grave, motioning into the expanse of the graveyard and added, "those same indentations continue on for some distance into the graveyard, growing fainter the further one goes. Whoever dug this poor woman up didn't use a cart to take her from here, Inspector. They carried her off."

"They wanted quiet," I said. "Or they couldn't afford a cart."

"Or they were quite powerful," the constable added. "Stronger than most men."

"Fair enough," I said. "Fine work," I added. I was thankful for the constable's steadying presence.

I then looked to the gravedigger and said, "My guess is that we are dealing with a band of pranksters. I can imagine no other rational scenario to account for this incident. And while this sort of crime does disturb one's sensibilities, it does not warrant the interest or resources of Scotland Yard." My head smarted. Neither the gin nor the laudanum had released me from their iron grip and the bilious yellow sun—reflecting against the smog sliding off the waters of the Thames—was drumming on my skull. "We haven't the resources to investigate this matter more closely, I'm afraid."

The morning air was heavy, treacly-sweet, tropical. It reminded me of my days in the jungles of Madras, my skin smarting from biting flies, sweat dripping from the tip of my nose. The summer of 1888 had been hot. The autumn promised more of the same. And as I well knew from my time on the beat, heat warps men's minds. It brings bottled rage to the surface. It makes madness seem sane.

The gravedigger was silent awhile, then motioned to a forlorn cottage at the edge of the graveyard and whispered: "I live close and I tell ye with all me 'eart, there is something rotten about this place, Inspector. I've seen things 'ere, shadows an' phantoms. Gliding shapes, lit by the moon, crossing the grounds in the dismal hours, when pious sorts are in their beds and dreaming. There are times, inspector, when I wake in the night to find shadows at my bedside, shadows that exude a feeling of indefinite evil.'Tis a wicked place, this is." His words melted away into the chill air.

Smyth asked: "You have seen men in the graveyard?"

"Shapes," the gravedigger replied. "Nothing more, I expect. The restless dead, unwilling to quit this world." The old man crossed himself piously. For the first time all morning I actually took a good look at the man. He was missing three fingers, his right eye was a yellowed orb, streaked with bursting pink veins—infected—and his left arm was withered to nothing, a brittle branch held close to his chest, barely peeking out of his shirt. The man wore a ring with a green stone—Chinese jade, dexterously carved—no doubt a trinket he'd purloined from one of the corpses he guarded with such care. He was a low, degenerated sort, another of London's shattered offspring, nursed on septic waters and poisoned air. He was another victim of a cruel and merciless city. As broken as that poor woman who'd been stabbed to death just a week before. She'd been gutted like a fish and left on the top of a flight of stairs, bleeding out in the dark. All these unfortunates—the gravedigger, the anonymous and now missing corpse, the murdered *dollymop* whore—all were beyond redemption. They were all damned.

I turned away from the gravedigger and said, "I must confess that crimes perpetrated against the dead do not hold much interest for me—or for Scotland Yard. They are beyond our humble jurisdiction. We have enough to worry about protecting the living."

I desperately needed a smoke. My hangover had been building throughout the morning, worsening as the sun ascended. I felt as if I might retch in the grass. My jaw clenched tight and my teeth ground together like gears in an old machine, holding back the hot bile bubbling in the back of my throat. Lights danced in the periphery of my vision. My hand squirmed in my coat pocket.

"Beggin' yer pardon, inspector, but that's a most

unchristian thought. Quite uncharitable to the dead."

"I suppose it is," I said, carefully extracting a cigarette from my pocket, lighting it and lifting it to my lips. I then tossed my flickering match into the empty grave, watched it die in the tea-brown muck. The sun's glow was warming the graveyard. Sweat was pooling around my neck and in my armpits, staining my shirt. I turned and fixed the old grave-digger with a withering stare. I saw a tarnished cross dangling from his spindly neck and smirked, amused by the man's sincere piety. How anyone could hold fast to the dream of a kindly, benevolent God in a city such as this baffled me.

All of us were silent for a while, lost in black thoughts, staring into the empty grave.

"She was such a pretty young thing," the grave-digger said, his words directed to nobody in particular.

I turned to leave. Church bells droned in the distance, their dense clamor strangled in the smog. As I began to follow the muddy path out of the graveyard, I turned and looked back towards the gravedigger and said, "Call on me if another grave is disturbed here. I'll see if I can have a man watch over the place at night. That ought to put a stop to it. I make no promises, though. Our men are—as I'm sure you understand—stretched rather thin." I finished my cigarette and tossed it in the grass. "Now, if you would excuse me, gentlemen, I must leave this place. I'm needed elsewhere." The part about posting a watchman in the graveyard was true; the part about being needed elsewhere was not.

As I departed from the graveyard I reflected on what had transpired. It was the footprints that troubled me most about the crime. They lent it a primitive, atavistic quality. It was the work of animals, not of men.

Rain was falling as I left the graveyard, filling the empty grave, making it seem as if the missing woman had never been there at all.

The little hand was reaching up from the mud, as if clawing at the impassive sky—or making a desperate last plea to a god who would not listen.

It was a wasted hand, brittle bones wrapped in a husk of skin. And it was missing three fingers. It was the gravedigger's hand, now blue-grey, gone cold.

The rest of him was nowhere to be found.

"Some boys found it this morning," Constable Smyth said coolly, eyeing the kinked and shattered hand without any evident feeling. His face was an impassive mask. He'd seen things as a beat officer, which would make the stoutest man swoon from fright.

The green ring was still on the old gravedigger's hand. It twinkled in the morning light. I felt instantaneous guilt for the rough way I'd treated the old man. I hated the aristocratic contempt I instinctively felt for him and his kind. It had been bred into me, but that was no absolution. The city had infected me with its own ugliness and it was growing in my heart, a cold detachment from humanity, a spreading canker of hate.

"Strange that whoever did this did not take that ring," I observed. "It's the only thing of value the old man had."

"I perceived that as well, Inspector. Quite strange."

It had been four weeks since my previous visit to the graveyard on Goulston Street, and it had been an exacting period. There'd been another woman murdered, in Buck's Row, near the London Hospital. She'd been carved up like a beef roast, nearly decapitated, and subsequently mutilated by a rampant, maniac's hand. I'd been assisting with the case, and the lack of suspects or evidence wore on us all. We were groping in the dark, trying to mine secrets from a city that guarded them jealously. A city where shadows ruled.

Smyth spoke again. "His hand is quite stiff, Inspector. I'd wager he's been dead since the early morning." He took his truncheon out from under his arm and pointed towards a collapsing tomb, nearby. "I also found the old man's shovel nearby, sir—snapped in two. Over there."

"It must have been broken by a very strong man. Any witnesses?" I asked.

"None. None of the lodgers in the adjacent common houses say they heard anything last night."

I thought awhile, listened to steamships churn through the briny water of the Thames. "The presence of the old gravedigger's shovel is significant," I muttered, talking through my thoughts.

My mind was less foggy today, more attuned to its surroundings. Proximity to murder sharpens the mind. As do tinctures of laudanum, tactically administered. "Surely, he did not come here to bury someone in the dead of night. I imagine he brought it with him as a way to frighten off an imagined intruder. He intended to use it as a weapon."

"He's dead, Inspector. I hardly think whoever he came to frighten off was 'imagined,'" Smyth said. His disdain for me was plain; it crackled in his booming baritone. He was a veteran on the force and I not more than a stripling, fresh from my studies. He was entitled to his scorn. "I suppose he saw someone in the graveyard and armed himself to confront them," he added. "He did say he had seen figures in the graveyard on numerous occasions."

"Quite right," I replied, deferential, cowed as a schoolboy before an exacting headmaster. "Anything left behind?"

"No, sir. Nothing. Whoever did this didn't open any graves last night. I should add, inspector, that I've interviewed the boys who found the ... *remains*. They had a most interesting story to tell, sir."

"Yes?" I asked.

"The boys—tough young lads, orphans all, from the Spitalfields Workhouse just across the way—were playing in the graveyard around dawn, staging mock battles with sticks and tossing bits of headstone at one another, as lads are wont to do. They said—and they uniformly agreed on all the following particulars—that, after they came upon the gravedigger's hand in the dirt, they saw dark figures crouched among the headstones. 'Living shadows' is how they described them. They couldn't make them out well, at that early hour, but they all said these figures were stooped, hobbling on their hands like apes are reputed to do, wearing nothing. 'Pale as ghosts,' they said, with hypnotic green eyes that shone in the fog."

I snorted. "Quite the imaginative boys!"

"They said they saw something else, Inspector. A 'Devil Ghoul' they called it. A gliding man who didn't make a sound. They said his eyes glowed like lightning. They said it was perched atop a tumbled-down tomb—balanced perfectly, like a great big tomcat on a wall—and that it had a set of green eyes that gazed and gazed and never blinked. They ran from the graveyard as quick as they could when they saw it. Filled the little runts with fright, whatever it was. When I spoke with them, they were hollering about it like they'd seen the devil himself. Some were still shivering from the scare." Smyth reported all this coolly, without scorn or mockery. Had I taken the boys' statements, I doubt I could have contained my laughter.

"A most fanciful turn of phrase. 'Devil Ghoul,'" I said.

"Yes, sir, fanciful indeed. But we must remember, these are mean streets and one matures quickly here. Those lads may be young, but they're no fools. I wouldn't dismiss them too hastily, Inspector."

"I had no intention of doing so," I replied, my voice testy and sharp.

I looked about the old graveyard. It might have

been beautiful once, but the inexorable forces of ruin had taken their toll on the old tombs, headstones, and crypts, leaving them fractured and broken, slowly disintegrating into the black soil. Moss draped the headstones, effacing the names they bore, and white mushrooms, glowing faintly in the gloom, peered out from the earth like the nested eggs of hidden creatures. The unkempt hedging rattled with the passing of the wind, and dead leaves were gathered in great piles in the nooks of the graveyard. Crows wandered aimlessly along the iron fencing that surrounded the place.

It was little wonder that imaginative boys, traumatized by their grisly discovery and goaded on by one another, imagined an evil spirit dwelling among the graves.

Smyth wrenched me from my reflections: "Inspector Marmont, shall I have a man stand watch over the place? The murderer—or murderers—may return."

"Manpower is not something the Metropolitan Police has in abundance, at the moment. However, given the circumstances, I do not think it unwise for us to post a man at the gate. And have a few of your men walk the surrounding blocks in rotations. With any luck, whoever did this will come back and we'll be able to snare them."

Smyth nodded in agreement and set off to relay my orders to his men. It was then that I looked at the ground where the old gravedigger's hand lay. There were footprints in the black soil.

The old gravedigger's cross lay stamped in the

mud. It was streaked with dried blood, the color of rust.

Shokol wiped dripping water from his eyes with one hand and tried to feel his way among the ranks of collapsing headstones with the other. He staggered, feeling the weight of his wet clothes, their chill creeping into his bones, the bite of the rain as it beat his bare hands and face, and the pull of the thickening mud as it oozed above his ankles. It threatened to suck him down and digest him in the earth below. He peered into the darkness but could make out nothing through the curtains of silvery rain. A white-hot lightning bolt arced in the sky, revealing hulking wharves and the spikes of factory spires along the Thames.

Shokol cursed and spat rainwater through his few remaining teeth. The water in this city tasted briny to him, sour. Not at all like the water in Lodz, his old home. He could make out nothing but the formless shapes of tombs and headstones all around him. Just black shapes against the deepening void of the cemetery. He trudged through the mud and the overgrown grass, running his fingers through his lank hair. He drained the last of the cheap gin he kept in his jacket. He tossed the bottle away, heard it shatter against stone. He heard other noises too.

He needed shelter from the storm. He felt in his pockets again, probed for the money he needed to rent a dosshouse bed for the night. He did not relish going back to one of those places. Gibbering madmen, loose women, and practiced throat-cutters alike abounded in the East End's lodging places, and the police avoided them as best they could, intent on letting the unfortunates housed there brutalize themselves without disturbance. Shokol had spent the night before in the same room as a glazed-eyed boy—he could not have been more than thirteen—who sopped bits of bread in a broth of halfpenny tea and sugar and an old man with a silvery beard who mouthed a gristle-caked ham bone like he was a hungry dog. He was certain both - were mad. Wretched as those places were—with their bedding that stank of dried rat shit, their tin teapots, all battered and stained, and their white-grey gruel that solidified in the bowl—he would have given anything for the coins to rent a bed in one of them.

And yet, he knew that he had nothing. He would need to make his own way tonight.

Thunder droned dully in the coal-black sky, like the tolling of an immense bronze bell.

Shokol spied a circular tomb in the furthest corner of the graveyard, towering above the surrounding headstones. He ran towards it, colliding with a grave topped by a headless angel. He cursed again, nursed the hurt in his foot, and then selected a heavy stone from the ground. It was covered in oily mud.

The graves were shallow here, shoddily dug. Skulls were peeking through the melting soil, grinning at him in the dark. Skeletal hands, freed from the mud by the heavy rain, clawed at the maelstrom in the sky.

Shokol approached the tomb, then hurled the stone at the door of the structure. It struck true, with a thick crack. The door splintered and cleft apart. Its verdigrised hinges, crumbling already, fractured and fell away, clanging loudly against the stone. The door hung on its crushed hinges for an instant, then fell inwards. Chalky dust billowed out from inside the tomb and radiated outwards among the surrounding headstones.

Shokol faintly heard screeching coming from somewhere near, and a sharp childlike wail, and hyena laughter. He paused at the entrance of the tomb, peered vainly into the blackness, then entered. His feet thudded heavily on the old stone floor. The sound reverberated in the silence.

It was quiet in the tomb, empty and still. Shokol could barely hear the pounding rain inside the thick stone walls. It was as if he'd been removed from the world—the crushing reality of fleas in his hair, of old shoes peeling apart, of begging for moldy biscuits—and transported into a different reality. A world of echo and stasis. He was safe now, here in this kingdom of the dead. Rainwater trickled from cracks in the ceiling of the tomb and ran down its sides, leaving rust-red streaks on the walls.

Inside, the tomb was perfectly black. It had been left undisturbed. Shokol knew this was unusual. He was savvy enough about London's alternative economy to know that grave robbers made a fair living by looting the dead. Pawning their precious trinkets for gin and rotgut and quick amours in alleyways. This tomb had been overlooked--or avoided. It was an ill-omened place. Shokol, thinking there might yet be valuables in the tomb, decided to explore the place. After wiping away snarled rat nests from the floor, he removed a filigreed iron grate and descended a short, snaking stairway into the crypt below. The stairs were slick with water and clumps of grey-green mold. Shokol slipped when he stepped on a rat's skull. He crushed it under his heel. Its orange needle-sharp teeth sank into his skin. He felt hot blood well in his shoe.

Reaching the bottom of the stairway, Shokol came to a small crypt, not more than a shallow pit. The earthen walls of the chamber smelled hot and putrid, turned. Rotten eggs. He gagged. Hunched low, he came upon a rough-hewn stone sarcophagus. Its lid had been removed. He felt inside but found nothing. When he retrieved his hand, he found it coated with wispy spider webs and grave dust.

As Shokol turned to make his way back up the steps and into the tomb's main chamber, however, the dense earthen floor of the crypt gave way, and he fell through a hidden wooden door. He tumbled into a chamber below, howling, feeling the cold soil on his skin and the old roots clawing at his clothes, and smelling the sickly-sweet tang of putrescent skin, like butcher's wares gone bad. The air was hot, heavy—poisoned.

He fell into a deep pit. It exhaled a dense miasma of venomous air, the uncorked reek of age-long rot. Screaming now, Shokol spun and swam in a deep pool of corpses. Bodies without number drifted listlessly in a lagoon of jellied gore. He felt them all around him, some sinking into the brown water, and others buoyed at the surface by their own gaseous bloat, their innards spilling out like swollen worms. Skeletal hands clutched his arms and feet and skulls beamed at him as he howled in the dark, gulping down the fetid water. His feet churned tangled bones, pounded them to dust and shards. Some of the bodies in the pit were far from skeletal, however. Rotten, with sunken features and shriveled skin that clung tightly to their bones, they wore ragged shreds of clothing—the finery they'd been buried in. Their eyes were blank, pitiless. They stared and stared, seeing nothing. He felt lifeless hands press against his skin.

An old man's body floated in the water beside Shokol. The man's eyes were wide with terror and his mouth was set in an endless scream.

And all around him, in the pit of bones and bodies, Shokol heard the same screeching he had heard earlier, but it was much louder now. And laughter too, the tittering of children. He sensed their joy. Their delight in his naked, animal terror. He saw eyes piercing the blackness, yellow and primeval: wolf eyes. And he saw teeth, punching through shriveled gums and cracked lips in rows, shark-like, all white as polished ivory. The teeth gleamed in the darkness.

And he saw another thing, pale and crouched close, atop a throne of knotted ribs and stacked skulls at the far edge of the pit. It was man-like but not a man. It was something incalculably ancient, something reptilian, primordial. Its eyes glowed like emeralds lit by candlelight, piercing the gloom with darts of liquid light. It beckoned Shokol come near. It invaded his mind, penetrating the webs of fear and revulsion that filled the man's mind. "Join us," it seemed to say--though it spoke not a word. "Come

"It cannot be!" Shokol shouted, gulping down fetid water. "Not here. Not here. The strzyga! The living-dead!"

Shokol grasped desperately at the roots in the tunnel above and managed to clamber out of the pit. He fled from the tomb, not stopping even when his head struck the tomb's entrance and blood drained from the wound and dripped into his eyes.

His wails tore through the night, echoed across the cobbled streets and the crooked, bent buildings of Goulston Street. They drowned out the quavering peals of thunder.

I had heard the story by now. It had made the rounds in every police barracks in East London. Only a few days before, a filthy, blood-crusted vagrant had been found, running in circles, his pants soiled, screaming in Yiddish and fractured, broken English about 'devils' and 'living-dead men' in a graveyard on Goulston Street. My graveyard. The one that had troubled my thoughts these last months, wrenching me away from pressing matters. From the Ripper.

Of course, I didn't believe a word of the man's story.

Or rather, I didn't believe in the particulars of

the man's story. I didn't believe the man had seen the 'devils' he so claimed. Smyth, who'd discovered the poor man, said his breath reeked of cheap gin, nasty stuff. A likelier explanation for the man's breakdown was that his imagination, fired by potent homemade spirits and filled with continental superstition, had gotten the better of him.

Still, I had to concede it was rare for one's sanity to be entirely blasted by drink, no matter how strong. Smyth claimed the man's last intelligible words were: 'the Prince of Hell is loosed on the world and has been crowned!' He was said to have repeated this many times before finally collapsing into an unblinking stupor, an idiot's grin plastered to his face.

The poor man had, unsurprisingly, been hauled off by the police and diagnosed with simple mania and acute imbecility by medical authorities. The last I had heard of him, he'd been shipped north, to the West Riding Pauper Lunatic Asylum. He would never leave there. Nobody did.

I was walking, sunk deep in melancholic thoughts, thinking of the dead old man and the boys who talked of monsters behind the graves, of the 'Devil Ghoul,' and the gibbering madman who talked of 'devils' and animate corpses. The footprints. The green eyes. And I thought of blood, pooled in alleyways under the carved-up remains of lost women, running in drains. I thought of eyes shining in the dark. Green as balefire. My hand twitched. I ached for a drink. No, for something stronger. One could not survive for long in this city without chemical reinforcement.

It was morning yet and the sun was high overhead, blazing, but mercifully smothered in clotted grey clouds. Smoke billowed from nearby factories, coiled in the sky, then congealed and grew thick in the summer air.

I walked awhile. The street was sticky with green slime. All around me, warped houses, rotten from chimney to cellar, bent low into the earth, as if they were being sucked down into it. And in every alley and court, furtive shadows huddled close to one another–human vermin, trapped together, close yet detached. Warming their hands beside low fires. Gambling away their last belongings. Auctioning themselves off for a crust of bread. This, then, was what the zenith of human progress looked like–an unfulfilled promise.

Across the street, a woman with sunken, coal-rimmed eyes looked me over and snarled wolfishly. She said something, but it came out choked and wet and I couldn't understand it. When she saw I didn't comprehend her words, she cackled darkly, showing her teeth. What few she had were yellow and broken. Her skin was pale, shadowed by an old bonnet hung with pink ribbons, and in the poison-hued twilight, she looked less like one of the living and more like a walking corpse. I looked away—too quickly—betraying fear. She laughed.

The street made me jittery. I was conscious of my distance from this world. My clean clothes. My shining shoes. My vulnerability.

I walked until the sun began to sink below the horizon and the moon sluggishly ascended into the black clouds. I stopped at a pub—the Gutted Pig—got one drink and then a few more. I left, my head heavy. My hand still twitched. I yearned for laudanum. I'd been gulping it down nightly. I needed it to sleep now.

As I entered the streets once more, heavily-muscled dockland thugs and grime-caked factory drones staggered in, all bellowing like maddened bulls for beer and gin, ready to throw away every wretched cent they'd earned.

I walked until I reached Goulston Street. It was quiet there. Few, save those too destitute to find shelter for the night, were on the street, and even they huddled together closely under gas lamps. Some carried sticks or held bricks in their hands. One, an old woman without a leg, clutched a rotten plank studded with rusty nails to her breast. They didn't pay me any heed, but instead watched the dark spaces all around.

The street was black, slick and glistening in the moonlight, and lit only by the dim coronae cast by the gas lamps.

Bats fluttered above me. Like ragged gloves, black and oily, tossed to the sky. They carved sharp runes in the air with their sickle-sharp wings.

I approached the graveyard. It called to me. I yearned to escape the pervasive ugliness of the realm of the living. I yearned to enter a reality that was not my own. I pushed open the iron gate, felt rust flake off in my hands.

I entered the graveyard and felt my feet sink into the sodden ground. I walked slowly, listlessly, as if my body was not my own. As if it were ruled by another, mastered by an intelligence greater than my own.

The graveyard was the darkest place of all on the street. I was swallowed by that darkness.

I heard a voice, faint yet coming closer, summoning me. I saw nothing. It was as if I were lost in a dawn fog, probing the air with my fingers like a blind man.

"Inspector Marmont," the voice said. It was a man's voice. I heard it clear now.

The darkness began to lift. I squinted, unused to the light, held my hand above my eyes. I felt the drool collected at the corners of my mouth, crusted over my scratchy, emergent beard. I felt weak. I felt sick.

There was a tall man standing before me, middle-aged, in a doctor's long coat. His spectacles hung precariously from the edge of his beak-like nose. His hands were clasped behind his back. His skin was pale. His hair was oily and neatly parted and beneath his physician's coat I perceived he wore a claret-red vest and a charcoal frock. He was plainly a man of condition and breeding. A gentleman. The sort of man I could have been.

"Inspector Marmont, it is a pleasure to make your acquaintance," he said, his voice silky. He was not smiling, but wore a mask of cool detachment, as if it mattered nothing to him whether I woke or not, whether I lived or died. "The nurses and I have ministered to you for quite some time. I feel we have come to know you well."

"Where am I?" I stuttered. My mouth was dry and the words came out cottony and jumbled, as if I had not spoken in a very long time and I'd lost the skill, as if I'd degenerated—gone feral.

"You are in a ward of the London Hospital, Whitechapel Road, Inspector, and I am your physician, Dr. Wallace. I must say, Inspector, you rather alarmed your colleagues. Rather upset them with your nocturnal adventures. Your wanderings in strange locales. You will need to exercise more prudence in your future investigative endeavors."

I stared blankly, uncomprehending. I said nothing.

"Didn't mother ever tell you to stay away from dark places, Inspector?" Wallace asked. His disdain, his contempt for my weakness, dripped from every syllable.

"What are you talking about?" I asked, alarmed now, my head smarting. A strange tannic taste in my mouth. The taste of blood.

"Do you have any memory of how you came here, Inspector?" The doctor thought I'd gone mad,and he despised me for it.

"No," I replied, my voice weak, sputtering. I wiped the drool from my mouth, felt the beard that ringed my face. It was thick.

My hand began to spasm, as if possessed of its own will. Wallace noticed this and smiled knowingly. He shook his head.

"Perhaps that's for the best," Wallace said.

"What do you mean?" I asked. My temple throbbed. Colors, nimbuses of pale light and cool shadowy orbs danced before my eyes. And I heard screeching—like metal grinding on metal—ringing in my ears. And deranged lunatic laughter—the glee of the insane. And I saw the pink petals of dying flowers, scattering, twirling in night air. And the blackness of the abyss, the total void. Green eyes, piercing the dark. Hot liquid dripping down my chin. An extended forearm, bleached-bone white, scrawled with spidery blue veins. I felt myself slipping, my mind recoiling from some veiled and obscure understanding.

"Can you tell me how I got here, Doctor?" I asked, growing weaker, consciousness ebbing.

The man studied me a moment and said: "No, I don't think that would be a good idea, Inspector." He waited a moment before speaking again and allowed his eyebrow to cock sharply. "I will say only that memories have a funny way of returning when they are least expected. Perhaps, one day, you will remember. For now, let's content ourselves with the official explanation furnished by your colleagues. You suffered an acute nervous collapse, brought on by overwork and by an imagination much given to morbid fancies." He was smiling now, but it was a smile devoid of warmth or feeling, the smile of a boy carefully plucking the wings from a moth.

He turned away and I heard him go and then the blackness returned. I was glad it did. I was returned to the world of dreams.

I was dismissed from the Metropolitan Police Force. I found I had been discharged on the same day I exited the hospital. I was provided with no rationale for my dismissal, though the inspector who delivered the news to me suggested my "melancholic and poetical temperament was, perhaps, unsuited to the rigors of police work in the capital." I did not protest.

That day, swaddled like a newborn in thick blankets, I was taken north by my mother, to our family home in Rosedale Abbey, a village on the northern moors. A gloomy and secluded place. Silent at night. Drowned in a silvery gossamer-thin mist in the morning. The wind howls there and the stunted trees writhe like dancers in the moonlight.

I was glad to be away from London, far from the rank hypocrisy of what learned men call civilization. Far from the blood-sport of men and women—all conscripted participants—clambering over each other to survive, while the fruits of notional progress heap up around them, visible but ephemeral. Eternally out of reach.

My mother tended to me throughout the winter months, nursing me on dainty cakes, sugared candies, and rich cuts of lamb and beef. These things, which had delighted me when I was a boy, brought me no pleasure now. My mother's food tasted chalky and I swallowed it only with a great effort. I felt it slide and settle in the pit of my gut and roil there. I longed for something more. My hunger went unsated. I was ravenous. I told my mother none of this.

I was forbidden to read the papers—most especially anything about the sputtering Ripper investigation. I was, instead, restricted to a literary diet of "wholesome and good" books. It ought to have been a happy time. Though my body grew flabby under my mother's ministrations, and my mind fell into a kind of drowsy torpor, the laudanum at least lost its taloned hold on me. Despite this, I did not feel as if I was growing stronger. I felt as if my strength was leeching away.

My mother was a kindhearted sort of woman and she thought it would benefit me to be among society. To this end, she organized a garden party at our home, extending invitations to all the finest families in the village. She orchestrated the gathering with the same will and vision as a general marshalling his troops for an attack, turning our weedy, overgrown lawn into a turf of velvet softness; pruning the knotted old oaks so they would form a domed corridor and shade our guests from the summer sun; planting arcades of blossoming rose vines, red as blood, with barbs that pricked the skin; and filling our gardens with blossoming pink flowers.

The party was charming. The guests were decorous and did not inquire about my misadventures in the capital, though I sensed that the preponderance of them were unsurprised that my experiment with employment had gone awry. The air was warm and heavy. Bees flitted among the flowers and people laughed. The birds sang fluted songs in the trees.

It was just as Dr. Wallace said; the memories returned when they were least expected.

I remember biting into a scone filled with ripe raspberries, not wanting to but doing so out of obligation. Forcing the chalky dough down. I felt the liquid from the fruits burst on my lips and stain and drip down my chin. I remember feeling sick then, and close to a secret. I sat in the grass, closed my eyes and hoped the feeling would drain away—and then I felt the dew in my fingers, the wetness. I lay on my back. I dug into the earth with my fingers—so cool—felt worms meet me. Felt tangled roots twine around my fingers. I became lightheaded, began to drift, to forget myself. I remembered Dr. Wallace— his cruel smile, widening and widening, extending from ear to ear—becoming a Cheshire cat grin. A madman's wild maw. Filled with rotten teeth.

Green eyes filled my vision.

And a mouth, brimming with teeth. Penetrating meat. Cutting skin and bone.

My mouth.

I opened my eyes and looked around me. I watched happy people biting into cakes and bits of dripping meat, blood glistening on their lips. I saw them sip wine. I heard them chew and swallow, their faces warping, becoming subtly wrong. The sun was high. I vomited in the grass. Green flies clustered around me, sensing sickness.

And then I saw the flowers under the oaks, their pink petals pressed into the moist ground. A little girl in a white dress tiptoed through the fallen flowers, smashing them into the earth. She was singing to herself. I remembered dark earth, cakey and wet. A wizened hand in the dirt. A green ring, shining like a beetle. An empty grave.

Blackness took me then. It was not like the blackness from which I'd emerged in the hospital. Rather than effacing my consciousness, leaving me a slumbering hulk and nothing more, this time I was forced into myself, into locked inner chambers where secrets festered, where they'd grown cankerous and strong. I wished to go there. To remember.

That day, lying in the grass, I became a spectator to my memories. I was outside myself, watching. Time slid beyond me.

I was in the old graveyard on Goulston Street. Crossing the cobbled path, my feet stamping in oily pools that reflected the carnivorous moon, the factory spires, and the black clouds. There was an icy wind in the air, gliding across space.

I pushed open the gate to the graveyard, winced at the scream of the old metal, and peered into the thickening, fluid darkness. The gas lamps had no purchase here. Black tendrils of shadow shifted and squirmed among the headstones. The moon was rising swiftly.

I walked in a landscape of weathered granite and dead flowers. There were open graves all around me, all empty. The moon, high now, conjured strange shapes in the darkness. Its twisted obelisks and statues into warped parodies of themselves. They seemed to move; to creep along beside me like black dogs of myth, driving me into the heart of the necropolis.

There were glittering eyes in the deep parts of the graveyard. And gamboling shadows imbued with life, blacker than the surrounding gloom. They were both near and far, form and void. Their eyes shone like icy stars. I heard voices, carried by the gathering mist, filled with joy and madness.

I walked among the shadows. They carried me to the heart of the graveyard.

I came to a circular tomb with high columns that was crusted with a skin of grey mold, its door smashed open, revealing nothing inside itself. Acidic air oozed from the entrance of the tomb. No grass grew near that place. It had all been strangled.

There was a girl, gaunt and squatting before the tomb. She had her back to me, and she was naked. She was small, half-starved. A runt. There were many such unfortunates in this city. I could not tell precisely how old she was, though I knew she was young. Her pale skin shone blue in the moonlight, marred by unhealed pink scars. It was drawn tightly around her ribs and spine. Her vertebrae—honed like sharpened spines—threatened to punch through her skin, and wiry purple veins rippled along her thin arms. She clutched something in her blackened hands.

I approached her. "What are you doing here?" I asked, trying to be gentle. I did not want to frighten her. She did not respond.

"Come with me. Let's get you home. It isn't safe here."

The girl turned, slowly, sniffing the air like a dog, snarling. Her face was wasted, skeletal, and her milky white eyes—sunk deep in the hollows of her skull—shone in the darkness like lanterns. They fidgeted, rolled wildly. She was clutching an infant in her hands; its white dress was caked with grave-soil and its skin was blackened with rot. Curdled treacle-thick blood oozed from its ravaged neck.

I faltered in my approach, gasped, and felt bile well in my throat.

The girl's nails were long. Viscid poison dripped from her every finger, hung suspended in the air, an expression of wordless threat.

The girl gazed at me and grinned wide—and growled—and revealed her blackened, oily teeth. Gelled blood coated her thin lips. She yelped and wailed, tossed the infant away and leapt into the tomb. I could tell from my brief glance at her swift body that she was immensely pregnant.

Skittering shadows gathered around me, chittered like rats. Pale shapes darted from the tomb's mouth and scattered around the graveyard. They crouched behind graves and tombs, lunged in the voids between, remained hidden beyond my sight. I heard laughter. A feral tongue. Then bones cracking and raw meat—wet still—tearing. The shadows slunk closer—ever closer. A tightening snare. I looked more closely around the graveyard. And I saw the bodies. They lay like dolls, but broken—as if they had been discarded by wanton children. They were strewn and opened over the grass, their limbs kinked at impossible angles, their heads missing, their blood seeping into the earth. The white shapes stooped above them, gaining form, becoming real. Men and women and children. Their skin fish-belly white. Their bile-yellow eyes shining and mad. Their teeth sharp. Their grins wide. All circling me like wolves bent on an ox, like practiced predators.

I now regretted my facile dismissal of the tale told by the orphans.

They licked their blackened lips. They hungered for me.

The earth churned beneath me, as if the splintered bones of the dead were burrowing from the grave pall, searching, as if their unseeing eyes would gaze on the world once more.

The tomb shook, exhaled green-grey dust.

I heard it first. The thing. Its howls were met by a chorus of delirious cries. The tomb buckled—stones cracked and fell—and columns shook. The earth trembled as if it were recoiling, disgusted by a foulness passing through it. I could not look away.

Before I saw the body of the thing, I saw its green eyes, dark yet burning with inner fire, like a pair of dying coals.

The thing staggered out of the darkness of the

tomb, slithered in the dirt like a snake, and then crawled on clawed toes, then flapped leathern transparent wings in the air—as if uncertain of its body. It was an abhorrence of conventional form. A being born of rogue biology, caught in the shadowy web between life and death. A thing that should never have been and yet was--and would always be. I gazed upon the thing and and knew it was the first man, molded from the primordial clay, ancient beyond reckoning and nursed on corpse-meat and the blood of the living. It was an eternal parasite, persisting by feeding on those who had once been its kin. It had conquered death.

Its skin was puckered like overripe fruit, the sallow hue of grubs and worms and newly-buried corpses. The stench of butcher shops and cadavers and stale blood suffused the night air. The thing was mighty, though. It roared like a caged lion and its jaws gnashed and frothed. Upright now, mastering itself, the thing's muscles swelled and rippled. Its face, falsely human, shriveled and old, trembled, and I gazed into the abyss of its biting maw, thick with needle-teeth. A diadem of finger bones, threaded with strands of white-gold hair and studded with teeth, crowned its skull.

The thing had been a man once, long ago. This I perceived. Like you and I. Imperfect. But it had changed, exceeded the boundaries of God's creation. The pale ghouls bowed low before it, in supplication—loving worship. It was father to them all.

I could not look away from the eyes of the thing! I

see them yet! I yearn to gaze upon them again. They burned with the chaos that preceded creation. Those beguiling lodestones penetrated me, searched out my innermost secrets, and broke open the shuttered chambers of my heart. I fell on my knees, knelt like a boy in prayer, and acknowledged a new patriarch. I became a toy. A puppet. Those eyes! They were set deep within his gargoyle face, an alabaster mask. Beautiful. Perfect. And alive, yes—rich with eldritch vigor—but old beyond all reckoning. Those eyes had looked out on the world when it was new. "Join us," those eyes pleaded. "Dwell with us, free in the ever-dark."

As I gazed in wonder at the court of ghouls, they huddled close to him, their father. He had transformed them, transfigured them with his carnivore essence. And they were his progeny, his warped brood and his wards. Their eyes were thirsting, avid, and filled with limitless love. As one, the members of that wretched and adoring throng fastened themselves to his bulging arms, jostled one another to drink deep from the open veins in his wrists—veins that wept like the stigmata. They gulped down his tomb-blood like it was sweet wine, and he gave it to them—a kind and loving prince. Their moon-mad, drunken eyes fluttered as they suckled. They were his children. And he was their father, their mother, their god and their king.

Here, at least, was a society that had evaded the sins of man, the vices of greed and pride and vanity. Here, in this stagnant patrimony, in this absolutist realm of the corpse-prince, had the most destructive impulses of our tormented species been conquered. Here, at last, was freedom.

"Join us," the being of the green eyes seemed to say. "Escape." He offered me his arm. Blood dripped from it into the wet grass.

I stood. And I approached, beguiled.

I hungered for his blood. I hungered for his promised gift. For escape.

That is, at least, what the doctors tell me when they come and visit. So be it. They are kind men, decent enough, though they are mistaken in their diagnosis. I am far from mad. I am caged.

I have been in my cell now for nearly a year, shackled to a wall like a brute beast. The doctors have explained to me on many occasions that I am 'prone to episodes of violent mania' and cannot be permitted even to leave my cell under armed guard. They are coy about my reasons for coming here, although a loquacious orderly once informed me--as he nervously fed me soupy porridge and worm-filled bread--that I was taken here from my mother's home after some sort of 'accident.' Evidently, after I stopped screaming and let go of the little girl at a garden party (I am told she is recovering nicely), I was brought to this place. My informant told me that I hissed like a snake and roared like an animal, that I seemed inhuman and monstrous.

He is half right.

I am told I will remain here for the rest of my days. My future thus consists of the following: a gloomy stone room, windowless, its heavy door studded with rusty iron bars and latched tight, and a hay strewn floor, concealing nested rats and spiders as big as shillings. This is what I get for disrupting mother's garden party.

I tried to break out of here once, but succeeded only in fracturing a wrist and cutting myself. The whole episode was most embarrassing, and I apologized to the doctors many times for my rudeness, though I must confess that I enjoyed all the blood very much. There was a lot of blood. It was warm, so very warm.

They say I will never leave. That I am a menace to the good and the innocent. Fair enough, though I cannot bear the thought of a life spent ingesting the gluey gruel they shove under my door. It turns in my stomach. I cannot eat it. I must have meat. I must have blood. I've told the doctors about this problem in the most diplomatic manner, and they have promised to rectify it in the future. They had best make good on their promise, else I may need to take more dramatic measures, for I have become very hungry in my cell.

I dwell now in a realm of endless half-sleep, awake, in a way, but removed from the world, aware of my dreams passing before me, my consciousness trapped—roaming—the wild space between sane and insane. I dream of my days spent in the kingdom of the dead, when I was free, a courtier of a generous lord. I dream of steaming blood, fed to me in bowls fashioned from human skulls, of banquets held beneath the flickering stars. I dream of another world.

I am unaware of my old self now, the man called Inspector Marmont. I am outside of memory; my edges are liquid, indistinct as autumn leaves, brittle and becoming earth. I am like the dead now, yet, unlike them, I wake and I want. I am forever liminal, a greedy and slavering child—unsatisfied. And the hunger remains—a gift of the patriarch; it waxes strong in me now. It will not be contained.

GRASP

JONAH BUCK

HENRI BLUM PUSHED THE SOLDIER'S PAYMENT across the table. Five brass rods for every hand he delivered. The *Force Publique* officer was maybe fourteen years old, and he gave Henri a big grin as he accepted his payment. This was probably the first time he'd ever been paid for anything. The brass rods weren't as good as genuine Belgian francs, but the boy would still be able to use them to go get stinking drunk in some dark corner of Leopoldville.

"Is that everyone?" Henri asked. He tapped the table with the butt of his walking stick, but no one else appeared to offer him more hands.

Lt. Rene Sax nodded. European officers were always in charge of the *Force Publique* conscripts. *Conscripts* was probably too gentle a word. The boy Henri had just paid had almost certainly been kidnapped from his home village somewhere deeper in the Congo basin, brutalized by the soldiers who took him away, and then given the option to either join or die.

The Gauss rifle Sax had in his hands made a constant humming sound that blended with the buzz of jungle insects and cawing birds. The big coil gun was heavy enough that Sax used a porter to carry it when his men were on the march. Of course, Sax's troops weren't issued with electro-magnet-powered weapons. They had to rely on old castoff black powder rifles the Belgian military had otherwise mothballed.

"Twenty hands. Not bad for a week's effort," Sax said.

"I've seen better," Henri said before handing over a pay envelope stuffed with francs. Sax's predecessor, who had been struck down by malaria and died in a delirium of fever and sweat a few months ago, had once turned in almost one hundred and seventy hands in a single week. No one said the process of civilizing this land would be easy or bloodless.

Henri took the bloody sack, being careful not to allow anything to dribble onto his shirt, and walked a short distance from the pay table. A large, metal bin stood far enough away that the smell didn't waft over to his station. Henri wrinkled his nose in anticipation of what was about to happen next.

He grabbed the bin's handle and held his breath. Moving as fast as he could, he whipped the lid off and tossed the sack of severed hands inside. He was too slow, though. A black cloud of flies buzzed out as if he'd summoned an evil djinn. The flies swarmed for a second before dispersing into the evening sky. Henri swatted them away from his face and took a few steps away before he dared suck in another breath. Henri knew from experience that a whiff of the hand bin from up close could be nearly overpowering. At least from a little further away, the odor wasn't so very different from the butcher's district on a hot day in Brussels.

The business with the hands was gruesome, but at least it was effective. Belgium's, or more accurately King Leopold's, colony of the Congo Free State consisted of an area almost the size of the entire Indian subcontinent right in the heart of Africa. Strictly speaking, the entire colony belonged to King Leopold. Leopold had to rely on a small number of military veterans to marshal the African "recruits" responsible for keeping some semblance of order. There were only a few thousand European colonists trying to keep grips on millions of Africans. The outflow of rubber and ivory made the effort profitable, though.

Even with a cadre of European officers, the *Force Publique* was barely a cohesive policing force. Left to their own devices, its soldiers tended to use their weapons to hunt game and supplement their meager rations or resort to outright banditry. Bullets were too expensive to be wasted like that.

Henri had helped develop the new policy to ensure that things went more smoothly. The soldiers were each given a set number of rounds, and they had to account for them at the end of each pay period. The best way to ensure that the bullets had been used to kill criminals or would-be rebels was to provide proof. Hands had become the most common way to demonstrate that the soldiers had shot someone. A soldier who couldn't properly account for his ammunition after an outing would get the *chicote*, a whip made from toughened hippo hide.

Of course, sometimes the soldiers would still shoot at game and then simply find a worker who hadn't met his rubber collection quota and take his hands. It was all the same to Henri, in the end. He was here to make sure the Congo Free State remained a profitable enterprise. If the *Force Publique* encouraged the local populace to turn in as much raw rubber and ivory as they could, that was all the better, actually. Hostages and the occasional razed village helped spread the message and encouraged work ethic, but nothing put the spring back into a man's step quite like seeing a handless neighbor or family member every day.

The biggest problem with the system was that Henri had to account for the hands, which meant he had to dispose of them himself. It was an unpleasant, smelly job, and sometimes he had nightmares that the odor would somehow cling to his clothes and refuse to come out. It was dreadfully expensive to import new attire down here.

He walked back to his pay table and packed everything up. When he was done, Henri stretched for a moment and took a deep breath of the warm, steamy air. There was barely even the hint of rancid decay.

Henri loved Leopoldville. Here in the European district, it was as if someone had lifted a few square blocks of Brussels and transported them to the edge of the Congo River. Despite the imported architecture and amenities, the place was nothing like staid, ponderous Europe. Even the air was different. The more equatorial climate thrummed with life and energy, and that vigor and dynamism found its way into the bones.

Men who would have been milquetoast administrators or dainty, second-rate cavalry officers came here and learned the meaning of getting things done. Nothing was done by halves here. Nothing.

In an hour, they would ignite the gas lights, and this area would become an island of light amid a sea of darkness. After dusk, the air would fill with insects of every size and appetite. Infection and disease meant a significant portion of the white administrative class died during any given year. Insect bites and tainted water were much more dangerous than any of the creatures huddled in the jungle.

"Care to join me as I walk back to the main plaza, Lieutenant?" Henri asked.

"But of course," Sax said.

Henri was about to set off toward his quarters when something rattled nearby. He looked around, thinking maybe a couple of Sax's soldiers had dropped their equipment, but he didn't see anything.

Then he noticed the bin. The lid was ever so slightly ajar. Henri stared at it for a moment. He was the one who had set the lid back down. Normally, he would be loath to leave it open, allowing more of that putrid stink to waft out into the open air. He must not have secured it quite properly in his haste to scurry away this time, though. Perhaps a rat had just pushed the lid aside and slipped inside the bin.

He looked around, hoping to spot a couple of Sax's soldiers. If they were nearby, he'd order them to drag the bin down to the river and empty it out. There was no one else to be seen, though.

No matter. Let the rats feast. He was done here for the day, and the breeze would carry the odor toward the African quarter anyway. It wasn't his problem.

A faint mist was starting to seep off the river and out of the jungle, and the warbling cry of the night insects was growing louder. Soon, the steamy night would be alive with bats and the shrieks of night predators. Henri grabbed his walking stick and soon forgot about the bin of discarded hands.

Night fell quickly over Leopoldville. Lights started to flicker on inside the buildings in the European sector. Aside from a few torches, the African quarter remained dark, its mud streets and shanty buildings fading into vague shapes in the moonlight.

Henri's walking stick tapped along the cobblestones as he walked toward the center of the administrative sector. People moved about on the streets, finishing their evening business. Clerks walked back to their quarters after tallying the day's haul of rubber and ivory. Steam boat captains meandered toward the seedy, makeshift bars set up near the river's edge. Big game hunters finished their arrangements to rent more porters for their next expeditions. There was even a small contingent of businessmen from some research company looking to lease land. It was all very lively, a blooming flower of trade and business in the jungle.

An autobuggy, one of only five such vehicles in the whole territory, trundled down the street. Its headlights snapped on as it hissed past, leaving behind an almost invisible trail of steam that quickly faded into the mist. That was the colonial governor's vehicle. It had arrived here before the latest railhead went through, which meant that it had to be disassembled, the pieces carried through the hill country by laborers, and then reassembled in Leopoldville itself. Henri had arranged the transportation himself, ensuring that the autobuggy was brought inland posthaste. Two porters had died of exhaustion, but Henri had foreseen that possibility and ensured there were enough extra hands to continue to carry all the parts.

Henri felt a certain pride watching the people conclude their business and slip away for the night. He helped keep the whole thing running. The entire system of unpaid labor would fall apart without him and the *Force Publique* to enforce the system of business.

Lt. Sax was in a cheery mood as well. "Say, it's been a rather successful month for my soldiers. We finally managed to capture a particularly nettlesome local chief who'd been agitating against us. About half the hands you took today came from him and his entourage of followers. Would you care to join me for a drink in celebration before we go our separate ways for the evening?"

Henri thought on it for a moment. He generally tried to return to his quarters as soon as dusk fell before the mosquitoes came out in force. A quick drink did sound nice tonight, though.

"Of course. I'd be happy to join you. It'll give me a chance to pick your brain about how some of the other pacification operations are going as well." Henri followed Sax as they made a short detour to the edge of the European district. The trip didn't take long. Even at its busiest, there were never more than a thousand or so white men in Leopoldville at a time. There was just the bare minimum required to run the administration and keep the flow of goods moving. It was only a few short blocks before they were on the edge of the section.

A small bar had been built at the juncture where the European section of town started to give way to the small manufacturing quarter. Steam spooled out of the vents of the manufactories as the night crews continued to work inside. Leopoldville imported most of what it needed, but it was useful to locally produce some of the battery packs that powered things like Sax's coil gun.

Henri had provided a grant for one of the local engineers to requisition a labor force to build something quite interesting, too. The man believed he could use an old steam boat boiler to power a sort of mechanical golem that could be used for security purposes. He wanted to attach a naval railgun to it and allow it to patrol Leopoldville's perimeter on its oversized legs. Henri wasn't sure the project would actually work, but he was undeniably intrigued by the thought of building a fleet of the mechanical giants, as tall as some of the jungle trees, to hunt down rebels.

Little Belgium's steam workshops were second to none, though. Even Britain and Germany were starting to convert their collieries and oil plants into steam systems and ferromagnetic engines. The massive infusions of raw material and cash the Congo brought in helped finance the new research and development and made Belgium into a very prosperous little country.

Of course, most of the people back in Brussels kept their eyes closed and their ears shut when it came to the efforts needed to fund these new advances. Henri was perfectly fine with that. He hadn't come here to win glory and accolades like a lot of the young officers leading the *Force Publique*. He was here because it was the only place on earth that afforded him the sort of opportunities he enjoyed out here. A man could become a hermit and go live in some cave somewhere to meditate on human nature his whole life, and he'd never truly know himself the way Henri did. The absolute free-for-all out here had a way of stripping away the unnecessary parts of one's self. Things like pity and shame fell away after a while, until it was obvious to men such as himself that they were simply social affectations for the belabored masses.

Fools. The lot of them.

He opened the bar's door for Sax, and the military man stepped inside with a quick nod of thanks. Henri was about to enter himself when he caught a glimpse of something out of the corner of his eye, no more than a flash of movement down the side alley. Twisting his head to see what had just moved, Henri caught a brief image of something scuttling out of sight.

Perhaps a large jungle spider or maybe even a rat. He hadn't gotten a good enough look to be sure, not that it really mattered. It was just some creature that had traded in the harsh life of scrounging through the underbrush for grubs and morsels for the easy option of scrounging through the garbage for tasty scraps.

Henri paid it no more mind and stepped inside the bar. He and Lt. Sax ordered a bottle of cheap but inoffensive wine and talked about the rigors of taming the land for first an hour. Then two. Then three. Henri barely noticed the other patrons slipping in and out around them and he and Sax discussed the merits of taking hostages versus razing a village in order to secure a tribe's cooperation with the colonial business system.

Finally, Henri checked his pocket watch and realized the evening was slipping away. Sax offered to buy another drink, but Henri begged off. He would need to help supervise labor procurement for a new railroad spur through the mountains tomorrow, and there was talk of upgrading the main line to a maglev system like the one connecting Brussels to Ypres. There was a great deal of work awaiting him, and he would need an early crack at it.

He wished Lt. Sax a good night and stepped out of the little bar. Taking a brief glance around, Henri started off in the direction of his quarters. The usually warm, steamy night air had taken on an unusual chill, and he adjusted his coat about him. A thin mist covered the ground, enveloping his boots and swirling over the cobblestones. The nearby lights of the European sector called to Henri though, and he picked his way toward them.

His walking stick tapped against the ground as he moved, creating a steady rhythm. Henri could hear snippets of conversation or music warbling from gramophones as he walked down the street. The boulevard was empty by now, everyone else having retired for the evening. His quarters were on the edge of the administrative zone anyway, which would be abandoned until the morning. It was a perfectly peaceful, pleasant evening.

A piece of glass shattered somewhere ahead, tinkling into the night. Henri stopped, the steady tap-tap-tap of his walking stick coming to an abrupt halt. What was that? Some sort of accident? Petty vandals from the African quarter? Some sort of jungle creature?

Henri took his next few steps with more caution. He was nearly to his quarters now. Up ahead, he couldn't hear any shouting or commotion, which seemed to rule out the notion of an accident or misbehaving conscripts. It would be unusual but not unheard of for a large jungle beast to wander this far into the town, but that would be a dangerous possibility. He reached into his pocket and pulled out a tiny pneumatic revolver. The gun didn't have a lot of stopping power, but it was sometimes a useful persuader.

Keeping a tight grip on the little gun, Henri started forward again. This time he kept his walking stick from tapping the ground, holding it up a little so he could swing it like a cudgel, if he had to.

He rounded the corner and caught sight of his quarters. The little apartment wouldn't have been anything special by the standards of the grand avenues in Antwerp or the capital, but the brickwork structure was perfectly adequate for his needs. Normally, there was a street light blazing into the night in front of his quarters, but tonight it had gone out. The lights to either side along the row were still functioning, which meant that his building was cast into a gloomy shade.

That must have been the source of the shattering glass he'd heard earlier. Something had busted out the lamp. Perhaps a particularly large bat had accidentally smashed into it, or maybe some fool had tossed a rock at it. Either way, Henri didn't see any immediate sign of danger. He tucked his pocket gun away and started through the shadows toward his home.

Something touched his foot in the mist. He leapt up in the air in surprise as it scurried over his shoe. Henri caught a brief glimpse of it as it disappeared into the darkness. It was a rat. A big one. He cursed under his breath at the jolt it had given him. The damnable creatures were growing bold, feeding off Leopoldville's detritus and the occasional dead bodies the *Force Publique* left in its wake.

The little creature tore down the street as fast as its little legs could carry it. Apparently, it didn't view Henri as much more than an obstacle in its way.

Henri looked down the street in the direction the rat had come. The remaining streetlights sent diffuse beams through the light fog, obscuring everything and turning the other buildings into nothing more than hazy outlines. In a few places low to the ground, the mist swirled and billowed in an agitated manner.

Maybe there were more rats out there in the gutter, carousing in the darkness. Henri was rarely out at such an hour. The thought that the outside world beyond his quarters might be enveloped in scrambling squirming rodent bodies was an unpleasant one.

He hastened toward his front door. His feet briefly crunched down on some of the broken glass from the street lamp, and he kicked it away. Unlocking the door, he stepped inside and shut it behind him.

Taking a deep breath, Henri rubbed his cheeks. The pleasant warmth of the alcohol he's shared with Sax was gone. The incident outside had burned it up like a bubble of swamp gas igniting. Now, all that was left was a sour taste in his mouth and a faint queasiness.

Looking around his dark hallway, he stripped off his jacket and headed for the bedroom. He'd experienced quite enough excitement for one night. It was time to retire for the evening. He knew his quarters well enough that it wasn't particularly difficult to maneuver around in the dark. Changing into his nightshirt, Henri peeled back the mosquito netting surrounding his bed and pulled the cover around himself in a warm nest.

He was nearly asleep when he heard the scuttling noise on the wooden floor. His eyes snapped open. Had one of those blasted rats slipped inside his quarters after him?

Henri reached out through the gauze of mosquito netting, fumbled around a bit for his lantern, and finally managed to spill some light into the room. The thing on his floor was no rat. It was a human hand.

It sat in the middle of his floor. Its dark skin was just starting to decay. The hand lay palm-down on the ground, the fingers slightly arched like the legs of a big, restive spider. After the heel of the palm, the hand ended in a ragged stump.

It was one of the hands the soldiers had collected. Someone had dug it out of the bin and dropped it onto his floor. Henri felt gooseflesh breakout all over his body, as if his skin had suddenly just cinched itself a size smaller.

Had it been here since he arrived back at his quarters? He hadn't turned the lights on when he arrived; the hand could have been here the whole time. But who would sneak into his home and leave such a thing? Were the soldiers playing some sort of petty prank on him? Was an African laborer trying to exact some act of trivial revenge?

Someone had been in his home, right in his bedroom, and they'd left this little macabre souvenir behind. But where was the culprit now? Would they come back?

A thought suddenly occurred to Henri. Despite the unusually chilly night, sweat started to pop up on his forehead. What if the perpetrator never left? What if they were still in the building somewhere, waiting for him?

He knew he couldn't just stay in bed and cower all night. He had to get rid of the hand and call in some of the night watch to scour his quarters. Henri's limbs felt suddenly leaden, though. Ancient animal instincts wanted him to hunker down under the blankets where he'd be hard to see rather than step out into the middle of the room, away from cover.

Ignoring the alarm bells going off in his head, Henri swung his feet off the side of the bed and dropped them down onto the cold floor. He stood up as quietly as he could and took a couple of little half-steps toward the severed hand. The soles of his feet padded against the ground.

A quick plan of action formed in Henri's mind. He'd creep out of his room and fetch his pocket gun before getting dressed in whatever spare things he could throw on. Then, he'd make his way outside and find the nearest guard and report this incident. If there *was* someone in his quarters, he'd bring a whole patrol of *Force Publique* soldiers down on them. Whoever was responsible, he'd have their head, and possibly their hands too, in due course.

Perfect. Now he just needed to get moving. Any vestiges of sleep had evaporated from his mind now that he had a course of action laid out for himself.

He heard another odd scuttling sound, this time from directly behind him. Henri spun around just a hundreds of human hands came boiling out from under his bed like bats shooting out of a cave. They pulled themselves across the floor by their fingers, moving like grotesque, broken insects. Some of them were little more than bones, creaking sinew, and leathery flesh. Others hadn't even begun to rot yet.

They'd been waiting for Henri, waiting for him to step away from his bed and into the middle of the room. Bone and fingernails scraped across the floor as the hands massed and came after him.

Henri leapt backward, crashing into the furniture behind him. He yelped and toppled onto the floor. The hands were on him in an instant, swarming over him like ants trying to overtake a beetle. Fingers danced over his skin, pinching and clawing and grabbing. They came for his face, latching onto his ears and probing into his mouth as he let out a scream. He could taste grime and rot where they tugged at his lips.

One of them poked him in the eye, and Henri roared in pain. He lurched up to his feet, swatting at himself. Hands tumbled off his nightclothes, but many more continued to swarm around his feet, trying to clamber up his legs or cling onto his robe. More hands were climbing the furniture or the mosquito netting on his bed and launching themselves at him, trying to land on him to continue their assault. Henri stamped his feet, snapping delicate finger bones and kicking some of the hateful things away.

That gave him just enough space to fight his way out of the center of the swarm. He lurched out through the bedroom doorway and into the hall, but there were more hands pouring in from the living room. They'd filled up his home, setting up an ambush for him.

One of them was on top of his head, anchoring itself in his hair. It swiveled down and started jabbing at his eyes. Henri grabbed it, feeling the ungodly thing squirming in his grip, and wrenched it away. He threw it as hard as he could against the wall before shaking off several more hands still clutching his clothing.

This couldn't be happening. This was some foul nightmare dredged up by the alcohol he'd enjoyed with Lieutenant Sax. It couldn't be real.

But it was. Henri could feel warm blood matting his nightclothes to his body from a dozen little cuts and punctures where the hands had latched onto him. He could still sense their rancid taste on his tongue. And the awful skittering noise they made as they marched *en masse* over the floorboards...Henri knew that he was not a creative enough man for his imagination to conjure such a terrible sound of its own accord.

The hands were coming after him again, regrouping into a frolicking, incoherent mass. The column coming down the hallway was maneuvering itself to cut him off while the hands from the bedroom came straight toward him. They moved over the floor like a wave of water from a burst dam, sweeping relentlessly forward in a shapeless, destructive swell.

Henri abandoned the idea of fetching his pocket gun. Maybe its bullets could sever some digits or cripple a few of his assailants, but his limited reserves of ammunition would barely make a dent before the tiny army was upon him again.

No, he had to flee and get help. That was his only option. Otherwise, the hands would trap him like Lilliputians ensnaring a giant. They would bring him down and pinion him, and then they would do unspeakable things to him.

His walking stick lay propped against the nearby armoire. Henri snatched it up and made a break for the front door. Sweeping the heavy wooden walking stick in front of him, Henri did his best to clear a path for himself as he ran. Even with his best efforts, leathery fingers still groped at his ankles as he moved, and he had to kick as he ran to prevent them from grabbing on. It was like dashing across a beach suddenly overrun with furious crabs.

Reaching his front door, Henri flung it open and slammed it shut behind himself. He dashed into the foggy street and feet cold cobblestones beneath his bare feet. There were still a couple of the severed hands grasping his sleeves and the back of his shirt. Henri ripped them off. They wriggled in his grip before he hurled them away into the night.

Henri's breath came in ragged, erratic bursts. He clenched his jaw tight and grimaced at the pain where rotting fingers had clawed at his skin and dug red furrows into his body. The devilish things had managed to scrape away more flesh than he'd realized. His legs below the knees looked like a spoiled cat's favorite scratching post, the skin raw and weeping. He could also feel a deep slash on his cheek pulsing with red fury in the night air.

It didn't take any great stretch for Henri to figure out where the hands had come from. The soldiers had been collecting them all month. Hundreds of them.

What the hands wanted was equally obvious. Revenge. Somehow, they'd formed a pact of fury and unholy retribution that transcended every law of nature, and now they were coming for Henri. Whatever cabal or ritual had animated the mass of hands, it would only be satisfied with blood. Henri's blood.

He looked around. Inside the nearby buildings, almost all the lights had been extinguished. Aside from the jungle sounds and the whistle of steam engines from the industrial quarter, the night was quiet.

"Help," Henri cried. "Help!" The cool night seemed to muffle his words, the mist strangling the sounds the same way the twisting jungle vines would loop around a tree and smother the life from it. No lights flickered to life at his cries. Most everyone in this section of the town was already asleep. The horror inside his quarters was his problem alone for the moment.

Suddenly, Henri heard a noise. It was a stealthy, creeping sound. Henri sucked in his breath, feeling his heart judder in his chest, as he strained his ears. Had someone heard his cry and come sidling through the shadows to see what was wrong? In the darkness where the street light was broken out, it was difficult to see.

He glanced around but didn't see anyone. Then, he noticed the ground fog seeping off the Congo. In most places, it was little more than a still blanket across the cobblestones. But coming around from the side of his building, it was positively seething. There was something coming toward him through the mist, something boiling across the ground under the cover of the night's gloom, and Henri knew exactly what it was.

Something touched his bare left foot and then clamped down on the already bloodied flesh. Henri shrieked and kicked it away. The hands had forced their way out of his quarters, and now they were coming for him again. He took off running down the empty boulevard.

Moving blindly through the night, Henri pushed through the low mist. He needed to get to Leopoldville's armory. There would be some officers on duty with their coil guns. Henri wasn't sure that a few Gauss Rifles would be enough to stop the vile things behind him, but there would be a cache of black powder too, for the conscripts' obsolete guns. Maybe they could use that to burn the hands or blow them up or *something*.

Henri moved as fast as he could. A dull throb of pain hit him with every stride forward as he jostled his wounds, and he could feel more blood dribbling down his side. The scurrying noises behind him were more than enough to keep him moving forward, though.

He could hear his heartbeat thundering in his ears, and his chest felt far too tight, but Henri kept moving. He shouted a few more times hoping to rouse help. A few lights appeared in buildings behind him, but never close enough for him to double back and try to seek some shelter. The lights were always back near where the mist started to shimmer with unseen movement below.

Wheeling back around, Henri realized he'd turned onto Leopoldville's main thoroughfare. He'd cut down a street too early. This would take him to the shuttered markets and river docks, not the *Force Publique* barracks. He needed to get to the armory.

A stitch burned in his side as he ran. Try as he might, Henri couldn't seem to force enough air into his lungs. His feet ached where they'd pounded across the cold cobblestones. Behind him, the sound of scrabbling fingers grew louder.

The river! Perhaps if he could just make it to the river, he would make it through this. Surely, the ghoulish hands couldn't swim. If he could just make it onto a boat and cast off until dawn, he had a chance to make it through this. The noises behind him told Henri that he no longer had the time to reach the armory. His only chance was to climb aboard one of the steam barges located at the docks.

Henri dashed down the street, passing the very spot where he'd awarded bonus pay to the soldiers for bringing him more hands. That very afternoon, he'd been the master of this land, carving it out as he saw fit. Now, he was just another hunted thing at the edge of the jungle.

Suddenly, something grabbed onto his heel from behind. Henri leapt up in the air, twisting and kicking in an attempt to shake the hateful thing loose, but he came down on a loose stone in the pathway. His foot folded under him with a loud cracking noise, and his ankle bent like a wet noodle. Henri collapsed under his own weight with a yelp, crashing down onto his chest.

He lay sprawled within sight of the can he used to dispose of the collected hands. He could see it now, flipped over onto its side, the lid lying nearby.

And then the hands were upon him. Henri had time for one final scream before the fingers found his throat and began to squeeze.

Enjoyed what you read? Don't forget to leave a review!

Visit us at:

deadsteam.wordpress.com

grimmerandgrimmer.wordpress.com

ACKNOWLEDGEMENTS

Bryce Raffle would like to thank William J Jackson and David Carlisle for their help with editing, proofreading, and selecting the stories for the anthology. He would also like to thank the members of the Scribblers' Den for their support in this endeavour. Further thanks goes to Derek Tatum and Leanna Renee Hieber for helping to get the word dreadpunk out into the world, in particular, to Derek "The Dreadpope" Tatum, whose correspondence regarding "dreadpunk" was particularly insightful; and to Leanna Renee Hieber, who went above and beyond by offering to write the foreword to DEADSTEAM. I cannot thank her enough for that.

ABOUT THE AUTHORS

LEANNA RENEE HIEBER
FOREWORD

Leanna Renee Hieber is the author of Gothic, Dreadpunk, Gaslamp Fantasy for Tor Books, Kensington, and other publishers. Her *Strangely Beautiful* saga (Tor Books) has been hailed as a foundation work of Gaslamp Fantasy, won numerous genre awards, and was a Barnes & Noble and Borders bestseller. Her *Magic Most Foul* saga, beginning with *Darker Still*, hit the Indie Next List and was a Scholastic Book Club "Recommended Read". Her *Eterna Files* saga is now complete with Tor Books and she launches *The Spectral City* (Kensington) this fall. Her short fiction has appeared in numerous notable anthologies such as *Queen Victoria's Book of Spells: An Anthology of Gaslamp* Fantasy (Datlow, Windling for Tor Books), *Willful Impropriety* and the *Mammoth Book of Gaslit Romance*. She is a frequent lecturer and guest speaker at conventions and institutions around the country and her books have been translated into many languages. A classically trained professional actress, she is a proud member of performer unions AEA and SAG-AFTRA, is a ghost tour guide in Manhattan, and works often in film and television in New York City, having been featured in shows such as Boardwalk Empire and Mysteries at the Museum. She is active across social media and has free reads, resources and more at leannareneehieber.com

BRYCE RAFFLE

EDITOR/BURKE STREET STATION

Bryce Raffle writes steampunk, horror, and fantasy. He worked as lead writer on Ironclad Games' online fantasy multiplayer game, Sins of a Dark Age, and is currently working on his debut novel, *Dead London*. His short story, *The Complications of Avery Vane*, was the winner of 2016's P&E Readers' Poll for Best Steampunk Short. His stories have appeared in numerous anthologies such as *Denizens of Steam*, *Den of Antiquity*, and *Hideous Progeny: English Class Goes Punk.* He lives in beautiful Vancouver, Canada, where he works in the local film industry. Visit him at **bryceraffle.com** and on social media @bryceraffle.

DAVID LEE SUMMERS
A SPECTER IN THE LIGHT

David Lee Summers is the author of eleven novels and over one hundred short stories and poems. His writing spans a wide range of the imaginative from science fiction to fantasy to horror. David's novels include The Solar Sea, which was selected as a Flamingnet Young Adult Top Choice, The Astronomer's Crypt, which is a horror novel inspired by his work at an astronomical observatory, and The Brazen Shark, which was voted best steampunk novel in the 2017 Preditors and Editors Reader's Poll. His short stories and poems have appeared in such magazines and anthologies as Realms of Fantasy, Cemetery Dance, and the bestselling Straight Outta Tombstone. In 2010 and 2016, he was nominated for the Science Fiction Poetry Association's Rhysling Award and in 2017, he was nominated for SFPA's Dwarf Stars Award. In addition to writing, David has edited five science fiction anthologies including A Kepler's Dozen, Kepler's Cowboys and Maximum Velocity: The Best of the Full-Throttle Space Tales. When not working with the written word, David operates telescopes at Kitt Peak National Observatory.
Learn more about David at **davidleesummers.com**
Facebook: **facebook.com/davidleesummers**
Twitter: **@davidleesummers**

DJ TYRER

SILENT NIGHT

DJ Tyrer is the person behind Atlantean Publishing and has been widely published in anthologies and magazines around the world, such as Tales of the Black Arts (Hazardous Press), Amok!, Stomping Grounds and Ill-considered Expeditions (all April Moon Books), Altered States II (Indie Authors Press), Destroy All Robots (Dynatox Ministries), and Sorcery & Sanctity: A Homage to Arthur Machen (Hieroglyphics Press), and in addition, has a novella available in paperback and on the Kindle, The Yellow House (Dunhams Manor).

DJ Tyrer's website is at **http://djtyrer.blogspot.co.uk/**

The Atlantean Publishing website is at **http://atlanteanpublishing.blogspot.co.uk/**

KAREN J CARLISLE

THE CASE OF THE MURDEROUS MIGRAINE

Karen J Carlisle is an imagineer and writer of speculative fiction – steampunk, Victorian mystery and fantasy.

She graduated in 1986, from Queensland Institute of Technology with a Bachelor of Applied Science in Optometry and lives in Adelaide with her family and the ghost of her ancient Devon Rex cat.

Karen first fell in love with science fiction

when she saw Doctor Who as a four-year old (she can't remember if she hid behind the couch). This was reinforced when, at the age of twelve, she saw her first Star Destroyer. She started various other long-term affairs with fantasy fiction, (tabletop) role-playing, gardening, historical re-creation and steampunk – in that order.

She has had articles published in Australian Realms Roleplaying Magazine and Cockatrice (Arts and Sciences magazine). Her short story, An Eye for Detail, was short-listed by the Australian Literature Review in their 2013 Murder/Mystery Short Story Competition. Karen's short story, Hunted, featured in the 'A Trail of Tales' exhibition in the 2016 Adelaide Fringe.

She writes full-time and can often be found plotting fantastical, piratical or airship adventures.

Karen has always loved dark chocolate and rarely refuses a cup of tea.

Webpage: **www.karenjcarlisle.com**
Facebook: **www.facebook.com/KarenJCarlisle/**
Twitter: **https://twitter.com/kjcarlisle**

ROB FRANCIS
B.A.R.B.

Rob Francis is an academic ecologist and writer based in London. He started writing fantasy and horror in 2014, and since then has had over twenty short stories published in various magazines and anthologies. Recent sales have been to Metaphorosis

Magazine, You Are Here: Tales of Cartographic Wonders, Syntax & Salt and Tales of Blood and Squalor by Dark Cloud Press.

He lurks on Twitter @RAFurbaneco

JAMES DORR

THE RE-POSSESSED

James Dorr's latest book is a novel-in-stories published in June 2017 by Elder Signs Press, Tombs: A Chronicle of Latter-Day Times of Earth. Born in Florida, raised in the New York City area, in college in Boston, and currently living in the Midwest, Dorr is a short story writer and poet specializing in dark fantasy and horror, with forays into mystery and science fiction. His *The Tears of Isis* was a 2013 Bram Stoker Award® finalist for Superior Achievement in a Fiction Collection, while other books include Strange Mistresses: Tales of Wonder and Romance, Darker Loves: Tales of Mystery and Regret, and his all poetry Vamps (A Retrospective). He has also been a technical writer, an editor on a regional magazine, a full time non-fiction freelancer, and a semi-professional musician, and currently harbors a goth cat named Triana. He welcomes readers to visit his blog at **http://jamesdorrwriter.wordpress.com.** Facebook: **https://www.facebook.com/james. dorr.9**

JAY SEATE
THE VELVET RIBBON

After Jay read a few stories to his parents, they booted him out of the house. Undaunted, he continues to write everything from humor to the erotic to the macabre, and is especially keen on transcending genre pigeonholing. His tales span the gulf from Horror Novel Review's Best Short Fiction Award to Chicken Soup for the Soul. They may be told with hardcore realism or fantasy, bringing to life the most quirky of characters. Novels include Valley of Tears, Tears for the Departed, And the Heavens Wept, and Paranormal Liaisons. His story collections are Carnival of Nightmares, Midway of Fear, Sex in Bloom, and A Baker's Dozen.
Links: **www.troyseateauthor.webs.com** and on amazon.com.

JEN PONCE
AGONY IN RED

Jen loves to read and that passion came from her mom, who valued books above all things (except, maybe, the Dallas Cowboys and Michael Jordan.) She has been writing since grade school, and has over 10 books published, plus numerous short stories in various anthologies. She lives in the Panhandle of Nebraska with her boys, her cats, her dog, her fish, her crab, and a large supply of books that helps insulate the house in the winter and expand her mind.

Website: **www.JenniferPonce.com**
Facebook: **www.Facebook.com/JenPonceAuthor**
Twitter: **www.Twitter.com/JenPonceAuthor**

LORI TIRON-PANDIT
A VISITOR AT SULTANA'S CASTLE

Lori Tiron-Pandit is a writer of Romanian extraction with a diverse background in editing, translation, and communication. Her work explores women's lives and universes, with the legends, dreams, horrors, and labors that shape them. Lori Tiron-Pandit self-published her first novel, Spell of Blindness, and is currently working on a second book. You can find out more about her work at **www.loritironpandit. com**.

Facebook: **https://www.facebook.com/ loritironpanditauthor/**
Twitter: **https://twitter.com/ LoriTironPandit?lang=en**
Instagram: **https://www.instagram.com/ loritironpandit/**

ALICE E. KEYES
EIRA ALBA AND THE SEPTUM SCIENTISTS

Alice E. Keyes grew up with one foot in Montana Rockies and the other foot in New England. Living in two different worlds gave Alice wonder lust. She now lives in Port Au Prince, Haiti with her husband, two children, and two Brittanys. She will move to Helsinki, Finland for her next adventure. When she is not writing, she enjoys getting out into nature by either bicycling or hiking.

aliceekeyes.blogspot.com
Twitter: @aliceEkeyes
Instagram: aliceekeyes

CC ADAMS
SANITY SLIPS THROUGH YOUR FINGERS

London native C. C. Adams is the horror/dark fiction author whose work appears in publications such as Turn To Ash and Weirdbook Magazine. A member of the Horror Writers Association, he also holds a 2015 Honourable Mention from the Australian Horror Writers Association for short fiction.

Still living in London, he lifts weights, cooks - and looks for the perfect quote to set off the next dark delicacy.

Visit him at **www.ccadams.com**

WENDY NIKEL
THE BOOK OF FUTURES

Wendy Nikel is a speculative fiction author with a degree in elementary education, a fondness for road trips, and a terrible habit of forgetting where she's left her cup of tea. Her short fiction has been published by Fantastic Stories of the Imagination, Daily Science Fiction, Nature: Futures, and elsewhere. Her time travel novella, The Continuum, is forthcoming from World Weaver Press in January 2018.

For more info, visit **wendynikel.com**

E. SENECA
HARVESTERS

E. Seneca is a freelance speculative fiction author with a strong affinity for urban and soft fantasy, as well as mild horror and soft science fiction. She has written original fiction since 2008, and has worked on novels, novellas, and short stories. She lives in the United States.

LAWRENCE SALANI
ODESSA

Lawrence lives near Sydney, Australia, with his wife and child. He has been interested in dark fiction/horror since his childhood, and draws inspiration from pulp and classic horror fiction of the past.

His interests extend to fine arts, drawing and painting.

His work has appeared in various anthologies, the most recent being:

"Danse Macabre" Edge Publishing.

"Darkness ad Infinitum" Villipede Publications

"Dark Magic," "Under the Full Moon's Light," and "Pick Your Poison" from Owl Hollow Press.

He can be found on Facebook and Goodreads.

Facebook: **www.facebook.com/lawrencesalani**

STEVE CARR

GRETA SOMERSET

Steve Carr, who lives in Richmond, Va., began his writing career as a military journalist and has had over 200 short stories published internationally in print and online magazines, literary journals and anthologies. He has two collections of short stories that have been published; Sand, published by Clarendon House Publications, and Heat, published by Czykmate Productions. His plays have been produced in several states in the U.S. He was a 2017 Pushcart Prize nominee.

He is on Facebook and Twitter @carrsteven960.

Ross Smeltzer
The Hunger

Ross Smeltzer is a social studies teacher and dabbler in dark fiction living in Dallas, Texas. His first book, a collection of dark fantasy and Gothic horror novellas titled The Mark of the Shadow Grove, appeared in print in January of 2016. Ross's fiction has appeared in Sanitarium Magazine and Body Parts Magazine. His short fiction has also appeared in anthologies by Egaeus Press, Dragon's Roost Press, and Hic Dragones.

Jonah Buck
Grasp

Jonah Buck wanted to learn eldritch knowledge and commune with pale, unspeakable beings that flit across the sunless landscape to terrorize the living, so he became an attorney in Oregon. His interests include history, professional stage magic, paleontology, and exotic poultry.
Author Site: http://www.jonahbuck.com

Made in the USA
Columbia, SC
08 September 2018